A Devious Plan

by

Michael S. Walsh

All of the characters in this book are fictitious, and any resemblance to actual persons, living or dead, is purely coincidental. The names, incidents, dialogue and opinions expressed are the products of the author's imagination and are not to be constructed as real. The events in this book are entirely fiction and by no means should anyone attempt to live out the actions that are portrayed in the book.

Copyright © 2015
California Times Publishing, Los Angeles

No part of this book may be reproduced, scanned, or distributed in any printed or electronic form without permission. Please do not participate in or encourage piracy of copyrighted materials in violation of the author's rights. Purchase only authorized editions. All rights reserved.

www.californiatimespublishing.com

Acknowledgements

FIRST AND FOREMOST, I'd like to thank my incredible wife, Joellyn, without whose love and support this book would not have been written. Thanks to my father, John, and his wife Anne, whose enthusiasm for the project was priceless. Your feedback and encouragement was tremendous, and your proofreading abilities very much appreciated. Thanks to my brother Kevin, my sister Tracy, and my sister-in-law Kitty for their enthusiastic support. I am deeply grateful. Finally, thanks to the friends who reviewed the book along the way. Your positive feedback gave me the courage to publish the book.

Chapter One

Saturday, March 14, 2009 – 12:00 a.m.

HE'D ALWAYS BEEN told revenge was a dish best served cold. True or not, tonight's entree was frigid. And the most delicious part was his wife had no idea dinner was even being served.

He needed to work quickly. The panel van was parked in the back yard, about twenty feet away from the back door. If it sat there for too long, it might arouse suspicion; someone might call the cops. That would be a disaster. If the cops arrived at his house right now, he would surely wind up going to jail. So, it would be better to avoid the cops this evening. And for the next few years.

He eased open the door to the panel van with his left hand while grabbing the duffel bag from the passenger seat with his right. He swiveled, and slid out of the seat until his feet gently touched the ground. While he wanted to be quick, it was even more important to be quiet. After six long strides he reached the back door.

The door was unlocked, just as he'd left it before leaving for work this morning. He entered the mudroom, pulled off the sweaty ski mask, and placed it over the doorknob. He hoisted the duffel bag, which contained about fifty pounds of gear, onto the mudroom workbench. Had he packed everything properly? Yes, the hot dog tongs, the tweezers, and the fishing knife were all in the duffel bag. He had tried to think of everything but he didn't have time to waste; he had to get moving.

Fuck! He'd left the trash bag in the van. *Should I just get a different one from the basement? No, asshole, stick to the plan. You'll just have to risk going back outside.* So, on went the sweaty ski mask as he dashed back out to the van, praying no one would see him. The bag, pre-weighted with about twenty pounds of rocks, was lying on the floor on the passenger side. He snatched it off the floor and hustled back inside.

Safely in the mudroom, he once again positioned the ski mask on the doorknob. He could not afford to leave it behind, plus, he wanted to make sure he wore it the next time he left the house. He didn't want any nosy neighbors to recognize him on the off chance they'd look out the window when he returned to the van.

With the duffel bag in the right hand and the trash bag in his left, he strode quickly out of the mudroom, through the kitchen and straight up the hallway into the front foyer, finally turning left into his home office. He knew his wife wasn't home, yet he stepped as lightly as possible. She had left in the morning for a business trip and wouldn't be back until sometime on Sunday. Still, he was loath to make any noise. He softly dropped both bags onto the floor as he entered the office, and then slid down the wall until he reached the pull cord for the office curtain. Gently and evenly pulling the cord, hand over hand, he watched the curtains sashay slightly with each tug as they slowly came together. Moving slowly was the key; he worried that a passerby might notice a quick jerk of the curtains. Not likely, but there was no advantage to rushing. With the curtains closed now, no one could see inside the office from outside.

He hustled back to the foyer and scampered down the stairs to the basement. With a flick of the switch at the bottom of the stairs, he had light. He jogged through the large finished rec room, through a door, and into the musty and cluttered storage room. There, hidden under a pile of large green trash bags, all filled with old clothes, was Grapple Man, exactly where he'd been left on Tuesday. Grapple Man was by far the most lifelike dummy one could find and had cost a pretty penny. Grapple was six feet tall, weighed 55 pounds, and was made of a sturdy polyvinyl compound. Designed to aid law enforcement during hand-to-hand combat training, Grapple Man would now aid Bill in executing his ultimate master plan.

The temperature in the house was an even seventy, yet perspiration dampened Bill's brow and palms. Squatting, he grabbed Grapple Man under the armpits, and flung him over his right shoulder. After taking a step backwards to gain his balance, he made his way to the bottom of the stairs and began his ascent to the first floor. It had been easier to get Grapple down the stairs than up. He carried Grapple Man back through the foyer and into his office.

The office chair was behind the desk as always, and Bill placed Grapple Man in the chair, sitting him upright as if Grapple was himself an insurance man reviewing documents on the desk. The dummy was looking quite dapper, sporting a fashionable oxford dress shirt, neatly pressed khaki work slacks, dress socks and Florsheim loafers. Bill had dressed Grapple just before hiding him.

Reaching into the duffel bag, Bill pulled out two scuba diver belts. Each belt had six weight pockets, and all twelve pockets were filled with four-pound weights. He wrapped both belts around Grapple Man's waist, bringing the dummy's weight up over one hundred pounds. Bill wanted Grapple Man to have a substantial weight, but not be so heavy as to be unmanageable.

With Grapple Man in position, Bill reached into the duffel bag and pulled out the bag of blood. It was a gallon bag, half filled, four pints of blood. His blood. He attached the gallon bag to Grapple Man's neck using duct tape. The house was so quiet it was unnerving. His heart was pounding and his mouth tasted like sawdust but he kept moving.

Next, he reached into the duffel bag and pulled out the gun. It was a Glock 17 9MM that he had selected at random. It was a nice-looking gun, with a great safety feature. If a finger wasn't on the trigger, the safety was automatically on. No accidents that way; Bill was no gun expert. Besides, he wasn't planning on getting into any gunfights. Far from it--he just wanted something that would work. He snapped in the ammo clip and screwed on the silencer. It would be a lot better if the neighbors didn't hear any gunshots. He would need some time after the shooting; he couldn't afford to have the cops arrive before he was gone.

Bill loved his Glock. Loved the feel of it in his hands. He enjoyed it much more than he ever thought he would. He had never really had anything against guns in the past, but also had had no desire to own one. Now it turned out, he was a pretty good shot. Kind of a natural. Since he'd had no experience, he thought it would be a good idea to take shooting lessons at a local gun range before using a gun tonight. He was right; it was a really good idea, and he had enjoyed the hell out of those shooting lessons and the subsequent practice. So that part of the plan, the shooting, was the least nerve-wracking part. Bill was very comfortable with the Glock. He placed it on the desk.

OK—everything is in place, it's go time!

Bill grabbed the knife from the duffel bag, removed the sheath, and placed the sheath right next to the gun on the desk. With the knife in his right hand, he walked over to the dummy and placed the point of the knife at the bottom of the bag of blood. With a short stroke he jabbed quickly upward, poking a small hole in the bottom of the bag. Blood began to trickle from the bottom of the bag onto Grapple Man's dress shirt. He shoved the knife in a little deeper, opening the hole in the bag a little wider. Now there was a steady stream of blood pouring down the front of Grapple Man.

Bill leaped backward, dropping the knife on the desk and grabbing the gun. He ran around to the front of the desk and quickly backpedaled until he was about five feet in front of it. He took dead aim at the middle bottom of the blood bag, left hand bracing his right wrist, right hand holding the Glock, index finger on the trigger. When just about half of the blood had drained from the bag, he fired one bullet, just like he'd been practicing at the firing range. The recoil kicked his hands up in the air about eight inches and the bag exploded, blood splattering everywhere. A chunk of the right side of Grapple Man's neck flew backward and hit the wall, leaving a spot of blood on the wall behind the desk. Grapple keeled over off the chair and onto the floor, landing on his right side, covered in blood. Bill fired a second shot just above the spot where Grapple Man's head would have been had he remained in the chair. No real reason, he just felt like it. He took a deep breath. Then another. His torso was clammy with sweat; the extra layer of the painter's suit didn't help. But the sweat was mostly from nerves. His knees felt a little weak. It had been the best plan he could come up with to simulate someone being shot in the jugular vein and create a confusing crime scene.

It had felt crazy at the time, but now he was quite pleased with himself for the night he'd spent in the woods, shooting bags of fake blood, the recipe for which he'd found on the Internet. You could make a liquid the same consistency as blood using corn syrup and water. By combining red and yellow food coloring, you could make it the right color also, but Bill didn't bother with that. He only cared about the realism of the blood splatter. He'd mixed five bags of "blood," tied each to a tree, and shot them, each in a different part of the bag, in order to gauge how the liquid splattered in each case. After the third one he'd realized that a full bag created too much splatter; the spray of the liquid was too wide and too wild. It didn't seem consistent with someone being shot in the neck. That's when he'd come up with the idea for stabbing the bag first. For some reason, the trickle combined with a bit less splatter looked more authentic to him.

He quickly unscrewed the silencer, removed the clip from the Glock, and put all three items in the duffel bag. He grabbed the knife from the desk and threw it into the duffel bag. The sheath followed the knife into the bag. His movements were faster now; he felt a strong sense of urgency. If someone happened in on this scene, there would be absolutely no way to explain it, other than he had gone completely and utterly loony tunes. And maybe he had. Reaching into the duffel bag, he pulled out the hot dog tongs and tweezers, grabbed the trash bag, and slid around behind the desk to where Grapple Man now lay on the floor in a pool of blood.

Using the hot dog tongs, he grabbed the blood soaked chunk of polyurethane compound from the floor, formerly part of Grapple's neck, and put in in the trash bag. That was the only big piece he saw. He didn't see any small pieces in the pool of blood on the floor or anywhere nearby. *I guess I don't need the tweezers!* He tossed the hot dog tongs and tweezers back in the duffel bag. He untaped the shredded plastic bag from Grapple Man's neck and put it into the trash bag. There was a lot of blood on the bottom of his boots now and it was being tracked through the office with each step. That was OK; it was part of the plan. He lifted both the duffel bag and the trash bag and took them out to the panel van, tracking blood from the front of the house to the back. After setting both bags on the ground, he opened both doors at the back of the van, and then flung both bags into the back.

Sitting down on the back of the van he took off the bloody size twelve fishing boots, and slipped on a pair of more comfortable size tens. Size ten was his size. He swiftly made his way back through the rear door, into the mudroom, through the kitchen, into the front foyer, returning to the office. He slipped behind the desk, making sure to step with both feet into a big puddle of blood. Grabbing Grapple Man under each armpit, with the dummy face up, Bill dragged him through the house, and out to the back door. Grapple Man weighed slightly over a hundred pounds with the weight belts, so it wasn't too bad dragging him. When he reached the back of the van, Bill plunked Grapple Man's shoulder blades down on the back edge of the van where he had just been sitting. He jumped up into the back of the van, reached down and grabbed Grapple Man under the armpits once again, and pulled him up over the bumper until the dummy was fully loaded into the van.

Bill pulled the panel van doors closed from the inside. Negotiating past Grapple Man and the other gear, he scrambled up to the front. An instant after turning the key in the ignition, the engine started with a slight squeal. Bill eased the van into motion away from the back door and toward the side yard.

It was okay if the neighbors had seen him load Grapple into the van. Grapple looked real enough that if someone was watching, they would assume it was a human being who was being dragged and loaded into the van. But in case a neighbor had been watching, he absolutely could not delay. The natural response of someone witnessing someone else being dragged out the back door and loaded into a panel van late at night would most likely be to call the police. At least he sure hoped someone would call the police if they saw something like that going on at his house! It would probably be better if no one had seen anything. He pulled the van through the side yard, onto his street, turned right, and began the short ride to the rendezvous point. Keeping his speed right at the limit, he continually scanned in all directions, happily finding no flashing lights coming into view.

Chapter Two

THE RENDEZVOUS POINT was seven miles away. In his mind, Bill referred to his destination as a rendezvous point, even though he wasn't meeting anyone. As parched as he was, he would have given his right arm for a bottle of water. But making a stop was out of the question. He steered the panel truck out of his subdivision and onto the highway, heading west. After about four miles, he veered right onto the second exit ramp and headed north on a two-lane road. After two more miles, he took a left onto a less traveled road into a wooded area, a road wide enough for two cars, but with no lines down the middle. There had been no sign of the police, no distant sirens, which probably meant no one had reported anything. And that was fine.

After another mile, Bill took a sharp right onto a narrow dirt road that carved its way through a heavily wooded area. The shock absorbers on the old van squeaked as she bounced along the tight passage. After bumping along deliberately for about a half mile, Bill headed left onto an access road that ran uphill into the woods. Calling it a road may have been generous. It was simply two parallel ruts with gravel and stones at the bottom of each rut.

Perhaps it had been a more proper road earlier in its life. It occurred to Bill that people with ATVs might use it in the summer months. At any rate, he had chosen the route because it was secluded and most people didn't know about the spot at the end of the road. It was highly unlikely that anyone would be around, at this hour, at this time of year. The left turn could easily be missed on a dark night such as this one. He wanted to kill the headlights, just in case, but it was too dark. The cloud cover blocked any moonlight, and without headlights to guide him he could easily veer off the trail.

The van was holding its own on the winding trail, even as the grade gradually got steeper. Bill was glad it wasn't raining. The van's well-worn tires would not have fared well going uphill in muddy conditions. It was slow going as the path wound this way and that through the trees. After what felt like an eternity, he finally emerged into a clearing at the top of the hill. <u>Bingo!</u> The 1995 Chevy S-10 pickup was still waiting for him at the far side of the clearing, right where he'd left it last night. He had not planned for the possibility that the pickup truck wouldn't be there, so he was very glad to see it! The clearing was about one hundred yards wide and at the far side there was a steep eighty-foot drop down to an old rock quarry, which was now a decent- sized lake. It was heavily used in the summer time as a swimming hole, but this was March; the water was much too cold for swimming.

Bill maneuvered the van across the clearing until it was right next to the car. He saw no one, hadn't expected to, and absolutely didn't want to. He ducked his head and moved from the driver's seat back to the bed of the van. Once in the back, he changed into a pair of khakis and a golf shirt, clean socks and sneakers. Glad to be out of the sweaty, bloody garments he'd worn while "killing" himself, he stuffed all the dirty clothes into the trash bag. He realized now that pre-weighting the trash bag had been a waste of time. *Oh well, no harm, no foul!* Now back in his normal weekend attire, he went to the front of the van and slipped on a leather jacket that would help fend off the night's chill.

He grabbed a manila folder from the glove compartment and got out. *Ooops, I forgot the keys.* He walked around to the other side of the van, opened the passenger door, and grabbed the keys for the Chevy from the glove compartment. After a quick look around, he opened the passenger door to the Chevy and tossed the manila envelope onto the front seat. Now things got a bit tricky. He jumped back into the van and drove up very close to the edge of the ravine. He hopped out. His plan was to drive the panel van right up to the edge and push it over, either by hand or by using the Chevy. He needed to gauge how much further he could drive the van, if at all, without it starting its descent with him still inside. He had to think for a second.

If I drive the van too far, I'm a goner. Better safe than sorry. I don't want to get into a situation where I'm leaping out of the van as it's starting its fall. I'll just leave it right here, five feet from the edge, put it in neutral, and use the pickup to shove it over. He judged that the van was close enough to the edge.

He knew from his days as a kid swimming in the lake that this part of the lake was very deep. Almost all the activity during the summer months was on the other side, where there were proper access points and life guards, places to rent paddle boats and buy ice cream. So he felt confident that the van would find a final resting place on the bottom of the lake and would remain undisturbed for many years. And that was what he needed. While there was nothing specific that would tie the stolen van to him, it wouldn't be a stretch for a sharp detective to put two and two together, linking all the evidence in the van to the "crime scene" back at the house.

He wasn't sure why, but he suddenly felt extremely nervous. *The die is cast, chief. Why be nervous now? It makes no sense; the hard part is done. I just need to make the van disappear and begin phase two of my master plan.* He hopped back into the van and moved the gearshift until the 'N' was backlit with green light. Wanting to calm down a little, he took several deep breaths. Then he jogged over to the Chevy, started it up, and swung it around to where its front bumper was touching the rear bumper of the van. He put the pickup in second gear and pushed the gas pedal about halfway down. It was enough power to get the van rolling. *Don't drive the pickup too far!* He pushed the panel van forward five feet, and it was just enough. It now had its own momentum, and disappeared over the side of the ravine. He heard some initial crashing sounds, and then a very loud metallic BANG, then some more crashing sounds, and finally a soft splash. He jumped out of the pickup, and looked over the ravine to try to discern whether or not the truck had actually sunk. But it was too far down, and too dark. Crap! Could he afford to drive off now, without being certain the van was completely submerged?

If the van was found with all that evidence in it-- Grapple Man, the Glock, two pairs of incriminating boots with blood on the bottom, and bloody clothing--his plan would be uncovered immediately. It dawned on him what a large investment he had just sent careening down toward the lake's bottom. Slightly over two thousand clams between Grapple Man and the Glock, not to mention the other odds and ends. But what was two thousand dollars compared to the three million in life insurance he would wind up with?

Screw it. I'm not waiting here all night so I can see whether or not the damn van sank. I'm thirsty, hungry, tired and cold. I heard the splash, good enough. The van has to be at the bottom of the lake by now. The panel truck is gone and so is Bill Ferguson.

So the newly minted Troy Stevens fired up his Chevy, registered to him, and drove it through the Connecticut countryside until he found Interstate 95. With his Wyoming driver's license in his wallet, he pointed the car south and began rolling toward Myrtle Beach, South Carolina.

Chapter Three

<u>About two months earlier</u>
Friday, January 9, 2009 – 7:05 a.m.

BILL FERGUSON TOOK a sip of his Starbucks vente latte as he read the latest headlines on Courant.com, the web site for *The Hartford Courant Newspaper*. He loved good coffee and was especially partial to Starbucks. He availed himself of the Starbucks drive-thru near his house almost every morning on his way to work.

It was a Friday morning just after seven a.m. Bill was almost always in the office by seven. Only a few others were on the twelfth floor at that time and he loved the stillness, the solitude. He felt this was the only part of the day that was truly his. Things were lousy both here at the office and on the home front. But for this one-hour or so, he could do just what he was doing, sip his morning coffee and read the newspaper, then ease into his day by catching up on his company emails and memos. By the time his boss rolled in around eight-thirty, he was ready to get to work. At least the work he felt like doing.

From his corner office Bill would occasionally hear a fellow early bird on his or her way to the copier. Or he might hear the low voices of other early risers conversing near the coffee machine. The tones were hushed, not because the conversations were especially private, but because those who arrived before eight a.m. understood the importance of preserving the solitude of the early morning.

Bill initially had loved his job. Fresh out of college where he'd studied economics, he kicked open the door to the Bedrock Insurance Company and dashed in, guns a-blazing. Somehow, Bill just knew he was going to thrive, and so did everyone he came in contact with. He came in early, stayed late, worked weekends, covered for colleagues, and within two years was running his own department. He wanted to be successful so badly he could taste it.

But as hard charging as he was, he was also willing to listen to the advice of the old guard. For instance, he had increased productivity for his department by thirty percent by automating some antiquated processes, but also sought advice from those more experienced when it came to personnel matters. He had trouble understanding how the guy down the hall could leave right at five o'clock when there was a mountain of paperwork still on his desk. The older guys helped him understand that some people also valued their life outside of work. For Bill, work was where he might become a king.

So, when the Investment Services Department thrived with Bill at the helm, he was fast tracked, and at age thirty-five became one of the youngest vice presidents in the history of the company. He was absolutely in heaven the day he was named Vice President of the Finance and Investment Division. And things went very well for a few years. Bill continued with his "work from dawn to dusk" ethos, and the Finance and Investment Division earned record profits under his stewardship. His work at Bedrock brought him a tremendous amount of satisfaction during those years.

Like most successful people, Bill didn't do it all alone. On his way up the corporate ladder, he had identified a couple of other go-getters who became his top lieutenants. Both Ed Simpson and Frank DeLuca moved up the ladder alongside Bill with each promotion. He could hand either any important assignment and trust it would be carried out as if he had done it himself.

While he had charged up the ladder two rungs at a time to become a VP, Senior VP seemed like the stratosphere. There was very little turnover among the Senior VPs; those were the ultra cushy jobs at Bedrock. Those guys were like Supreme Court Justices; most of them treated their positions as if they were lifetime appointments. He had reached VP with determination, ingenuity, and a tremendous work ethic but reaching Senior VP was more of a waiting game. Bill didn't like waiting--it was boring. He wanted to crash the party, not sit around until the engraved invitation came in the mail.

Over time, things began to change. Bill settled into being a VP. He was making a huge salary and enjoying lots of company perks. So, he relaxed a little, knowing he'd have to bide his time to become a Senior VP. He leaned more and more on his "right hand men," trusting them fully with big accounts and important meetings. His executive assistant Jennifer was a dynamo, and over time he gave her more and more responsibility. With increasing frequency, Bill played golf on Friday afternoons, or would take an extra long lunch on a Wednesday. He worked late in the evening less often and came in on weekends even less. Eventually, the one afternoon off a week to play golf became two.

When he had first joined the company, he was the young buck, able to outthink most and outwork everyone. But now at age forty, Bill mostly delegated big assignments and decisions to his trusted lieutenants. Having convinced himself the next big promotion was essentially unattainable, he lost his drive. He had become content.

Then, in the summer of 2006, Alan Madigan, a Senior VP and trusted mentor retired. And in the fall of 2007, Sam Worman, another influential Senior VP and mentor left for a competing company. In late 2007, Bedrock was acquired by Greystone Mutual Insurance, and suddenly Bill had a brand new boss, who had no notion of him being the fair haired boy. Quite the contrary, Bedrock had paid its employees quite a bit more generously than Greystone Mutual. So right out of the gate, Philip Axelrod, Bill's new boss, was subconsciously thinking, okay hotshot making such a huge salary-- show me. Show me you are worth that kind of money. And this spelled trouble for Bill, who'd been coasting for the last two years.

Axelrod was a Senior Vice President and CFO for Greystone. He was results-oriented, with a no-nonsense attitude. After majoring in Economics at Stanford, he followed up that act by getting his MBA at Harvard. He entered every room assuming he was about to be the smartest guy there. He often was, and as a result was one of the most respected figures at Greystone. Many of the other Senior VPs sought Axelrod's counsel regarding important corporate matters. His word was often the de facto law for Greystone.

After the acquisition, the Bedrock executives were rolled into the flatter corporate structure of Greystone, meaning fewer top managers working under the executives. So just when Bill was getting used to the good life, delegating all kinds of important work, his top guys were both reassigned. Frank DeLuca got a promotion to VP of the Claims Services Division, while Ed Simpson was moved laterally to Risk Management, where it was assumed he was the heir apparent to be VP when his boss retired within the next year. Had Bill been as driven as he was six or seven years before, this scenario would not have been a big deal, but now he was in a position where he had to prove his worth all over again to brand new bosses, in an environment where no one was coddled. There were very few left who had witnessed his meteoric rise and would go to bat for him now. The company had been significantly streamlined to be more profitable, yet the profits of Bill's division began declining with each passing quarter after DeLuca and Simpson left.

At eight o'clock, Bill started looking over the fourth quarter numbers for his division. <u>Hmmm, these numbers don't look so good. Axelrod won't be too happy about this</u>. Bill studied the reports and came up with some ideas on how to improve the weaker areas.

<u>It's eight-fifty now, time to head upstairs for the nine o'clock meeting with Axelrod. Probably just a quick meeting about some ideas to make the Finance and Investment Division more profitable</u>.

Chapter Four

BILL WAITED PATIENTLY in a snazzy chair outside Philip Axelrod's fourteenth floor office. As Senior Vice President and CFO for Greystone, Axelrod oversaw three divisions, including Bill's Finance and Investment division. After several minutes, Axelrod's secretary spoke. "You can go in now Mr. Ferguson."

With two quick knocks on the door, Bill entered Axelrod's posh corner office. The door split the huge corner office in two, and even though it was an open room, it was in fact two distinct spaces. To the left was the traditional office space, complete with a grandiose mahogany office desk, executive chairs and floor to ceiling built-in bookcases. The other section was a meeting area, with a couple of nice chairs, a sofa opposite them, and a glass-topped coffee table in the middle. The windows beyond the meeting area revealed a spectacular view of the Connecticut countryside.

"Have a seat Bill," Axelrod said sharply, motioning to the chairs situated on the opposite side of his desk.

Bill was a bit surprised by his boss's tone.

"I'll get right to the point. The board feels that they'd like to see Anderson have a crack at running the Finance and Investment Division."

"Excuse me?" blurted Bill, taken aback.

"Let's face it, the profit margins for Finance and Investment have been in decline since the acquisition. The board feels it's time for a change. And I just don't have any ammunition to fight them with."

Yeah right. Like you'd go charging right into the breach for me if you had any "ammunition." Bastard. "The numbers aren't really that bad. We can recover. I've got some good ideas I'd like to go over with you."

"Not really that bad is NOT what we expect from someone as well paid as yourself, Bill. And you've had three full quarters to right the ship. But not only hasn't the ship been righted, in fact, it's listing badly. It's too late for ideas to improve now. In the board's view, you've had plenty of time to make improvements. We feel it's time for a change."

A Freudian slip. "We" feel its time for a change. Not that it mattered if Axelrod had made the decision himself or was simply going along with the board. Bastard. "This is crap. I took that division from almost nothing to what it is now. Remember, I lost two top guys at the beginning of last year also. So that made this year tough."

"And that's part of the problem. Those two get promoted and suddenly your division isn't doing so hot. Kind of makes us think those other guys were doing all the work. Did you really think they were going to be yours forever?"

"It takes time to train up new people. Ed and Frank were with me for years. And now you're giving my division to that idiot Anderson? Give me a break!"

"Oh, come on. If you were worth all that money, you'd have anticipated that they wouldn't be there forever and would have made sure their replacements were ready. And this conversation is becoming very revealing. It was never YOUR division. It was always the company's division, even when it was part of Bedrock, and you had the good fortune to have stewardship over it."

Axelrod paused for just a second. "And let me say this before you go any further with your indignation there, Bill," said Axelrod, through clenched teeth. "I'm one of the main reasons you didn't get bounced out of here entirely. OK? A couple of the board members wanted you out completely. Gone. OK? But I talked them down. Out of respect for what you did pre-acquisition. I convinced them that I could light a fire under your ass, and maybe you'd be able to pull it together and get back to the kind of employee you used to be. Under the old management you probably could have gotten away with coasting until retirement. But the folks from Greystone, we're kind of funny that way, we actually want some bang for our buck."

After another brief pause, he continued. "We are reassigning you to the Claims Division, as the deputy VP under Melissa Jones. And we'll see how it goes. You'll keep your office and executive assistant for the time being."

Bill was steaming, but was able to hold his tongue, just barely. Without another word, he left Axelrod's office with the blood in his veins at the boiling point. <u>How dare they do this me? I built that division from the ground up!</u> But he knew deep down that Axelrod was right. He had, over time, lost his drive and acquired a sense of entitlement. He had been coasting, a little more each year. And he had never really admitted it to himself. So, this meeting was like getting hit in the head with a two by four. It was humiliating to be called out like this. Since Bill had faked himself out, he had assumed everyone else had bought into his rationalizations and excuses.

The hard truth was, simply put, embarrassing. Bill had no one to blame but himself for his situation. He had always assumed it was just a matter of time before he would occupy a senior VP's office just like Axelrod's, if not the very same office. Now that dream felt as distant as the horizon he had seen out the window of the beautiful corner suite.

Something Axelrod had said towards the end of the conversation stuck in Bill's craw--the way he had said "employee." It had never really occurred to him before, but to the Senior VPs and board of director's, that's ultimately all he was, just another employee. Just another employee who, if he didn't toe the line, could be simply "bounced out" at any time. Yet somehow in his mind, because of his VP title, he'd felt like he'd already made it, like he was untouchable. And now he was disgusted with himself for having thought that way.

He took the stairs down to his office on the 12th floor in no particular hurry. Angry and humiliated, he sauntered past his executive assistant, Jennifer, his only acknowledgement of her a quick, "Jennifer, please hold my calls for the next hour." He took off his suit jacket and slung it over the first guest chair he came to. His own office was nothing to be embarrassed about, it was also a very nice corner office, just not as large or nicely furnished as Axelrod's. He slumped down into his desk chair, closed his eyes, and imagined he was standing on the eighteenth tee at Pebble Beach, overlooking the glorious Monterey Peninsula.

Chapter Five

AFTER COLLECTING HIMSELF for the better part of thirty minutes, Bill realized he was going to have to do some soul searching regarding his career. Did he really want to try to reestablish himself in the Claims Division, working for Melissa Jones? He didn't know her very well, he'd heard good things, but what did that matter anyway? The real question was what did he want to do? Bedrock, and now Greystone, was all he had ever known.

He slipped on his suit jacket and his overcoat. As he left his office, he called, "Jen, I'm taking an early and long lunch. No meetings this afternoon, right?"

"There's nothing on your calendar."

"Thanks, please keep it that way for the rest of the day. I'll be back this afternoon."

He took the elevator down to the lobby and a stern blast of cold air hit him in the face as he stepped out onto the sidewalk. It was brilliantly sunny, twenty-five degrees, and a slight breeze made it that much more brisk. It was refreshing. The air quality was always good on days like this. It was only about ten-thirty, so there wasn't much action on the street yet. The streets would start coming alive just around eleven o'clock, as the early lunch folks would begin making their way to the numerous restaurants, pubs and eateries in downtown Hartford.

Bill didn't want to eat just yet, and he decided a walk would be a good thing right now. He'd always liked Henry's Bistro, about a ten-block walk, roughly fifteen minutes by foot. There was a bookstore on the way; he could browse there for a few minutes and time lunch for around eleven. By then he'd be ready for a hot bowl of soup and a sandwich.

He reached Henry's about ten minutes after eleven. The browsing in the bookstore had morphed into a purchase. He wound up buying a murder mystery novel by his favorite author. When he thought about it, it was kind of amazing he even had a favorite author. He'd put in so much time at the office, nights, weekends, especially early on, he'd barely had time to say hello to his wife. He sighed to himself. The wife. He'd have to address that "situation" when he got back to the office.

Hungry now, Bill took a seat at the bar so he could watch ESPN while dining. Many in Bill's shoes, having just been demoted, might have ordered a drink, but he wasn't much of drinker. Iced tea was his usual drink when eating out. He'd had his share of cocktails, but usually in social settings, and very rarely would he drink this early in the day.

Henry's had a killer lobster bisque, so he ordered a bowl of that along with a French dip sandwich. He ate slowly, with one eye on SportsCenter, but he was mostly lost in thoughts about his work life and his home life.

It was twelve-thirty now according to Tag Heuer. Time to get back to the office. He decided he didn't need another walk and stepped out into the brisk weather and hailed a cab. The high- rise office building that housed Greystone Mutual appeared in no time. He hopped out of the cab, generously tipped the cabby for the short ride from Henry's, and headed inside.

The high-speed elevator reached the twelfth floor in a matter of seconds. Bill stepped out and headed for his corner office.

"Jen, can you set up a meeting with Melissa Jones for Monday morning, assuming she's got time?"

"No problem, I'll set it up."

He didn't bother to tell her the purpose of the meeting; he figured he'd fill her in on the demotion on Monday morning. No point in ruining her weekend, too. Even though it didn't reflect on Jennifer in any way, he knew she would take it hard. She had been his assistant ever since he became a VP.

Bill felt tired now. He wanted to close his eyes for an hour. But there was an important matter to attend to first. Leaning back in his executive chair, he let out a deep sigh while staring down the phone. *You've put this moment off long enough. You've GOT to make this call.* But, it was difficult. He didn't want to believe this was happening to him, of all people. So he just sat there, paralyzed, staring at the phone for a few moments longer.

If the call he was about to make had been a business call, then, no problem. He'd made plenty of tough choices and tough phone calls over the years. Business was business, and he had never had a problem getting the job done, at least not until recently. For much of his adult life, his career had been his focus, his passion. And he wasn't quite ready to admit that the very same dedication to his work, which had led to all the success, was also the reason he had to make this next call.

But he could ignore his instincts no longer. He was certain of it now. Laura, his wife of thirteen years, was having an affair. The signs had been there for months and months and months. But until now he had preferred to keep his head in the sand, not wanting to believe what his eyes, ears, and gut had been telling him. *Things aren't great between us right now, but she would never do THAT, would she? Of course not!*

He had known Laura for twenty years. They first met at Yale when Bill was on the golf team, and after a good match some of the guys had a party at their off-campus apartment. Laura showed up with some girlfriends and Bill was instantly smitten. She was blond and thin, about five feet six inches, weighing about one hundred and ten pounds. She always looked sharp. Her clothes fit perfectly, almost never a wrinkle. And in addition to her looks, Bill was attracted to her personality. She was smart, funny, and sweet.

They dated for the next year until Bill had a dalliance with someone else while away at a golf tournament. Division I golf teams do a great deal of traveling and wind up in all sorts of fun college towns. One night after a match with Clemson, Bill had a little too much fun, at least in terms of his relationship with Laura. The beers and shots were flowing, and Bill had always been taken with those Carolina accents. Eventually, one thing led to another with a shapely co-ed whose name he had forgotten long ago. After he sobered up the next morning, feeling terribly guilty, Bill told Laura about his one-night stand. She dumped him immediately. He was shocked. Before fessing up, he hadn't considered the possibility that she wouldn't forgive him. And he hadn't realized that he really loved her until he got dumped. He barely ate or slept for weeks, his golf game suffered, and so did his grades. He realized he'd made a huge mistake, but there wasn't anything he could do about it. She wouldn't even talk to him.

Over time, Bill was able to get back in her good graces again, at least as a friend. Bill dated others but never let things get too serious, because in the back of his mind he always held on to the dream of getting Laura back some day. He kept in touch and kept tabs, but had lousy timing. After a breakup she'd be on to the next guy before he could pull the trigger on trying to date her again. This continued for a couple of years after college. Finally, right after her twenty-fifth birthday, and after a recent breakup for Laura, Bill "happened by" the bar where Laura and her fellow law classmates hung out on Friday nights. And over the next few months he got her to fall in love with him all over again.

He thought back to how happy they'd been when they were newlyweds. Laura was a law student, and Bill was working a lot. It worked for them back then. Even though they learned early on that Laura couldn't have kids, it didn't matter much. They met for late dinners, would go for midnight walks, and stay up extra late watching movies on the weekends. They were young and free and in love. But, as the years passed, their love slowly eroded. His memories of the good times began to fade. When he recalled the early days, it was as if he was watching a movie with an actor that resembled Bill Ferguson, but it wasn't really him. Someone that happy had to be someone else. In many ways, he was a different person now.

Someone who was pretty sure that, in terms of his marriage, things had reached the point of no return. He just needed some proof.

The moment had arrived. Bill opened a desk drawer and pulled out a number he'd looked up a few weeks before. Another deep sigh. He picked up the telephone receiver with his left hand, and slowly punched in the numbers with his right.

After three rings, a woman's voice on the other end of the line answered, "Stapleton Detective Agency, how may I help you?"

"Yes, hello, may I speak with John Stapleton please?"

Chapter Six

Monday, January 12, 2009

JOHN STAPLETON WAS the CEO, CFO, CIO and chief cook and bottle washer at the Stapleton Detective Agency. He had built the smallish agency from the ground up with nothing but gumption and brain cells, and was very proud of it. He wasn't a millionaire, but wouldn't trade being his own boss for all the money in the world. And now after thirteen years in the PI business he had office space, a secretary, and five detectives working for him.

As a kid John was plenty smart, but not one for "hitting the books." He mostly hit opposing lineman and linebackers as the right guard on the high school football team. A bit undersized to play college ball, and with no other incentive to go to college, John joined the Marines right out of high school. He liked being a Marine, but decided in year number two that he didn't want to make it a career. But he also never saw himself as a traditional nine to fiver, sitting behind a desk for thirty or forty years. So after an honorable discharge from the Marines, John came home to Hartford and went to work for a local private detective firm. He saw it as a way to use the brain/brawn combo he'd begun developing while playing high school football and enhanced as a member of the Corps. Plus, it simply sounded exciting.

John quickly learned that private detecting did not consist of the dangerous stakeouts, high-speed chases, and occasional gunplay that he had envisioned. There was a lot more legwork, research, and time spent on the phone than he ever imagined. Still, the work was challenging and interesting, and John worked hard. As his skills developed, he fashioned himself into a very competent detective.

He became the agency's "go to" guy when it came to finding people. When he felt like it, John was capable of charming the pants off people. He could get them to make admissions without realizing they were giving away crucial information. He learned how to talk to the relatives, the ex-lovers, the friends, and the ex-friends until he began to get a complete picture of his quarry. He used public records, credit information, and real estate databases. Eventually he'd learn enough so he would be able to pinpoint a location.

His reputation began to grow when, after two other detectives had failed to find a client's brother, who had been missing for a few months, John was able to find him. He turned over the one rock the other two hadn't thought to turn over—he found the guy in jail. The man had been arrested and jailed after multiple DUIs, and had been too embarrassed to tell his family.

But at thirty years old, John started to realize he'd never make a lot of money working for someone else. If he ever wanted the big house in the burbs with the SUV in the driveway, he'd better hang out his own shingle. So he did just that. He worked solo for five years, using the second bedroom of his apartment as an office. Eventually he saved enough money to rent a small office in an inexpensive downtown office building. And then he brought in fellow ex-marine Hank Slater as a junior detective.

Seven years later, the Stapleton Detective Agency had five full-time detectives, not including John, who at the age of forty-two had lost his zest for the fieldwork. He was content to run the office, talk to the clients, and dole out the cases to his detectives. He had a secretary to answer the phones and do the filing. He was happy with his work and his station in life.

Home life was good too. John had a very cool wife, Amy, and two great kids, Susan, ten and Steven, eight. Both kids loved sports as much as their father did, so weekends generally centered around the kids' sporting events. Susan loved soccer, while Steven was into basketball. When the family wasn't scurrying around the county to various games, they were enjoying life at their fine house in the suburbs. The only "problem" was that a nice new minivan had replaced the SUV.

And John had the perfect man for the Ferguson case. His most experienced and best overall detective was Slater but he had someone more suited for the Ferguson job. Not that Hank would have done a bad job; on the contrary, he was very skilled. However, Andy Jacobsen had nearly made an entire career out of getting the goods on cheating spouses. Andy was a master at "getting the shot." So Stapleton figured he'd use Andy for this case. Besides, Andy had just wrapped up another case last week, and was waiting for his next big assignment.

Chapter Seven

ANDY JACOBSEN LOVED his job. He loved just how creative and devious his chosen career allowed him to be. He couldn't think of any job he might enjoy more, perhaps with the exception of being a professional ballplayer. As a seasoned private detective for the Stapleton Detective Agency, his nickname was the Kodak Kid. Give him an assignment involving taking photographs of a particular target, and he would get them. Every time. Usually with the target having no idea he or she had been photographed, and with no one suspecting it was Andy who took the pictures.

As Andy drove home from the gym after his evening workout, he recalled his first assignment for John Stapleton. A woman had suspected that her husband was cheating on her, and Andy was given the assignment of tailing him for a couple of nights in order to check it out. He was to get pictures if possible. The wife said she suspected, when her husband went out after dinner and said he was going back to the office, that he wasn't actually going back to work at all. Instead, he was seeing another woman and she was stuck at home with the kids.

On the first night of the assignment, Andy arrived at the couple's street around six p.m. and parked several houses down just as he'd been taught. He wanted to get there early enough so if the dude left right after dinner, he'd be in position to tail him. This was very exciting stuff. This was his very first night as a detective. He was stoked! Adrenaline pumped through his veins, and he sat literally on the edge of the seat of his Ford F-150, ready to pull out behind Mr. Cheater's vehicle as soon as it left the driveway. John Stapleton had taught him that pickup trucks were good vehicles for detectives in suburbia because they didn't stand out too much. If he was going to be on a case that took him downtown, he'd probably rent a commuter car for the job.

As neighbors happened by, he pretended to be reading a map, or just talking on his cell, hoping to blend into the background as much as possible. But six o'clock quickly became seven, and then eight, with no one entering or leaving the house. As it got to be nine o'clock, he had become quite disappointed. It was fairly obvious this prick was not planning on seeing his girlfriend that night. Crap! Andy was quite irritated. He had gotten all geared up, and then, nada. Zilch. A big fat goose egg. At ten o'clock, he finally called it a night, forcing himself to drive away, fighting off the temptation to hang around, "just in case." He was going to have to dial it back a bit or else this new job could drive him nuts. The only consolation was he was paid for four hours.

On the second evening, Andy again arrived around six. He told himself, over and over, you've got to be patient. *If he doesn't step out for a second night in a row, you can't let it get you down. It's not personal, it's a job, potentially a great job, but a job none-the-less and you can't take it personally if the targets don't do what you want. You can't will them into sleeping with their girlfriends on Tuesday instead of Wednesday just because you're ready and looking for some action on Tuesday.*

Yet despite his self-talk, the first hour felt like three. Andy second-guessed his new career choice. *Waiting around like this is sheer torture. Do I really have the patience for this?*

And then at seven fifteen—bingo! Mr. Cheater was on the move! Backing his nondescript Ford Taurus out of his driveway, his evening of debauchery began. Andy waited as his target drove two or three houses down the street before pulling out to follow, staying back as far as possible, while still maintaining visual contact. After Andy followed him onto the Interstate and then off the second exit ramp to the north, he continued following Mr. Cheater into a quiet little tree-lined neighborhood of Cape Cods, built back in the 50s. While driving slowly behind, at a distance of about a hundred yards, Andy watched as Mr. Cheater pulled into a driveway. As Andy drove past, the philanderer got out of his car, walked up to the front door, and was greeted with a big sexy kiss from a comely young woman. Andy just kept driving as the cheating husband pulled into the driveway. He got a great look of the two of them smooching, but he wasn't in position to capture that ever-so-touching moment on film. He circled the block and parked across the street, a couple of houses down.

Andy sat in the truck, window rolled down, as dusk descended on that sticky July day. There wasn't much activity on the street. Andy pretended he was looking over a map for the benefit of a man walking his dog. But of course, he was casing the house, trying to figure out where the master bedroom might be, and if there was any way to gain visual access. The dog walker didn't even look Andy's way. Excellent! The last thing he needed on his first assignment was some neighborhood watch-type questioning his presence.

At around nine p.m., when Andy was certain that no one was active on the street, he made his move. He remembered quickly and stealthily moving to the backyard of the house, all the while checking to make sure no one was watching. He noticed his breath was quick and shallow. This was the real thing! It was one thing to be sitting in his car, where if someone challenged him, he could just drive away. But if someone saw him now, he'd have a hard time explaining what the heck he was doing in this broad's backyard! *Focus on the assignment. Don't get distracted with random thoughts.* There was only one window in the back of the house with a light on, a second floor window, so he guessed that was a good place to start.

Looking around, he noticed a fairly large shed in the corner of the back yard. Moving slowly towards it, he visually swept the backyard as he moved. He glanced at the windows of the neighbors' houses, as well, to make sure no one was watching him. He could practically taste the cotton in his mouth, feel the sweat of his palms, and hear his heart pounding in his chest as he gently opened the door to the shed, praying for the old hinges not to squeak. The door easily swung open without a sound. He let out a huge sigh of relief. He glanced back toward the house. No movement, he was still undetected.

Andy stepped into the shed and closed the door behind him. Using a small flashlight he retrieved from a front pocket of his jeans, he discovered a ladder lying on the floor against the wall on the right hand side of the shed. Tall enough for him to get a look inside that window, he hoped. He grabbed the ladder and turned off the flashlight. Ever so slowly, he pushed open the shed door, and eased into the yard. His heart practically pounded out of his chest while walking back across the yard to the house, where he leaned the ladder against the bricks as gently as humanly possible, just to the left of the illuminated window.

A famous actor was once asked, "How are you able to pull off all those difficult stunts? Aren't you afraid of being injured?" The actor replied, "You can do anything when you're in the character." Andy was in full PI character now, and scampered up the ladder without hesitation.

After he reached the top of the ladder, he decided instead of leaning over and looking into the window directly, he would try something else. He reached into the front pocket of his jeans with his hand, and pulled out his brand new Mini HD Spy Camera, which had cost him one hundred bucks online. Shifting the camera he extended his arm and angled it to get a picture of most of the room. Click! Balancing atop the ladder, he quickly pulled his arm back to inspect the picture.

Whoa! When seeing the two lovers entangled nearly made him fall off the ladder. He quickly extended his arm and positioned the camera again. Click, click, click. He clicked away continually, getting as many shots as possible in rapid-fire succession. Suddenly, a light flashed across his face. Then he heard a booming voice, "Hey you! What the hell are you doing up there?"

A DEVIOUS PLAN 45

Andy turned to see a rather portly man, not very tall, whose backyard was directly behind him, making his way down his back steps, a flashlight in his hand, a baseball bat in the other. Andy quickly scrambled down the ladder. Luckily the neighbor was not fit, and seemed to forget this as he was running after Andy. Apparently he was overcome with excitement when faced with the prospect of catching his first Peeping Tom.

"Hey you, get back here! You sonofabitch! You freak!" Andy made it to the side yard before giving one last look backward. The neighbor decided to end his pursuit when he reached his back fence, realizing he would never catch the youthful Andy. Plus, with a forty-pound beer gut, it would have been quite a chore for this guy to negotiate the four-foot high fence that separated the two backyards. But by that time, other neighbors heard the yelling, and were alerted to the fact that something was happening. Lights flicked on in the windows of all the nearby houses.

Andy sprinted full-tilt to the pickup truck; his feet barely touching the ground. He jumped in and fired up the engine, threw it in drive, and jammed down on the gas pedal. The truck's tires skidded and squealed for a full two seconds before they finally caught traction. The door of the neighbor's house across the street flew open, but the truck had already torn past him, moving too quickly for the neighbor to see a license plate or get a good look at Andy.

When Andy reached the highway, and realized no one was chasing him, his heartbeat returned to a normal rhythm. He took a deep breath. He'd never had such an adrenaline rush in his life. He felt like Carl Lewis in the Olympics as he ran from that yard. He was extremely lucky. What if that neighbor had been in shape? Or what if he had decided to sneak up on him, instead of yelling out? Or what if he'd simply called the woman who lived in the house? Or what if he had called the cops?

As Andy drove on, and realized that he only knew what the first picture looked like. Pretty damaging, but not a great view of the guy's face. What if the other pictures were crap? Would the first one be enough? He urged himself to calm down. The first one was probably plenty. The wife would know her husband's body well enough to know if it was him or not. They didn't need to convince a jury here, just deliver proof to an already suspicious wife. When he got home, Andy was able to verify that there were some wonderful "action" shots, shots that left no doubt as to who was the star of the show.

The next morning Andy reported to John Stapleton. He tried not to smile as he walked into John's office, but he couldn't help himself. As a matter of course John asked, "So, how did we do?"

But he knew by the look on Andy's face he was about to hear good news.

"Well, I think there's really some great Kodak moments here, boss," Andy replied dryly.

"Oh really?" John asked as he started laughing. "Kodak moments, eh? Let me see." John taking the camera from him, and scrolled through the digital pictures. "Yes, these really are quite touching," he joked. "Kodak moments indeed. Congratulations Andy, I think you just became the Kodak Kid."

That was five years ago. Now Andy was handed his latest assignment, to get the goods on a woman named Laura Ferguson. She was an attorney who worked in Hartford, and travelled often for business. Her husband told John Stapleton she would be heading to Boston this coming weekend. So Andy would head to Beantown on Thursday and start making preparations for catching his quarry.

Chapter Eight

Monday, January 12, 2009 – 11:30 a.m.

THE HOSTESS AT the Wicked Onion Grill led Bill and Jennifer to their table for two. Bill made it a point to take Jennifer out to lunch on a monthly basis, as sort of an added bonus for her hard work. She had always done a great job for him. Supremely organized, she was always able to quickly find that important file. She kept Bill on schedule with meetings and reminders of key deadlines. Hence, the monthly lunch was his way of showing his appreciation, beyond making sure her excellent work was acknowledged in her annual reviews and yearly raises. And, in addition to the fact it seemed like good employer-employee relations, lunch with Jennifer was fun. Jennifer had a spunky personality, and in social settings her quick wit could have Bill in stitches.

She was attractive, five feet seven and slender, with blonde hair that was always well-groomed. Bill guessed she was in her early thirties, but wasn't quite sure. It was one of those things you didn't dare ask a female co-worker straight out in 2009. He knew she wasn't married. He didn't think she was dating anyone, but that was the kind of thing that could easily change from month to month. From their casual conversations Bill knew she was in the market for a husband, and wasn't into investing too much time in guys who didn't have the potential to be Mr. Right.

This lunch wasn't going to be anywhere near as lighthearted as their normal lunches. Bill needed to tell Jennifer about the demotion. He figured she had a hunch already. She was uncharacteristically quiet this day, almost subdued. Plus, the river of gossip that flowed through the executive assistants' offices ran swiftly. As soon as they placed their lunch orders, Bill got to it.

"So, I've been demoted. I've been reassigned as the deputy under Melissa Jones."

"That's the Claims Division, right?"

"Yes."

His response was angrier than Bill intended. He was doing his best not to lash out. Jennifer didn't have anything to do with his demotion. Meanwhile, it seemed to Bill that she was taking this pretty well, as if she had already made peace with it. Bill was wondering if she hadn't found out before he did. She must have gotten a heads up from one of her cohorts.

"So, how do you feel about all this?" Bill asked.

"I'm okay. It's a little surprising I guess. How do you feel?"

"Pissed off."

Ugh. Bill felt like he needed to lighten the mood somehow. "I guess every career has hiccups at times. At least I'm still employed."

"I heard Melissa is a good boss."

"She seemed okay this morning when I met with her. And Jen, you know, even if they were to can me, I'd make sure they found a spot for you. You're a dynamo."

She smiled at the compliment. "They'll never fire you Bill. You're a legend in that company. This is just a hiccup, like you said."

"Well, it's a new ballgame now with these Greystone cats." He stopped himself from saying anything more. This whole thing was his fault, and he didn't want to appear to be wallowing in self-pity. Especially not in front of Jennifer, who probably needed to hear from him that everything was going to be all right. Even though she was a much less endangered species.

"Well, no matter what happens, I'm here for you, Bill." She said it very softly and her tone caught Bill's attention. Did she have feelings for him? He had often gotten that inkling, but had dismissed the idea. He was married and he was her boss, after all. So he'd never allowed himself to think of her in that way but things were changing now with his marriage, weren't they? Jennifer was attractive, smart, fun. Maybe if he wound up getting divorced …

Their food arrived and they ate their lunches with minimal banter. Bill got his usual steak sandwich, while Jennifer usually enjoyed the Wicked Onion Grilled Chicken Caesar Salad. The mood was lighter now, the bad news having been officially announced. They could both breathe a sigh of relief, and enjoy being away from the office for a few more minutes.

Chapter Nine

Wednesday, January 14, 2009 – 12:00 p.m.

IT WAS LUNCHTIME and Bill found himself sitting at the bar at Henry's again, waiting for a bowl of French onion and a chicken salad sandwich. He caught himself tapping the bar with his fingers-- an old nervous habit he had mostly broken that still manifested when he felt especially stressed out. He had been anxious for several days now, ever since he had hired the Stapleton Detective Agency to find out if his wife was in fact having an affair. And he was still coming up to speed as to what his responsibilities would be in the Claims Division, so there were a lot of new acronyms and terminology to learn. The walk to Henry's helped clear his mind. He didn't need the exercise, he worked out regularly at the gym most mornings before work.

As he waited for his food, Bill couldn't help but think about the Laura situation and what Stapleton might be able to figure out. And he thought about what had gone wrong. Very early in their second relationship, Laura had hinted she was hoping to marry someone who was successful. She wasn't interested in the day-to-day struggle to make ends meet that many families endured. She was in law school, after all. Bill, who had no problem with hard work, took Laura's attitude as a mandate to work as much as was needed to become a corporate success, and it became his life's mission. He felt he had been tasked, and he was not about to fail the girl he was in love with, the one he was going to make his wife. Laura simply assumed there would be a certain degree of work/life balance during his climb up the ladder of success, but Bill made no such assumption. Bill figured he'd take time to smell the roses after he "made" it, but the definition of success was never clearly defined. Thus the seeds of marital destruction were sown. Bill charged ahead, working maniacally day in and day out in order to further his career, but with no real goal, and no real buy-in from Laura.

Early in the marriage, while Laura hated that Bill was a workaholic, he did compensate with lots of little gestures. He routinely brought home flowers on nights he had worked late, and took her out for late, expensive dinners on the Saturdays he spent at the office. Once a season she'd wake up on a Saturday to find her husband gone to work, but on the kitchen counter would be a note, "Sorry honey, had to work today. Enjoy this spa gift certificate; I want you even more beautiful when I come home!"

As Bill advanced in his career, the little gestures became less and less frequent. One spring, Bill bought Laura a BMW as a present, then proceeded to work eighty-hour weeks for the next two months. During that stretch, they never went out to dinner, hardly spending more than an hour together in the same room. By the time Bill's workday was done, all he wanted to do was come home and "veg." They rarely made love; Bill was too tired and Laura was too pissed off. In Bill's mind, he was just doing what he had to do to complete a crucial project, and hey, I just bought her a BMW, so that proves how I feel. By the time I get home from work, all I want to do is sleep, but I'm sure she gets that.

At this point, the Fergusons were doing quite well financially. They had joined the local country club, wore the finest clothes, and ate at the best restaurants that Hartford had to offer, when Bill made himself available for dinner. Bill assumed all those perks were keeping his wife happy. Meanwhile, Laura was absolutely miserable. Of course, she enjoyed the country club and nice clothes, but she was starting to wonder if Bill really cared about her anymore. All those hours at work … he *was* working, right? A hairline fracture had cracked the foundation of the marriage.

The following year Bill stopped calling all the time if he was going to be home late. He'd think to call, but then get engrossed in his work and forget. What the heck, Laura knew the deal, right? She knew how dedicated he was, and that he was working like crazy so they could have the good things in life. But he didn't know that Laura was starting to hate her life. Sure, she thought it was nice that Bill was making great money, but what she really craved was his companionship and his love. That was why she had married him. But she felt him to be more and more distant with each passing month. The fracture in the marriage was expanding into a crevice.

About three years ago things started to really go downhill for Laura. Bill failed to show up for a birthday dinner for her father and never called. Laura put on her best face during the dinner, but her blood was boiling. It wasn't until Bill had gotten home later that night, and Laura had given him a frigid shoulder, that Bill had finally remembered the dinner. It was way too late to do him any good. For Laura, the flowers the next day seemed like an empty gesture and Bill didn't get it--why was she so pissed? She knows we're working on a major proposal. But he didn't understand that Laura's anger had been slowly building for years, and now she'd had just about all she could take. The crevice in the foundation was widening into a canyon.

For the past two years, there was a tension just under the surface that neither could deny, nor was brave enough to address. When Bill and Laura were home at the same time, which wasn't very often, they were polite to each other but the passion was lost. Each was waiting for the other to do something magical to make it all better. In Bill's mind, as soon as the next big project was finished, he'd take Laura on a huge trip somewhere tropical and rekindle things. As soon as one big projected ended, another one started. Meanwhile Laura had resigned herself to the fact that her marriage was never going to be what she had expected. She stopped feeling sorry for herself and angrily waiting for Bill to come home, or for Bill to have a day off, or for Bill to notice her, and she started simply assuming he wasn't going to be there. She went to the gym, taking art classes, and joined a book club. She worked more and accepted a promotion at her firm that would involve a lot more travel--a promotion she probably wouldn't have taken had things been better at home.

Laura's promotion had her working shoulder-to-shoulder with some of the more powerful men in Connecticut. Men with money, looks and brains. More important, she liked the way they ogled her, they way they desired her. She felt special again, for the first time in quite a few years. Working more and traveling, she was having fun, while the only thing waiting for her at home was a broken heart.

Bill was jolted from his thoughts when the bowl of French onion was placed in front of him. He slurped it leisurely and his attention was drawn to a story on CNN. *Wow, they caught that guy already?* Bill had been following the story of a pilot who tried to fake his own death by purposely crashing his plane. He was fascinated by stories like this, and had watched his share of late night detective shows. Shows like *Forensic Files* and *City Confidential* were among his favorites. The pilot in question was a financial manager who actually owned three companies. But he had, unfortunately, been defrauding his investors for quite some time. His wife had filed for divorce, the law was closing in on him, and in a panic he had quickly thrown together a plan to try to fake his own death. Bill was assuming he must have been in a panic because, after the fact, the plan turned out to be so lame. The guy just made a number of really stupid moves that could not have been very well thought out.

I really didn't want the guy to actually get away with defrauding people who trusted him, but couldn't he have at least given the cops a run for their money? He wasn't sure why, but he had been rooting for the guy to elude capture for at least a couple of weeks before being taken into custody. Surely, that would have been more fun. But almost immediately after the plane crashed, the police surmised that the pilot had jumped from the plane.

And they also knew he had traveled to Alabama ahead of time and stashed a motorcycle in a storage unit as his getaway vehicle. How did they know that so quickly? Bill decided he would do some Googling when he got back to the office and get more insight into what had gone "wrong."

The chicken salad sandwich arrived, and Bill dug in, quickly forgetting about the pilot and his feeble plan. After polishing off the sandwich and his iced tea, Bill left his usual big tip and headed back to the office by cab.

Chapter Ten

Thursday, January 15, 2009

IT WAS AROUND ten a.m. and Bill had just finished a meeting with his new boss Melissa Jones and other senior managers in the Claims Division. He was kind of enjoying the lack of pressure associated with being the new kid on the block. Not much was expected of him yet. With only four days in the new position, it was still okay to be "coming up to speed." So, while he was still smarting from his demotion, he was starting to accept that a fresh start may not be the worst thing in the world.

In between meetings, he had a few minutes to himself and decided to follow up on the pilot story. He had been really curious as to why the guy had been caught so quickly. This was the beauty of the Internet. Information about anything was right at your fingertips, especially recent events.

One of the very first reports he found mentioned the pilot had made a distress call from the plane, saying the windshield had been destroyed and he was bleeding profusely. So military planes were scrambled in order to locate the damaged plane and try to assist. But by the time they got to the Piper PA-46 Turbo Prop, the pilot had already parachuted out. The military planes were flying next to his plane and could see the door wide open. Authorities knew before the plane ever crashed that he had parachuted out. Ouch! Then when the plane finally crashed, there was no cracked windshield, no blood, and of course, no body. But worse was the fact that the guy had left a trail of breadcrumbs leading right to his own capture. He'd left information on his escape plan, including the name of the campground he planned to hide in, right in the cockpit of the plane.

<u>Note to self. If I plan to fake my own death by crashing a plane, at the very least I'll aim it so it crashes in the ocean. Wouldn't it be a lot harder to determine whether or not anyone had been in the plane at the time of the crash? At least it would take a lot longer to figure it out. And no distress calls! If you want to disappear, wouldn't it be better to have the plane disappear as well? And for crying out loud, don't leave an escape plan in the cockpit for the police to find! What an idiot!</u>

Bill was chuckling to himself when he was jolted back to reality as the phone on his desk rang. The caller ID revealed it was a call from home.

"Bill, it's Laura. I'm calling to let you know that I'm leaving on that trip to Boston this afternoon instead of tomorrow-- the client requested we come up a day early so we can have some meetings tomorrow morning. I know, the whole trip, it's kind of weird, but the customer wants us to meet with him on Saturday also, because someone he wants us to meet can only be there then."

Yeah right, well I don't suppose we can disappoint the "client," now can we? "Oh, okay. Sorry to hear it. I guess I'll have to be the Lone Ranger until Sunday."

"Yep. Okay—good bye, I'll call you tonight."

It was weird, for a couple that wasn't really a couple anymore, Bill and Laura were strangely cordial to each other. It was just habit really, neither had grown up with much drama, so it was normal for them to be polite. Bill was conflicted--part of him hoped things would ultimately work out, but deep down he didn't believe there would be a happy ending.

Bill picked up the phone and called the Stapleton Detective Agency. "John Stapleton, please."

After a short time on hold, John Stapleton came on the line. "Yes Bill, what can I do for you?"

"I'm just calling to confirm that Laura is going to be in Boston this weekend. If fact, she's leaving today."

"Ah, okay, thanks for the info. Stay tuned, I'll give you a call early next week."

John asked for a quick call once Laura's plans were confirmed. Bill took that to mean that they might try to catch her in the act this weekend. *Wouldn't that be awesome if I got results that quickly? Because waiting for more info is driving me nuts!*

Chapter Eleven

Friday, January 16, 2009

IT'S A PRETTY easy two-hour drive from Hartford to Boston. Andy began the trek in the early afternoon so he'd get to Boston before rush hour. His adrenaline was pumping, he was about to go to work, and few were better at his kind of work. As he headed for the luxurious Concord Arms Hotel in Boston, he silently reviewed what he knew about the case.

His new target was a woman named Laura Ferguson, a married litigator who often took business trips with her boss, Jonas Worthington. Laura's husband Bill had hired the Stapleton Agency to find out if his wife was having an affair. He claimed to be ninety-percent sure, and really just wanted the Stapleton Agency to confirm his suspicions. Andy had learned over the last five years that most people who suspected something was amiss regarding a loved one were usually dead on. The client didn't know who his spouse might be having an affair with, but cold logic suggested it was someone at Laura's firm since she was spending so much time at work. That included at least a couple of evenings a week, and occasional weekends, plus traveling. Bill had mentioned Laura took frequent business trips to Boston where her firm had a major client. He also was pretty sure she usually stayed at the Concord Arms Hotel.

John Stapleton had suggested they wait for Laura's next trip to Boston and do surveillance there. John's theory was that lots of people were more discreet in their hometown than when traveling, where fewer people knew them. Their behavior would be much more guarded at home, where the possibility of running into a neighbor or a friend was always a risk. Early in his career he had been taken aback by how brazen the public displays of affection by cheaters became when they took their show on the road, assuming no one was watching them in a distant town. They think, "Here where no one knows us, we can behave like, well, like us." John's firm had brought its clients the goods many, many times using this simple principle.

Andy had started off peeking in windows in order to capture his Pulitzer-worthy images. But in the intervening years, he had acquired much more sophisticated techniques and equipment for recording extracurricular activity on film. He relished the successes of his devious ploys.

A quick phone call to the hotel revealed that Laura was in fact booked into the Concord Arms. There was nothing worse than staking out a hotel lobby for hours on end only to find out it was the wrong place. The next step would be to get her room number, and that of her probable partner. If he knew for sure her room was where any misdeeds would occur, then his job would be easier. But what if they mostly stayed in his room, assuming of course there was cheating going on? Why assume the cheating was with a man, thought Andy, lightheartedly scolding himself for his own assumption. He'd seen it go that other way a couple of times, women leaving their husbands for other women, and men leaving their wives for other men. Not too often, but it did happen.

At about four p.m., Andy pulled into the hotel parking lot and fetched his bags from the car. He had two suitcases, one with his clothes and the other with some special equipment. He walked to the front desk and checked in. His reservation was for two nights, just in case he needed the second night to get the goods. Usually, he didn't. He wanted to be in the lobby by about four-thirty in case the lawyers knocked off early and came back to the hotel to freshen up before dinner. So he unpacked, and helped himself to a beer from the mini-fridge. What the hell, it was on the customer's dime.

At about four-twenty, he headed back to the lobby. Before doing anything else, he checked in with hotel security, making it known that he was a legitimate PI working a case, so when they noticed him hanging around he wouldn't be hassled. John Stapleton trained all his detectives to always check in with local law enforcement or security whenever appropriate. Andy had learned the hard way the pain involved with ignoring that particular guideline. As a relatively green detective, Andy had once decided to stake out a hotel lobby sans communication with hotel security. After three patient hours, the subject finally arrived in the lobby, and almost simultaneously, the hotel dicks swooped in on Andy, hauling him off to a back room for lengthy questioning. He had blown the case because the hotel would not cooperate with him after that. They didn't trust him. And when Stapleton found out what happened, he hit the roof. Andy nearly lost his job. He never made that mistake again.

At any rate, Andy needed to find out who the lover was, and his or her room number, in order to cover his bases. He decided to stake out the lobby and wait for Laura Ferguson. He found a chair in the lobby situated so he could see anyone entering the building and heading for the elevators. He would watch for Laura, and hope she had lover boy in tow when she came back from wherever she was. She had checked in yesterday according to her husband. Andy found a spot near a wall outlet, plugged in his laptop, and brought up the photo of Laura that Stapleton had emailed to him. He studied the picture for a minute or two, then minimized it so he could quickly display it if he wanted to double-check anyone in the lobby against the picture. Laura was comely, so he was pretty sure he'd recognize her.

Around six p.m., Laura arrived but unfortunately, she was alone. Andy recognized her immediately--she looked even better than the picture. *Well, she's probably coming back from work or something.* He decided to stay put for a while and see what happened. There was an excellent chance she'd simply get cleaned up and then head out for dinner with her beau. *Even cheaters on business trips need to eat, Andy chuckled to himself.*

Ha! About an hour later Laura entered the lobby from the elevators, accompanied by a distinguished-looking man who appeared to be in his mid-forties. Jonas Worthington I presume? He wasn't sure, since the law firm Laura worked for didn't display photographs of the attorneys, only short bios listing credentials and experience. Andy slipped the laptop into its carrying case and sauntered off toward the couple, pretending to be buzzed.

"Excuse me—Roger? Aren't you Roger Jones from Milwaukee?" asked Andy, beaming from ear to ear.

The startled man answered, "No, I'm sorry, you've got the wrong guy."

Andy faked being crestfallen. "Oh, oh, okay—you look just like my old friend Roger ..." Then Andy smiled and asked again, this time with a wink, as if he was just kidding, "You're sure you're name isn't Roger, right?"

"Yes, I'm quite sure. My name is Preston."

"Preston Jones?"

"Preston Malloy."

"Well have a nice evening, sorry to have bothered you."

Andy made his way to the bathroom, amazed at how often that little trick worked. The problem now was - who was Preston Malloy? Of course, just because Laura had met this dude in the lobby didn't mean he was her lover, but he was a wild card now. Was there a Preston Malloy at Hutchins, Bronson and Wilder?

Andy went back to the lobby and got the laptop out of the case. Bringing up a web browser, he clicked on his bookmark for Laura's law firm. *Hmmm.* There was no Preston Malloy listed in the company's online directory. No Prestons at all. Well, if he was a prominent attorney, he would come up in a Google search for Hartford. Bingo! Whoa, Preston Malloy was listed as an Assistant District Attorney for Hartford County. A mildly interesting tidbit. Was Laura sleeping with a semi-celebrity?

Now that he had both names, he needed the room numbers in order to really get the goods. He dialed the number of his favorite caller ID spoofing service, a service that allowed his call to appear to come from any number he chose. He dialed the service, and when prompted for the number he wanted to call, he entered the hotel number. Next, he was prompted for the number he wanted to appear on the caller ID display at the hotel. He entered 555–763–4000, the number for the Boston Police Department. He had tested this number before making the trip, so he was confident the caller ID would display "Boston Police Dept" as expected.

"Hello, this is the Concord Arms, Joann speaking, how may I be of assistance?" said the polite, but slightly nervous-sounding voice on the other end.

"Yes, hello Joann, this is Detective Corcoran with the Boston Police. We are conducting a routine investigation and I need your help with a couple of room numbers of two persons of interest presently staying at your hotel." He paused for a couple of seconds and there was dead silence on the other end. Andy smiled. "Now Joann, just for my records, could I trouble you for your last name please?"

"My last name is Williamson."

"Got it, Joann Williamson. Thank you so much for your cooperation. You are really saving me some valuable man hours on this one." He paused again. Silence, Joann was listening intently. *This is too much fun.* "Now Joann, I need the room numbers for Mr. Jonas Worthington, Mrs. Laura Ferguson, and Mr. Preston Malloy. And while you're at it, can I get the name of your supervisor? I want to make sure I let him or her know just how much help you've been."

"Okay, I'm going to place you on hold for just one moment Detective and retrieve your information."

This was always a tense moment for Andy. He could never be sure if the receptionist really bought his act. So far, he had gotten full cooperation from any woman that he had talked to, but a few guys had been more "by the book," not willing to give up room numbers without first seeing a badge in person. There was a small chance that Joann was on the other line to the Boston Police Department, verifying that there was in fact a Detective Corcoran, or that her supervisor was intervening behind the scenes. And sometimes, the targets would check into the hotels with different names, although Andy didn't expect that in this case because the probable affair was being "covered" by a legitimate business trip.

"Detective?"

"Yes, I'm still here."

A DEVIOUS PLAN 71

"Okay, first my supervisor's name is James Stanley. And the room number for Mr. Malloy is 1218. Mrs. Ferguson is staying in room 1230. We have no Worthingtons listed at this hotel."

"Excellent work Joann! I really appreciate you taking the time to help me out; I'm sure you're quite busy. I'll make sure I put in a call to Mr. Stanley to let him know what a great help you've been!"

Andy hung up, beaming from ear to ear. He could probably get in a lot of trouble for stunts like this, claiming over the phone to be a police detective, but there was very, very little chance anyone would ever connect the dots and figure out how he had gotten the room numbers.

Chapter Twelve

THE NEXT PHASE of the operation required fairly precise timing. Andy had one male and one female operative at the ready. Both were very attractive, and dressed to look like successful corporate lawyers. Each was to wait for instructions at a Starbucks about a block from the hotel. Steve, the male operative, was about forty-five, and he was to get the first call. Andy dialed Steve's cell phone number.

"Hello, Steve? Okay, here's what I need you to do. For the next fifteen minutes, you are Preston Malloy, a hot-shot attorney. So go to the front desk, introduce yourself as Preston, and explain that you left your room key in your room, room 1218, and you need a duplicate. Then bring me the key in room 1114. Oh, and also, make sure you are helped by someone other than Joann, and get that person's name."

"Preston" attempting to get the key from Joann would probably be okay, but Andy felt it was prudent to avoid her since she might remember the name and associate it with his fake police inquiry. In Andy's experience, a well-dressed, attractive person who knew his or her room number wouldn't have to verify whom they were to score a duplicate key from a member of the opposite sex. Only the hotel guest was supposed to know the room number. Andy wasn't too worried; Steve had served in this capacity before and had been successful.

About ten minutes later, Steve knocked on the door of room 1114, Andy's room. He walked in, produced the key to room 1218, and collected his cash. Andy smiled, thanked him, and then placed his call to Cindy, his second operative. He gave her the same spiel, asking her to get help from a male at the front desk, but if that wasn't possible then try to avoid being helped by Joann or Kathy, the woman who had helped Steve.

Timing here was critical. Andy had to get the room numbers, secure the keys, and plant the cameras before the targets got back from dinner. He was never sure just how much time he was going to have. In most cases there was sufficient time, but sometimes the targets went out for a quick slice of pizza and were back within the hour. Sometimes they didn't come back until the next day.

After twenty anxious minutes, there was a knock on the door. Finally, it was Cindy, key in hand. Andy was relieved, and Cindy volunteered she was just getting ready to ask for help from one of the women before a young male manager finally started helping at the front desk.

"Good work, excellent job. And yes, any longer would have been too long, so it would have been the right thing to do to just get help from one of the women. We do this kind of operation fairly frequently, so I'm sure I'll use you again."

Andy handed her the money, bid her a fond adieu, and got moving on the next step.

The next phase of the operation would be quick and easy. He left his room carrying a Macy's shopping bag, as if he was a tourist who had just returned from shopping. He started up the stairs toward room 1218, Preston's room. As he walked up the stairs, he pulled out his cell phone and asked for room 1218. The front desk put his call through, and just as he expected, no one answered. If someone answered, he would have to abort the mission, of course. At that moment, it occurred to him that he should have also made that call using the spoof service. If someone did answer, his cell phone number would be on the caller ID. Not good. Since he started using the spoofing service, he didn't bother with a second cell phone for operations. But he had to remember to use it!

Andy entered the hallway and leisurely strolled toward room 1218, making sure not to make eye contact with the woman who passed on her way to the elevator. He opened the door to the room. Moving quickly, he went to the bedroom of the two-room suite, and pulled a completely innocuous-looking potted plant out of the Macy's bag. He placed it on the dresser, angling the plant toward the bed. He had done this kind of thing many times. This was no ordinary potted plant. He really didn't know what kind of plant it was supposed to be, nor did he care. It was attractive and looked real. There was a tiny camera hidden in flower petals that would transmit a video feed over the Internet to a pre-specified IP address. So Andy could be anywhere in the world that had an Internet connection and watch the video. In this case, he'd simply be watching from his hotel room on the 11th floor.

Once the camera was situated in Malloy's room, Andy made the call to Laura's room to make sure no one was there. This time he made sure he used the spoofing service when he made the call. As expected, there was no answer. He hustled down the hall into her room and put the camera plant in a strategic spot. With both cameras in place, he walked quickly back down the stairs to his room on the 11th floor. Outwardly he appeared to be very calm, but on the inside he was very excited. Things had gone extremely well!

Back in his room, Andy got situated. First, he booted up the laptop, and set up a browser for each of the plant cameras. He placed the browsers side by side so he could see Ferguson's room and Malloy's room simultaneously. He set things up to record the videos to the laptop's hard drive as well. That was critical, there had to be a copy to show the client. It was also good, in case he fell asleep; he could review things on fast-forward in the morning if it was a late night for the cheaters. He set the laptop off to the side where he could see it out of the corner of his eye.

With the surveillance in order, Andy called room service and ordered dinner--prime rib with potatoes, a Caesar salad and a beer. Then he ordered up the movie, "The Dark Knight." He was ready to hunker down and wait for the festivities. It was always more exciting to witness the cheating live then to have to review the video in the morning.

Chapter Thirteen

Saturday, January 17, 2009 – 1:00 p.m.

"BILL, YOU PLAYED great today; let's add these up and get an official score," said Barry Wilkins, a long time golf partner of Bill's. They had played many rounds together over the years at Mohegan Country Club.

"I'm pretty sure I was four over, but you can double check my math," replied Bill.

"Yep, four over, seventy six. Great score for this time of year. I shot an eighty on the nose."

"Laura has been out of town a lot, so I've been playing some, and hitting the range a lot, weather permitting."

"Yeah, we got lucky today, mid-forties, can't beat that in January."

"And no snow on the ground."

The golfers clinked their beer filled glasses in minor celebration.

Bill glanced at his watch, seven minutes after one. "Not too bad—played it in three hours. You slowed us down a bit when you hacked up number eleven with that triple."

"Yeah, well, you know … I got behind that tree and … eh … yep, pretty well hacked it up."

They both chuckled. The lunches they had ordered while sitting in their golf cart at the eighteenth tee arrived. And they ordered another round of beers. There were a few moments of silence while the hungry golfers attacked their food.

When the hunger began to dissipate, Bill asked Barry, "So, how is the family? How is Celeste?"

"Celeste is great. We are doing well. The kids are growing like weeds."

"Is Philip still playing baseball?"

"No, he's more interested in lacrosse now. So any golf I get to play this spring will be snuck in, in between lacrosse practices and tournaments. And Janie is into soccer now, so we'll be running around doing that too."

"Sounds like fun," said Bill, realizing he was a little jealous.

"It is fun. Hectic, but fun." said Barry with a smile.

"How is your, eh, situation," asked Barry.

"It's weird. And it's probably coming to a head soon. Something has to give I guess."

"Well, hang in there man. If you need anything, don't hesitate."

"Thanks man, I appreciate that. I'll let you know."

Then, out of the blue, Barry asked, "Have you been following this crazy story about the pilot who crashed his own plane?"

"Yes, I did see something about that, what an idiot!"

"I can't imagine what motivates people to do stuff like that."

"I guess things have gone badly for them and they are looking for a fresh start."

"I guess, pretty lame plan though."

Bill laughed heartily. "Yes, I agree one hundred percent. Terrible plan."

It had been nice for Bill to forget about his own problems for a few hours, but for some reason, talk of the pilot brought him right back to his own ugly reality. He'd been embarrassed at work, and now believed his wife was having an affair. The idea of starting over somewhere else wasn't the worst one he'd ever heard.

"All right man, I've got to roll. Got to get Janie to a birthday party this afternoon."

"I think I'm going to hang out and have one more beer. Say hello to Celeste for me."

The friends shook hands, and Barry scurried back to his busy life.

The fourth round of five of the Bob Hope Desert Classic was being played on the flat screen above the bar in the grill room of the club. Bill decided to have one more beer and watch for a while. He knew he was just delaying the inevitable, heading home to the empty house. There was no rush. He was halfway through his third beer, which was a lot for him, when his mind began to wander. He thought it was weird that Barry had mentioned the pilot story again. It seemed like every day something brought his attention to it.

Hmmm. If I wanted to fake my own death, how would I go about it? I don't have my pilot's license, so there would be no plane crashes! What about a car explosion? Or maybe a car fire? I could get the same kind of vehicle I have now, and blow it up in front of my house! Or set it on fire! No, that wouldn't work. It would have to be my actual car. A duplicate car would have a different VIN. But then there is still the issue of a body. Even if I somehow "acquired" a body, wouldn't the police be able to figure out pretty quickly that it wasn't actually me? I've heard the phrase "body burned beyond recognition," but what about dental records? Hmmm. Do teeth burn in a really intense fire?

And say I solve the "body problem," then I still have issues. Okay, I'm alive, everyone thinks I'm dead, now what do I do? I'd have to have a new identity already in place. With enough planning, maybe I could already establish a new identity, with all the paperwork, before I "died." There is a lot of insurance money, but that would all go to Laura. I'd have to partner with her in order to get the money? Or steal it from her after the insurance company paid off? How cruel would that be? Let her think I'm dead, and then steal all the money ...

Bill chuckled for a few seconds at that one. He was pretty sure she was having an affair, but even under those circumstances he wasn't sure he was capable of being that much of a dick.

Chapter Fourteen

Tuesday, January 20, 2009 – 10:00 a.m.

"BILL, I HAVE a Mr. Jones on line two." Bill's secretary Jennifer's voice came through over the phone, sounding puzzled.

"Okay, put him through."

This was a call Bill had been both anxiously waiting for and dreading at the same time. It wasn't actually Mr. Jones, but John Stapleton, the private investigator Bill had hired to find out if Laura was, in fact, having an affair.

"I've got some information for you, Mr. Ferguson. I think we should meet in my office. I'm free until about two-thirty, can you make it in by then?"

"How about in half an hour?" Bill replied. "I'll take my lunch now."

"Works for me—see you then."

Bill pushed the button on his phone to reach his secretary. "Jennifer, I'm going to be out of the office and unavailable for an hour or two."

"Oh, okay, Bill."

John Stapleton's office was just a few blocks away, so Bill decided to walk despite the cold weather. His heart was pounding, his mouth was dry, and he figured the walk would do him some good. He was pretty sure he knew what the information was going to be. Part of him wanted to be right, and a part of him wanted to be wrong. But mostly, he wanted to be right. Being right would confirm his instincts had been correct. He hadn't really thought that much about how he might feel if Laura wasn't having an affair. Now as he was walking along, he realized he'd probably feel relieved, and also pretty foolish. It would be a bit embarrassing, but only on the inside as he had not confided his suspicions to anyone other than John Stapleton, who was mostly a stranger. His pal, Barry, knew things weren't great, but Bill had never gotten into specifics.

Bill looked up at 2022 Amherst Street, an old brownstone that had been converted into a small office building. The building housed just a couple of tenants, including the Stapleton Detective Agency. Bill fought off a slight temptation to put the meeting off. *Don't think, just go.* He opened the door to the brownstone, walked up the stairs to the second floor, and knocked on the door to suite number five. An attractive young lady answered the door. Bill had been to the office once before, but didn't recognize her.

"Oh hello, you must be Mr. Ferguson. Mr. Stapleton is waiting for you."

Bill followed her back to Stapleton's office.

It was the office of a very busy man—not dirty, but it was cluttered. It wasn't dingy, but the cinder block walls could stand a new coat of paint. Three bookshelves dominated the wall to the left, and were completely filled with books, manila folders, and knick-knacks. There were cardboard boxes stacked on top of each bookshelf. A sad-looking plant sat on the windowsill behind Stapleton. Three filing cabinets were lined up on the wall to the right. All were bursting at the seams, if the one open drawer was any indication of what the other drawers contained. And there were files stacked on top of the filing cabinets. No room inside, Bill guessed. Or no time to organize them. And Stapleton's desk had three separate stacks of files on it.

"Bill, please come in, have a seat. Would you like water or coffee or anything?"

"Water would be great," said Bill, whose mouth was as dry as sawdust.

"Jill, could you bring Bill a bottle of water please?"

Bill took his coat off and slung it over the back of his chair. He smelled coffee, there was some freshly made, and poured, probably into the coffee cup in front of John Stapleton. Before he was seated, Jill was back with the water. She closed the door gently behind her as she left the office. But to Bill, it was a very loud click. His senses were heightened.

With only a nod, John slid a business-sized brown envelope across the desk to where Bill could reach it. He took a deep breath.

Go on, already. You know what's in it.

He undid the metal clasp that bound the envelope shut. He reached his hand in and pulled out a stack of photos. He rifled through a few of the photos, which clearly showed his wife and another man ... together. It felt like he had been punched in the gut. Suddenly, he felt kind of dizzy, kind of queasy. He was surprised at his physical reaction, since he had pretty much known what to expect. Yet it was one thing to believe your spouse is having an affair, and another thing entirely to be hit between the eyes with physical, tangible, undeniable proof.

John had learned long ago not to say too much, there was really nothing he could say to make the wronged spouse feel any better. He always gave his clients some space so they could process what they were seeing. His policy in this situation was to let the client speak first.

After a few minutes, Bill finally muttered, "That bitch. That fucking bitch. I suspected something was going on, but it's different to actually see it," said Bill, not looking up from the photographs.

"I understand. It's kind of like the death of someone close to you who has been ill. Even if you expect it, it's still pretty shocking when it actually happens."

Bill muttered, "Death is right. I'm staring at the death of a marriage right here." There wasn't a clear picture of the guy Laura was with, but somehow he looked vaguely familiar.

"Who's the guy?"

"Honestly, I don't know. He could be anybody, really. Finding that out would be a separate job. And maybe not the best thing? You're the client, I can't tell you what to do, but focusing on your situation first might be better."

"Meaning you don't want to be party to me shooting the fucker after you told me who he is?"

"Well, something like that. If you really have to know and haven't found out in a week on your own, then we can talk. If you kill the guy in cold blood after some time goes by, well then, that's really on you at that point."

"Point taken. Well, I guess there isn't much more to say is there? You did an excellent job, John."

"Thank you. And thank you for saying that. It's surprising how many people want to shoot the messenger."

The Stapleton Agency had done a very good job. They had confirmed Bill's suspicions quickly and efficiently. And as he shuffled out of John

Stapleton's office, Bill began wondering what the hell he was going to do next.

Chapter Fifteen

BILL LEFT STAPLETON'S office in a fog. What to do now? Part of him felt he wasn't ready to confront Laura yet. This was obviously going to end in divorce. Maybe it was better to keep his knowledge of the affair quiet for now as an ace in the hole. He wasn't sure that made sense. Another part of him wanted to simply explode. Go get a shotgun and smoke them both, the fuckers. No pun intended.

I'm not thinking clearly at all. I better go somewhere and just relax. No way can I work right now.

Bill pulled out his cell phone and called Jennifer. "Hey Jen, I've got a personal matter I have to attend to this afternoon, so I won't be back in the office today. I should be back in tomorrow, though."

"Uh, okay Bill, I'll let everyone know. Is everything all right?"

"Yeah, everything is fine, I'm just a little under the weather."

Standing on the sidewalk outside of Stapleton's building, he realized he was only a couple of blocks from the Blarney Stone, a fabulous Irish pub. And he suddenly realized he hadn't eaten yet either. He sauntered the two blocks and entered the pub with two goals in mind. First, get something to eat. Second, get absolutely smashed.

Bill sat at a table near the bar. The lunch crowd was starting to thin. He ordered a shot of Finnegan, his favorite Irish whiskey, a Smithwicks draft, and a plate of bangers and mash. As much as he liked Guinness, he absolutely loved Smithwicks straight from the keg. Famished, he polished off the food and drink in front of him in no time. Not ready to leave, he ordered a second shot and a second Smithwicks. Needless to say, he was feeling considerably more relaxed. About half way into his second Smithwicks, the "wonder pilot" story flashed on the TV above the bar.

Bah, this moron again. Okay. I'll bet I could fake a death ten times better than that idiot.

He began pondering what it might take to actually pull something like that off. There were several challenges. How could he make it so everyone assumed he was dead, including any insurance companies, when there was no body? And what would he do afterward? Obviously, it would be best to have an identity already established. Hell, if he was organized enough, and timed things right, could he even have a job under his new name, in his new city, waiting for him when he "died?" A place to live already established? Maybe he'd have to lead a double life for a couple of weeks to really get things set up.

He could have a bank account, car, an apartment already established. But first things first, how do you establish a new identity? Is that the kind of thing you can Google? Or maybe there were ads in the back of *Soldier of Fortune*. Is that still a magazine? He had heard of people establishing new identities by using the name of someone who had died as a baby, but would be about the same age as the identity "borrower." But he had heard those stories years ago. All those loopholes had been closed already—right?

But the key question is this. Say I manage to pull it off, fake my death, and establish a new identity in a new city. Say the insurance company pays off. Could I make a deal with Laura to split the money? And if so, could I trust her to deliver? To keep quiet? Of course, I'm in a position of power at the moment, with my proof that Laura is cheating. But even if I blackmail her into cooperating, she might eventually spill the beans ...

"Oh yes, another Smithwicks, thank you."

Without a plan for getting the money, there doesn't seem to be much point to all this.

He pulled out the notepad he kept in the inside pocket of his suit jacket. He began scribbling his "to do" list.

A DEVIOUS PLAN 91

1. Figure out the appropriate "death."
2. Establish a new identity in a new city.
3. Figure out how to get the money from Laura after the insurance pays off.

Bill noted his list was not necessarily in order of action or importance. It was a pretty short list. And yet, it was a daunting one. But ultimately, what did it matter? It was a fun afternoon, getting drunk and scheming and plotting. He knew he would never actually do any of this.

Chapter Sixteen

BEING QUITE DRUNK, Bill decided to leave his car at the office and take a cab home. It was around five p.m., and it seemed very strange to be home this early on a weekday. He rarely got home before dark, even in the summer. Laura was not home, which was not surprising. Up until this past year, Bill rarely got home before eight p.m. So, even before her affair, Laura had learned how to fill up her early evenings by taking classes, working out, and any number of other activities. *How long has the affair been going on, anyway?* Bill went to the kitchen and grabbed a bottle of water. *Better hydrate.*

He sat down in the kitchen and noticed the stack of bills on the table. It struck him that he hadn't really sat down and written out many checks in the last ten years. Managing the couple's monthly budget had been Laura's job. *Well, I guess I better start thinking about that. Of course, you can do that sort of thing all online now. But Laura still writes checks out every month doesn't she? I guess when you've been doing it that way for that long, you just keep doing it unless something forces you to change.*

He picked up the stack of envelopes and began sifting through. They had all been opened. Laura had obviously given them a once over before she went out. There was the electric bill, the cable bill, the telephone bill, etc. He was glad Laura had been taking care of this mundane stuff all these years. When he was single, it bored him to tears to write out the checks. So he put it off. And as a result, his payments were sometimes late. Laura was definitely better at the day-to-day minutiae of life. He had really needed a partner like that.

Just beneath the Nordstrom's bill were three statements from the bank. One was the statement for their joint checking and savings accounts, the second was Bill's personal checking account, and the third was Laura's checking account. Most of Bill's pay wound up in either the joint checking or the savings account. He kept a balance of around two thousand dollars in his own checking account for incidentals or emergencies. It was a relatively modest amount given the fact that he was a vice president at a successful insurance company. Bill slid Laura's checking account statement out of the envelope. *Hey, you gotta do what you gotta do. There may be a war coming. This is my chance to get some information before she knows I'm wise to her.*

Bill's jaw hit the floor when he saw the balance, $75,634.83. He looked again, it wasn't $7,000?

Nope. No doubt about it, 75K. *Holy crap. Wow, I've really had my head up my ass on this one.* Not only was she having an affair, but it appeared that she was squirreling away money as well. Apparently she was taking full advantage of the fact that he really didn't pay attention to the day-to-day business of the household. Bill had always been content to simply watch their quarterly net worth statements increasing regularly. The big picture stuff.

So, not only has she been cheating on me, but also the bitch must be planning to leave! Bill was sobering up now, fast. Their system had always been if too much money wound up in one of the checking accounts, they would invest it in one of their mutual funds, or at least put it in the savings account. And it was Laura who had always initiated these conversations, naturally since she was aware of the amounts in the checking accounts on a day-to-day basis. And now it hit home, there had not been a conversation like that in, what? Two years? Bill had been so detached he rarely talked to Laura about much of anything. *Okay, maybe I haven't been the greatest husband but I don't deserve this!*

Suddenly, Bill noticed that he felt awful. His buzz had worn off and he was tired and had a headache from the booze. Plus now he was half-crazed with anger. *I better not be here when she comes home, which might be soon. I need a place to rest and think. If I'm going to somehow use this information as leverage, I'm going to have to keep it close to the vest. But if she walked through that door right now, I'd explode.*

Bill took the bank statement and made a copy of it on the printer in his home office. Then, heading back to the kitchen, he placed Laura's bank statement into its original envelope, and then put all the bills back into a stack resembling the one he had originally found. He grabbed another bottle of water from the refrigerator and quickly bounded upstairs. Finding the Motrin in the medicine cabinet in the bathroom of the master suite, he took two for his headache, and then dumped a pair of pajamas, some assorted casual clothes and his travel shaving kit into a duffel bag. Not wanting to be sitting at home waiting for a taxi cab when Laura arrived, he headed on foot for Tammy's, a local restaurant a few blocks away where he and Laura went for dinner occasionally on Saturday evenings.

Bill got to Tammy's and headed straight for the bar. It felt a little odd walking into the restaurant carrying a duffel bag, but no one seemed to notice.

"Hi, how are you? I'd like a menu and a Coke please."

He thought he'd eat first, and then call a cab to take him to the Yorkshire Hotel, right across from Greystone Insurance downtown. *Gotta remember to call home in an hour or so and say I'm working late, maybe really late.* He had stayed in the Yorkshire Hotel a couple of times after some very late nights at the office. So his not coming home once in a while wasn't unprecedented. And with what he knew now, he doubted Laura would care anyway.

Bill ordered a club sandwich and another Coke to wash it down. He tried to remember what he had been working on at the office before his meeting with Stapleton, but it felt like several days had gone by since then. He was beginning to think he'd had enough of that place, but he had no idea what he might do instead. The insurance business was all he knew at this point. After polishing off the sandwich, he was beginning to feel better.

"I'm ready for the check, and could I trouble you to call me a cab?" Bill asked the bartender.

"Yeah, the cab is good idea, you were hitting those Cokes pretty hard," joked the bartender.

They both chuckled.

Bill arrived at the hotel lobby with just his duffel bag and the suit he had been wearing since the morning. *If I go to work tomorrow, I'll just have to wear the same suit. Ah, no problem, I can just iron the shirt if I have to and no one will notice. Besides, I'll probably blow off work tomorrow anyway.*

Still kind of looped when he packed the duffel bag, he really hadn't put much thought into what to bring. It was about six-thirty in the evening. Using his cell phone, he called the house and left the "I'm going to be working very, very late and may not even make it home" message. Not surprisingly, he got the answering machine.

Bill changed out of his suit and into a tee shirt and sweat pants. He hung his suit up in the closet, just in case he decided to go to work in the morning. As he was hanging up the suit pants, he found the copy of Laura's checking account statement he had made before leaving the house. He looked at it once more in disbelief.

Tomorrow is Wednesday, right? Laura goes to work around nine-ish, maybe I'll just go home and do some snooping. I wonder if the password to her Yahoo account is still the same? I could always test that now with the laptop ... but, probably best to wait until I'm certain she won't be near the computer ... patience! Gotta wait until tomorrow.

Over the course of his gut-wrenching afternoon, Bill made a decision. Obviously, Laura was over. She had decided it, and now he concurred. And his once stellar career was now in shambles as far as he was concerned. He had no interest in working doggedly again to regain his stature at the insurance company. Been there, done that. It was time to create an easier life. And a detailed plan began to germinate in his mind.

Chapter Seventeen

THE PLAN STARTED coming together when Bill realized he knew Laura's Yahoo email password. He had set up all her online accounts and passwords. As intelligent as she was, she wasn't very computer savvy. She had just never bothered much with technology. So, Bill was pretty certain he still knew her banking password. He would, of course, test this theory in the morning, but if she hadn't changed her passwords, then he'd have access to her bank accounts.

And the point, of course, was if he successfully faked his own death, and Laura collected the life insurance money, he could access her account online and set up a transfer to another bank account. Bingo bango, he'd be rich. Like many forty-year-old guys, Bill was worth more dead than alive. There was a three million dollar life insurance policy on him. With that money, or at least some of it, he could move to an island somewhere in the tropics. A place with lots of sun, lots of boats, and lots of tiny umbrellas that go perfectly in fancy drinks. And lots of golf courses—don't forget the golf!

Bill wanted something sweet to eat now. He called room service and ordered a piece of chocolate cake and a bottle of water. He was fried, and he didn't want to think anymore. Conveniently it was eight o'clock, and the old movie, *Die Hard*, one of his favorites, was just coming on. He hadn't watched it in quite some time, so he figured 'what the heck.' Have dessert and vegetate watching one of the modern classics. Well, at least it was a classic to him.

Wednesday morning, he awoke to an infomercial hawking the latest abdominal workout machine. The last thing he remembered about the movie was Bruce Willis saying Bill's favorite movie line of all time, "Yippee-ki-yay, motherfucker." Great line in the context of the movie. He grabbed his watch; it said seven a.m. Wow—it was late, he'd slept for ten hours!

Jennifer got in around eight a.m.; he'd call to let her know he wasn't coming in to work because he was "sick." So he had an hour to kill. He took a shower, threw on some jeans and a golf shirt, and headed down to the hotel restaurant for some breakfast.

Just after eight he went back up to his room and called Jennifer, who wasn't surprised by the call because on a normal day, Bill would beat her to the office. So she knew something was up. He said he had a stomach "thing" and thought it would be better if he just stayed home.

Laura left for work around nine a.m., so he figured he'd go to the house around ten. She'd be gone to work by then for sure. His plan was to test and make sure he still knew her email and banking passwords. He'd check online and look at all their bank accounts. There could easily be more he didn't know. Also, he would search the house for anything that might be of interest with respect to his wife.

What about this evening? It'll be weird if she comes home and I'm already home. I'll come back here, put my suit back on, and head home at my normal time.

Bill called the front desk and booked his room for one more night, even though he'd only need it until about eight this evening.

And he'd had a new thought regarding the fake death. He wondered if it wouldn't be easier to stage a foul play situation, as opposed to a case where there really should be a body and there wasn't one. Or somehow use a different body. His instincts told him it would be really hard to trick a forensics team into concluding that someone else's charred remains were actually his. But what if the police happened upon a scene where there had been a struggle, and there was a blood trail? All his belongings would be left behind, and it would appear that someone had taken him by force. Or killed him and transported his body elsewhere.

Hmmm. Could he somehow systematically "gather" his own blood over a period a time, and then use it for a really bloody crime scene? Can you freeze blood to keep it "fresh?" They could tell if the blood was old, couldn't they? There could be a concentrated puddle where he'd been killed, then a trail leading to some tire tracks. He could use an old carpet, put a bunch of blood on it, and then drag it to where a fake vehicle would be, as if his body had been dragged. Freaking brilliant! He was enjoying this idea immensely.

Of course, there were other problems to solve. How to get the blood from himself safely? And what about storage? But these seemed solvable. If he was able to create a really bloody crime scene, then maybe the police wouldn't necessarily need a body to conclude that he was dead. If you lose a certain amount of blood, you have to die right? So part of the puzzle was to figure how much blood was too much to lose and still survive.

Another question: Who was going to kill him? He really didn't have any enemies. And although he was doing very well as a VP at a large insurance firm, he would hardly be the target of any underworld types. Could he manufacture a fictitious "beef" with someone, which eventually escalates into murder? That seemed a bit farfetched. It would probably be pretty easy for the authorities to see through a fake beef. It would probably be better just to leave it a mystery as to who killed him. Even when the police failed to discover any known enemies or motive, they wouldn't be able to ignore a bloody crime scene that pointed to his death.

With roughly two hours before he felt comfortable going home, he figured this was a good time to start laying out the plan that was in his head. He noted to himself that he'd need a base of operations to collect his blood, etc. Bill figured he would need to acquire, or do, the following things, in order to carry out his master plan. He jotted them down:

- an apartment as a base of operations
- a gun, and learn how to shoot it
- several pints of my own blood (need to figure out the right number of pints)
- a life-sized human dummy
- a truck to transport the "body"
- a plan to get rid of the "body"
- a new identity ready to go

He knew there were many details to work out, and the list would grow over time. But his mind was set, he knew what he was going to do, and had a general idea of how he was going to do it. Now that he knew Laura was not only cheating on him, but also socking away money, for the purpose of leaving him, or so he assumed, his feelings had changed. He would brilliantly fake his own death, then steal the insurance money from his wife, and move to somewhere warm and sunny where he could play golf every day.

Chapter Eighteen

Wednesday, January 21, 2009 – 8:00 a.m.

STILL AT THE hotel, Bill realized he was hungry. He called room service and ordered breakfast; the western omelet with toast and hash browns. No Starbucks today, he'd have to settle for whatever coffee came with the room service.

Bill decided to check his own Yahoo account and discovered mostly spam--he didn't get much personal email these days.

With time to himself, he thought this might be a good time to do some research. He typed, "How to create a new identity" into Google. But he stopped himself just short of hitting "Enter." *I don't want to leave any kind of a trail ... I could always do that kind of a search at the public library.* So he decided not to perform a search like that on his laptop.

Bill remembered there was a public library just a few blocks from his house. Why not go there first? Then he realized his car was still across the street at Greystone. Grabbing his coat, and leaving everything else behind, he headed for the elevator. After reaching the lobby, he dashed across the street to the Greystone parking lot, retrieved his car, and drove toward his neighborhood.

As he pulled into the parking lot of the public library, he realized he hadn't been there in quite a long time. He imagined that was true for a lot of people. With so much information online now, only those few holdouts who refused to get Internet access would use the library for general information.

Bill entered the library and sat down at one of the public computer terminals. Internet Explorer was already up and running. "Creating a new identity." Wow! Forty two million, three hundred thousand hits! Amazing! Bill looked through the titles of the web pages that came up in the search. He was astounded. There was a Yahoo discussion group on the subject. Many of the sites seemed to be existential in nature; "be the person you always wanted to be" kind of thing.

But as he scrolled through the pages of links, he discovered that many of the web pages discussed the nuts and bolts of how to get new documents to support a new life. He clicked on one link where someone had posted a question regarding taking the identity of someone around your age who was dead. The responses were quite funny, including the one that simply asked, "Have you been naughty?" Bill got a nice chuckle out of that one. Other web sites discussed the legality of creating a new identity.

Wow, I didn't know what to expect on this, looks like I've got a lot of reading to do here. Maybe one of these web sites will give me some insight ...

One particular site offered practical, high level, advice regarding creating a new persona. According to the author of this article, the guy who asked the question about taking the identity of a dead person was on the right track. In many cases, birth and death records in the U.S are held by local governments and municipalities, and there is often not a strong correlation between the two types of records. And if someone is born in one place, establishes a residence in a new city and eventually dies there, then there is an excellent chance there would be no record of the death in the town where he was born.

So obtaining a copy of the person's birth certificate is the way to get started. The site went on to suggest a number of ways to obtain, "identity replacement candidates," as Bill referred to them in his head. According to one author, the best possibilities were people you already knew something about. The ideas included childhood friends, acquaintances, etc. The person had to be a good fit; you wanted to be able to establish an entire background for them if possible. College records, job history, etc. Things Bill had never thought about. But then again, how much background would he need if he had three million dollars? It's not like he'd have to work unless he felt like it.

Hmmm, I'll bet there are all kinds of records at the company. Ah, but that's a slippery slope. Probably better to leave the company out of it—that way there is less of a chance I'll leave a trail. There is probably a way to search through death notices to find a likely match. Anyway, I might not have to be too detailed on my background since it won't be important that I get a job.

Bill then noticed a site with links to guides and books about creating a new identity. It was a site by a publisher who seemed to specialize in publications about fake identities. The title of one book in particular intrigued him, *Escaping Your Past.* He was starting to realize, while this effort might be worth the payoff in the end, in order to really get away scot-free with the money, he'd have to be smart. Very smart. The book was geared toward those who felt they needed to go underground for personal safety, such as a woman trying to escape an abusive relationship. He figured he could use advice on this level, as he was going to be looking to completely disappear. He wanted the book! The question was how could he obtain the book without it being traced back to him?

Well, I could probably just get a cashier's check and send it to the company. But I'd need an address to send it to, so there wouldn't be a way to connect the purchase of the book back to me.

Next, Bill Googled "blood storage." He got roughly 2,500 hits, and the first page was all companies that offered blood storage services--not what he was after. He was just wondering, once he "got" the blood from himself, in a yet to be determined manner, if he could refrigerate or freeze it so it would be "fresh" on the day he staged the crime scene. He then tried "blood storage refrigerate." The first link was for a blood storage refrigerator, with a temperature range of thirty-four to forty-two degrees Fahrenheit. Interesting. So, what is the range of an average refrigerator?

Another quick Google revealed that an average fridge operated at thirty-eight degrees, right in the middle of the range of the blood storage version. There was nothing special, temperature wise, about the blood storage fridge, so a standard one would do just fine for storing his blood. What made the blood storage version unique were the trays inside designed to hold vials of blood. And of course, Bill had no need for that feature.

A couple of more Googles revealed blood stored at that temperature had a shelf life of thirty-five days, at least according to the Blood Bank Wikipedia page. So he'd have to figure out how much blood to collect for the crime scene, and he'd have to collect it and use it within about one month's time. That didn't sound too daunting, except he was expecting to create a pretty bloody crime scene, one where the authorities would conclude he was dead if they didn't find him pretty quickly.

He remembered he had seen a sports documentary about a hockey player who had had his jugular vein cut by a skate during a professional game. It was a freak accident that quickly developed into a ghoulish scene as blood gushed from the poor guy's neck. A quick acting trainer saved the man's life by applying pressure to the vein, stemming the flow of blood. The documentary went on to explore just how close the guy had come to dying. Bill was trying to remember the details. He had seen the show a number of months before. Was it forty percent blood loss and you'd be in serious danger? And the body had, what, six quarts of blood? He'd have to research that in the coming days. He needed to get over to the house now while he was sure that Laura was out.

Chapter Nineteen

IT WAS ABOUT ten-thirty in the morning when Bill got home. Laura's car was not in the driveway. Good. It was very strange to be arriving home at this time of day on a Tuesday. But of course, every bit of normalcy in his current life was going to be blown out of the water in the coming weeks.

Plopping down in front of the workstation in his home office, he brought up a web browser. He fired up Yahoo mail and typed in Laura's ID. Then, taking a deep breath, he typed in her email password. Success! Of course, this wasn't the critical account, but he was pretty sure if she hadn't changed this password, she hadn't changed any of them.

He scanned the titles of the emails in her Inbox. He read a couple of emails from someone named Preston. *Okay—this is the dude she's sleeping with.* But the emails were fairly benign, 'what time do you want to meet for dinner,' stuff like that. He didn't come across anything racy, thank goodness. But he didn't look too deeply, no reason to, the affair wasn't new news anymore.

He exited Yahoo mail and brought up the website for the bank. This was the moment of truth.

Then, after typing in her online banking ID, he typed in what he knew to be her password. There was a split second of panic while a spinning icon indicated his request was under consideration. Finally, after a few nanoseconds that felt like a millennium, Laura Ferguson's banking information came into full view on the monitor. Including the absurd 75K balance in her checking account.

Bill's plan had been to systematically search the house for "evidence." Evidence of what, he wasn't quite sure. He knew she was sleeping around and stockpiling money. What else did he need to know? The search now seemed like a waste of time. Instead he went upstairs and went to bed. Even though he'd gotten ten hours of sleep the night before, he felt tired.

Before he lay down, he had set the alarm for three p.m., just in case. That move proved to be fortuitous. When the alarm woke him up, it took him a full minute to get his bearings. He decided to take a quick shower. At around three-thirty, now fully rested, he headed back to the hotel.

Having skipped lunch, Bill went for an early dinner around five at the restaurant at the Yorkshire Hotel. He ordered an appetizer, a full dinner, and dessert. He was in no hurry, after dinner he'd change back into his suit, pack up, check out of the hotel and head home, pretending he was arriving home from work.

It was just after eight when he arrived home. Laura was there. He'd been wondering how he would react at seeing her for the first time after his suspicions had been confirmed. He found that, because of his plan, he was able to keep his emotions in check. After a day to get used to the idea, he was able to act as if nothing had happened, all the while knowing he'd have the last laugh.

"Hello," said Bill coolly, as he came through the front door. He noticed Laura looked very tired.

"Hello," said Laura, equally detached.

"Have you eaten yet?" asked Bill.

"Not yet. Can we just order a pizza and watch a movie?"

"Sounds perfect."

And they did just that, ordered a pizza and watched a mindless romantic comedy on the flat screen. They sat on the sofa together, but watched the movie separately, each barely watching the movie, each lost in his or her own thoughts.

That night as Bill lay in bed, unable to sleep because of the long nap he'd taken earlier, something occurred to him. The insurance policy on him was, of course, held by Greystone. Now, if things went off as planned, he'd be living in another city under a different name, waiting for the money to reach his ex-wife's bank account before he stole it all. But it might take months before his death became official. Maybe longer, he'd have to research that. That was something he wanted to understand before he actually left town—how long would it be before he was declared dead, if there was no body?

At any rate, maybe he could set up an account that would let him access the company computers remotely after he'd "died." He could set up a fictitious employee who had remote access. Then he could still receive company email and perhaps set it up so he could check on the disposition of his own case. It was a pretty big company; maybe he could even have the new guy draw a paycheck and use that for his seed money! He smiled at that one. Stealing the insurance money from his adulterous ex-wife was one thing. But steal from the company? Could he do that? Did moral questions like that even apply anymore?

Okay, let's get real. Email idea, good. A fictitious employee drawing a paycheck, bad. That kind of greed could help me get caught. I really don't need the "seed" money anyway.

And another thought occurred to him. When the insurance money comes through, he would conceivably transfer the money from Laura's bank account to an account he controlled. But his new identity would be well-established, he'd have a job, a residence, a bank account. So, of course, the bank transfer could be traced right to him. He'd be caught within the hour. So … the only conclusion was that he would need a second fake identity in order to actually keep the money. And some kind of anonymous offshore account. A place for the money to go before his second persona could then stash it in a real account. He'd have to acquire a second fake identity while waiting for his big payday.

Man. There were so many details to attend to while trying to do this correctly it was astounding! If I had put this much thought into my job this last year, I'd be a Senior VP by now.

But there was one thing he could not deny. He was suddenly having a blast. This was the most fun he'd had since college. He felt alive again. He woke up in the morning with a vigor he hadn't had in years. He attacked the day now, loving the idea of his plan and the new excitement it would bring him.

Chapter Twenty

Thursday, January 22, 2009 – 12:00 p.m.

IT WAS LUNCH time and Bill decided to head to the public library to do some research for his "project." He walked the five blocks to the downtown branch of the public library and secured the last Internet terminal. He wanted to understand exactly how much blood he would need to collect in order to make the crime scene bloody enough. He'd have to collect it within roughly one month's time, as that seemed to be the max time for storing it.

He found this information on the Wikipedia page about bleeding:

Types of bleeding:

- Class I Hemorrhage involves up to fifteen percent of blood volume. There is typically no change in vital signs and fluid resuscitation is not usually necessary.
- Class II Hemorrhage involves fifteen to thirty percent of total blood volume. A patient is often tachycardic (rapid heartbeat) with a narrowing of the difference between

the systolic and diastolic blood pressures. The body attempts to compensate with peripheral vasoconstriction. Skin may start to look pale and be cool to the touch. The patient may exhibit slight changes in behavior. Volume resuscitation with crystalloids (Saline solution or Lactated Ringer's solution) is all that is typically required. Blood transfusion is not typically required.

• Class III Hemorrhage involves loss of thirty to forty percent of circulating blood volume. The patient's blood pressure drops, the heart rate increases, peripheral perfusion (shock), such as capillary refill worsens, and the mental status worsens. Fluid resuscitation with crystalloid and blood transfusion are usually necessary.

• Class IV Hemorrhage involves loss of greater than forty percent of circulating blood volume. The limit of the body's compensation is reached and aggressive resuscitation is required to prevent death.

Bill also found an article that described a crime scene expert's testimony at a trial where the accused was acquitted of murder because the victim hadn't lost enough blood to cause his death. He learned an average person carries around about twelve pints of blood, and it would take the loss of around four pints of blood to cause death. So that was thirty-three percent, or a Class III Hemorrhage, per the other web site he had found. So, that made sense. But how long would it take someone to die if he or she lost four pints of blood?

He seemed to remember from the documentary about the hockey player that it wouldn't be too long, maybe even minutes? A quick Google revealed that you bleed to death in just a few minutes if the wounds are severe enough. That's all he really wanted to know. If someone lost four pints of blood quickly, he would not have very long to live. So the trick would be to create the illusion that he had lost four pints of blood, and then had been transported somewhere else. From those "facts," investigators arriving the next day would have no choice but to conclude he was probably already dead.

The next question was how long would it take him to collect four pints of his own blood? He read on the Red Cross web site that the average blood donation is about a pint of blood. He had given a few times over the last few years and had felt no ill effects. The Red Cross FAQ also said that the average person replaces the fluid within twenty-four hours. But there was a regulation that you had to wait fifty-six days between donations. The FAQ indicated if someone gave two units of red blood cells, they would have to wait one hundred and twelve days to give blood again. So, his guess was that, fluid replacement aside, the fifty-six days was about replacing red blood cells. *Hmmm. I need to understand this better.* He was going to need to collect three to four pints of blood in a four-week period. One pint per week. But was that going to be safe?

Next, Bill Googled "Effects of giving blood too often." Amazingly, the first link he clicked took him to the famous Dr. Andrew Weil's website, where he read the following statement as part of an answer to his very question:

"Your body replenishes any plasma you donate in forty-eight hours so it is considered safe to give more as soon as two days after a first donation. However, the American Red Cross limits plasma donations to twelve a year, so you're better off donating once a month rather than once a week. Some blood centers impose longer waiting times between donations."

That was good enough for Bill. Not surprisingly, the Red Cross was extremely conservative with the amount of days they made you wait between donations, at least according to what he had just read. His plan now was to extract a pint of blood once a week, somehow, and if he felt lousy the second or third week, he'd worry about that then. His instincts told him he would be just fine.

Bill now knew he was going to collect the blood and store it for a staged crime scene. He envisioned dragging a life-sized dummy through the blood and then out the back door to a waiting truck. The "killer" would shoot him, and then take the body somewhere else. But why? He couldn't come up with a good reason for that. If you are going to conceal the crime by hiding the body, then shouldn't you clean up the "murder" scene? But his plan was the opposite; he wanted to create a very bloody crime scene. He was starting to realize there was simply no way to think of, or control, everything. His working assumption was if there was enough of his blood at the scene, the police would have to conclude he wouldn't have survived. If other things didn't make sense to the investigators, so what?

But, what was the best way to disperse the four pints of blood and make it as realistic as possible? One thought was to strategically place several pouches of blood on his dummy, shoot the blood pouches, and let the platelets fall where they may. But did this really simulate how a person who had been shot would bleed? Bill decided that for the killer's actions to make any sense at all, he'd have to simulate being shot in the jugular vein. That would lead to a quick death. Otherwise, why would the killer still be at the scene? Who would shoot someone, wait around for a slow bleed out, and then move the body without cleaning up?

So, simulating the hockey injury, or something along those lines, seemed to make the most sense. As far as Bill was concerned, it was okay for the police to be confused about certain details as long they ultimately concluded that he must be dead. The jugular vein idea gave him a clear vision of what he was trying to accomplish, so there was a better chance he'd actually be able to pull it off.

As Bill was walking back to work, he noticed Borders Books and got an idea. Entering the store, he went to one of the store terminals that allows one to search for books based on title, author's name, and/or a keyword. A search on the keyword "identity" brought back a surprising number of titles. There were actually books you could buy about creating a new identity, and they were in stock! Who would have thunk it? He paid cash for a book titled, "Create a New Persona."

When he got back to the office, he asked Jennifer to hold any calls for about an hour. He closed his office door and eagerly began reading. Based on the current plan, establishing a new identity was something he needed to do right away. He would use the new persona to rent a small apartment, which would function as a base of operations, a place to collect and store the blood, keep the gun he'd use for the shooting, and perform any other activities related to his plan.

Chapter Twenty-One

Thursday January 22, 2009 – 6:00 p.m.

BEFORE HEADING HOME, Bill decided to go to the library and do some additional research. A key chapter in the "Persona" book was titled, "Identity Documents." In the chapter, the author described techniques for obtaining birth certificates, driver's licenses and social security numbers. He explained that for daily use, by far the most important document is the driver's license.

The author advised the easiest way to obtain a driver's license for someone over eighteen is to go the old-fashioned route-- get a learner's permit and then go to driving school. It's elaborate enough that it masks the true intentions of the person creating a new identity. The book also mentioned an adult going to driving school in an urban area would look a lot less suspicious than in a rural area. It's a lot more plausible for an adult to have never driven before in a place like Manhattan, for instance, where one can easily survive without a car.

While all that made sense, the whole idea of going back to driving school seemed truly bizarre. He'd been driving for almost twenty-five years for crying out loud. On the other hand, whom was he kidding? The whole plan was absolutely nuts to begin with, wasn't it? Of more concern than the apparent weirdness of a forty-year-old suburbanite going to driving school was the amount of time it might take. The process of getting a learner's permit and driver's license in the traditional manner could take months. Bill's timetable didn't allow for that. He definitely needed more information.

At any rate, it seemed like a good idea to try to obtain a birth certificate from New York State, so he could tell the bureaucrat in Albany, or Binghamton, or wherever, that he'd lived in Manhattan all his life and was getting his driver's license for the first time. In case anyone cared.

But Bill quickly got discouraged when looking up the requirements for obtaining a New York State learner's permit. Based on what he'd read, he had envisioned a scenario where he could waltz in somewhere with a birth certificate and maybe a Social Security card and immediately get a learner's permit. But that wasn't going to happen in New York. New York required LOTS of documents to prove you are who you say you are. Massachusetts had a similar set of requirements for proving one's identity. Apparently, it would take a tremendous amount of effort to create a new identity in the northeast.

Frustrated by what he was finding out by targeting the neighboring states, Bill decided to try a different tactic. In the Google search field, he typed a very broad search, "Obtain a driver's license." The results were surprising, and quite encouraging. The information posted on one link implied that if one was willing to drive south down I-95, things would be a lot easier. Another link indicated that North Carolina specifically was a very easy state in which to get a license. Accessing the North Carolina DMV website, he looked up the requirements for getting a North Carolina learner's permit. It looked like all you needed was a birth certificate and a Social Security card. <u>Now this is more like it! Birth certificate from New York, driver's license from North Carolina?</u>

He then discovered that he should be able to get a Social Security card with a birth certificate. <u>So there you go. If I can get a birth certificate, I can create a new life in the south.</u> And then with a valid driver's license with a new name, he could eventually go anywhere. He vowed to check out other southern states learner's permit requirements as well.

There was another reason to look south to the Carolinas. There were tons of golf courses. His plan was to become an assistant golf pro somewhere down there while he waited for the big insurance money to come in. It would give him something to

A DEVIOUS PLAN 125

do and bring in a few dollars. Plus, he loved the game and was still a very good player. He'd just have to plan on living lean for those months, however many they turned out to be.

Then his plan hit a snag. According to the North Carolina Motor Vehicle Administration website, it looked like you had to have a learner's permit in North Carolina for six months before getting a license. Yikes! That was way too long before getting a driver's license. I'll need a different plan. I want to create a new identity ASAP.

It was eight p.m.; the library was open for another hour. After another half hour of Googling, Bill finally discovered that Wyoming only required adults to hold a learner's permit for ten days, AND, you only needed a birth certificate, no other documentation was required. Woo-hoo! He guessed he could probably just get the learner's permit and then show up for the driving test ten days later, having "skipped" driving school. But he would make that call when he got his learner's permit.

So the new quick plan was to get a New York birth certificate, and then "move" to Wyoming so he could get a Wyoming driver's license. Why was he moving to Wyoming? He'd need a story for that. To escape the rat race in New York? He should probably do some research on Wyoming. But Wyoming wasn't going to be long term. He would head to the Carolinas soon after getting his Wyoming driver's license.

Chapter Twenty-Two

Friday, January 23, 2009 – 12:00 p.m.

BILL COULD HARDLY believe it as he glanced at the white envelope sitting on the passenger's seat. He was halfway home on his way back from Poughkeepsie, where he'd just visited the satellite office of the New York Department of Vital Records. The advice in the 'Persona' book had worked like a charm. His immediate questioning of the thirty dollar price tag for the copy the birth certificate had led to a detailed explanation of the fact that what he was about to receive was not just a photo copy of the birth certificate, but an official New York state document, with an official stamp and seal. The debate regarding the price had completely distracted the harried desk jockey from questioning Bill's right to obtain the birth certificate. Instead he got to flex his bureaucratic muscles regarding the price, asserting his power over all things birth certificate, at least for the Empire State.

So once Bill sheepishly agreed to go the whole thirty dollars, even though he didn't think it was really worth it, his order was processed. An hour later, he was called back to the front desk, and handed the magical white envelope that was going to be the key to his future, at least for the next several months.

While part of him felt elated, another part was utterly disgusted. Not disgusted with the fact he'd been able to easily dupe a distracted government worker into giving him a document he wasn't entitled to but what he'd just done felt incredibly sleazy for a different reason.

When Bill was a junior at Yale, one of his teammates on the golf team had died in a horrific car accident. It was messy; the kid was out joy riding with one of his roommates one Saturday night and both were drunk. Like many kids at Yale, the roommate had rich parents, and had the use of a very fancy, very fast Porsche 911. On that cool April evening in 1989, they got into a drag race, and at 110 mph the roommate lost control of the car. The Porsche smashed into a telephone pole, and ultimately there wasn't much left to recognize of the Porsche, or sadly, either student.

Troy Stevens was the first person Bill actually knew who had died. They hadn't been close friends, but Bill had gone to Troy's funeral. There was a huge turnout. Several of Troy's close friends got up at the service and told stories about how much they loved Bing, how much they would miss him and why the world was much worse off because of the loss of Bing. Bing? It was the first time that Bill had heard Troy referred to as Bing. He discreetly asked about it at the reception and discovered that Troy's nickname was Bing because he came from Binghamton, New York. For some reason, probably because it had been his first funeral, Bill had always remembered that.

So Troy would have been about the same age, and was from the right state. While Bill felt like he wanted to throw up, he also felt like he'd done what he had needed to do. And the truth was, despite its slimy feel, this move was a major step forward. Bill had no plan B had this tactic failed. Now there was an excellent chance he would succeed in Wyoming as well, and would be on his way. Really, how could someone working at the Wyoming DMV possibly question that he had lived in Manhattan all his life, and now was moving away from all that congestion in order to get a taste of fresh air.

I like that, I'm moving to get a taste of fresh air. I might use those very same words when charming the pants off Cowboy Clay, or whoever, from the Wyoming DMV.

Chapter Twenty-Three

Sunday, January 25, 2009 – 8:15 a.m.

"BARG BAGS ARE under the seat, looks like you're going to need one."

Bill agreed, and was able to grab one and maneuver it into position just in time. No small trick considering how violently the small plane was bouncing and pitching. But even after regurgitating his sausage McMuffin, he didn't feel much better. He couldn't remember ever feeling this sick. Dizzy, off-center, nauseous. He guessed this might be what vertigo felt like.

"Once we get through this turbulence and get to our cruising altitude of eight thousand feet, the ride will smooth out and you'll be fine. At least most people start feeling better."

Bill had never experienced airsickness before, but he had never been in a plane this small either. It was a ten-year old Cessna 172, a single-engine plane built for four passengers. The plane was being tossed around by the turbulence as if it were a kayak caught in a hurricane. Bill's only comfort was the pilot seemed unfazed. His demeanor suggested nothing in the world could be wrong and his face appeared to be as calm as if he was guiding the Queen Mary across a placid lake. He had obviously flown in these conditions before, and had obviously survived.

Bill hoped the flight would get better. He could not envision surviving twelve-plus hours in the air feeling like this. It was probably a fourteen-hour trip all told, including two stops for refueling. But however long it took, and however bad he felt, it beat driving twenty-nine hours each way to Cheyenne. It beat having to take all kinds of time off from work just to drive back and forth. And unless he stayed in Wyoming for ten days, which was the interval between securing his learner's permit and driver's license in the Cowboy State, he'd have to drive it twice. So he'd found this alternative, because taking a standard commercial flight was out of the question.

Like many of the things he'd be doing in the coming months, this flight was technically illegal. Private pilots were forbidden from taking payments for flights. Passengers could only share expenses with the pilot. But Bill figured that if he found the right guy, there was probably a deal to be made. A lot fewer people were dabbling with flying as a hobby in this economy. He had guessed, correctly, that there were probably some struggling flight instructors out there, guys who'd be happy for his business. Guys who wouldn't ask too many questions if enough greenbacks were on the table.

So Bill had been strangely confident as he entered the parking lot of Kissinger Field just yesterday morning. Kissinger was a small regional airport about thirty miles outside Hartford. He didn't know exactly where he was going, or exactly who he was looking for, so his situation reminded him of a quote he'd heard years before regarding hard-core pornography, "Difficult to actually describe, but you know it when you see it."

Bill had skirted the terminal and strode purposefully to the hangar area where passengers boarded the planes. He had wanted to give the appearance that he knew exactly what he was doing. Luckily, there hadn't been too much security at an airport as small as Kissinger. Despite the thirty-five degree temperature, there had been a decent amount of activity. The hangar doors were wide open and Bill could see half a dozen small planes, three of which were being tinkered with or repaired by men Bill guessed were the pilots. Just outside the hangar a guy had been loading luggage into the cargo hold of a small Cessna as a well-dressed couple watched.

The guy furthest to the right, inspecting the older plane, had caught Bill's eye. He was young and trim, maybe twenty-six or twenty-seven? Roughly five feet nine inches tall, he was sporting a tee shirt, jeans, and sneakers. None of his apparel appeared to be new. On the surface, he seemed like a good target. A young guy eking out a living by working at the hangar and giving the occasional flying lesson.

Bill had waited until everyone's attention was diverted and had approached the young man.

"Hello there—are you a pilot? Do you give flying lessons?"

"Yes," said the pilot, carefully eyeing Bill. "What are looking for?"

"Well, I've never flown before, so I thought I might want to take a few lessons and see if I liked it. How much does it cost?"

"Plane rental runs about eighty an hour, and since I'm a certified instructor I charge forty an hour. But before we get up in the air, you should take the ground school course, about one hundred and fifty bucks. And there are also books and stuff you'll need, that costs around two hundred."

"Well, I guess that doesn't sound too bad. What's ground school?"

"In ground school you learn the basics of the airplane, where all the instruments and controls are, and a little about navigation."

"Oh, okay, I guess that makes sense. So, what, is there a waiting list for this kind of thing?"

It was all the pilot could do to not burst out laughing. He quickly regained his composure and explained that while he did have quite a few clients, which was an exaggeration, he could probably find a way to squeeze in just one more. And Bill knew from the instant smirk on the pilot's face that he wasn't busy at all. But he appreciated that the guy recovered quickly and tried to play the game; it showed he had some brains and some moxie. Bill liked him instantly, and was hoping this would be the guy.

Bill did some quick calculations in his head so as he wound his way, conversationally, to his real objective, he could make a reasonable offer. He had already calculated that in a small plane it would take about twelve hours to fly from Hartford to Cheyenne. He knew a Cessna 172 burned about eight gallons an hour while cruising, and the current cost of aviation fuel was about three dollars per gallon. So the cost of fuel for the trip to Cheyenne would be about three hundred bucks each way, six hundred total. If he paid the guy his forty an hour, for the twenty four hours it would take to fly to Cheyenne and back, that would be nine hundred and sixty dollars for the whole trip. He figured he'd leave out the "plane rental" fee in his offer. He simply wasn't willing to pay that much.

"You aren't with the FAA are you?"

"Oh hell no! I'm just a guy who wants to get to Cheyenne quickly and quietly, and then get right back."

"What's this trip all about, anyway?"

"My reason for the trip is private. But I'm willing to work something out with you, from a bonus perspective if you'll take me." Bill reached into his pocket and scooped up a crumpled five hundred dollar bill into his palm, and then closed his fist. He pulled his hand out of his pocket and shifted his clenched fingers just enough so the pilot could see the cash.

"Okay, okay, put that away. Meet me at Harry's Diner across the street in an hour and maybe we can make a deal."

Harry's was a traditional '50s style diner. Neither the menu nor the decor had been updated since it opened sixty some years earlier, yet it did a brisk business for breakfast and lunch. The food was cheap and tasted great, mainly because most everything, with the exception of possibly the toast, was cooked in bacon grease. But those who availed themselves of Harry's cuisine weren't there because they were counting calories. The pilots and mechanics frequenting this joint just wanted something quick and hearty to go with their regular old cup of joe. Harry's proudly served old-fashioned creamed chipped beef, otherwise affectionately known as "shit on a shingle," and you would never find a scone there. There were no lattes, espressos, or cappuccinos within a half a mile of Harry's. It was practically a city ordinance.

So at roughly eleven-thirty a.m. on Saturday, Bill left the airport and jogged across the highway to Harry's Diner. He wasn't that hungry, but decided to kill the hour by having an early lunch. As he entered the diner, there was a sign next to the entrance podium that stated, "Please Seat Yourself." He chose a booth to the right, one with a window. He situated himself facing the entrance, so he could see the pilot enter. Soon after he sat down, an elderly woman shuffled over to his booth. She was short and rotund, with gray hair. Her nametag read, "Agnes."

"What can I get for you, darling?"

Bill ordered a Reuben, knowing a place like this would make a great one. Noticing an unclaimed newspaper sitting on the bar, he jumped up and grabbed it. He wanted something to read to help kill some time. As soon as he flipped open the paper, the iced tea he had ordered to accompany his Reuben arrived. He sipped his cold beverage and leisurely read through the paper, looking for anything of interest at all on each page. A slow read was in order.

Having made quick work of his delicious sandwich and running out of interesting articles to read in the paper, Bill was grateful when the pilot arrived about fifteen minutes early for their meeting. Bill waved him over as soon as the pilot entered

Harry's. The pilot sauntered over and Bill motioned for him to sit down.

"Hungry?" Bill asked?

"Very."

"Sorry, I never got your name back there."

"It's Adam. Adam Wherling"

"I'm Troy Stevens," said Bill, reaching out to shake hands.

Just then Agnes appeared, eager to serve an additional customer. "Can I get you something, darling?"

Adam looked at Bill with raised eyebrows, asking non-verbally, "this is on you, right?"

Bill got the hint. "Please add what Adam wants to my bill."

"I'll have a club sandwich with fries and a Coke."

"I'll be right back with the Coke, sweetie." And with that, Agnes scurried off.

"Okay, start from the beginning, what are we talking about here?" said Adam.

"I need to make a quick trip to Cheyenne, Wyoming. Leave one day, come back the next. I just have a quick business meeting, and I don't want to fly commercial."

"Why not fly commercial? It would be a lot faster."

They both went silent as Agnes arrived efficiently with the Coke. She sensed she wasn't needed further and quickly departed.

"Faster, and cheaper," said Bill. "But I have personal reasons for not flying commercial this time. Nothing you need to worry about. I figure my half of the expenses for a trip like this is about thirteen hundred dollars."

Adam sat back and didn't say anything for a full two minutes, as he calculated his expenses and weighed them against Bill's offer. He figured that Bill offering thirteen hundred really meant he was willing to pay fifteen. With gas for this trip costing around six hundred, that meant he'd get nine hundred to keep for two days worth of work. He tried not to show his excitement. "No drugs or guns involved?"

"Absolutely not. I'll just have a change of clothes with me for the overnight and some documents."

"The numbers really don't work at thirteen hundred. I get it, I don't need the whole thing for plane rental and everything, but I think eighteen hundred is fair."

Neither said anything for about thirty seconds, both waiting for the other to blink.

Finally, Bill spoke. "Fifteen then?"

"I can live with that."

The two shook hands just as the club sandwich arrived.

As luck would have it, Adam just happened to have a break in his schedule for the next two days. They would meet at the airport at seven forty-five the next morning, Sunday, with the take-off scheduled for eight a.m. The plan was to spend Sunday night in Cheyenne, then Bill would take care of his business early on Monday, and they'd fly back late Monday morning.

Bill was quite surprised when he got to the passenger area the next morning, with one overnight bag as promised, and there to greet him was Adam alongside a gnarly, tall and muscle-bound TSA agent with a drug sniffing dog. But of course, the dog found nothing, and Bill was allowed to board the plane without further ado. Still, Bill took note. Despite his apparent youth, Adam was not to be trifled with.

Chapter Twenty-Four

Friday, February 6, 2009 – 10:30 a.m.

THE DRIVING TEST had gone fairly well, despite the fact that Bill was exhausted. He'd slept little the last two nights. And he was feeling especially groggy because he'd decided to skip breakfast and hadn't had his morning latte. It had taken two cracks to get the parallel parking right, but he was happy he'd been smart enough to practice. Had he tried to just wing it, he surely would have flunked. And that would have been a relative disaster, as his whole plan hinged on this move. Obtaining his license was critical. As he sat, waiting in the lobby of the Cheyenne DMV, he felt exposed, naked. What if someone was in a back room, trying to figure out why a forty-year-old man was just now getting his driver's license? <u>Oh, quit being paranoid. These folks are bureaucrats, they don't care that much.</u> But Bill wouldn't be comfortable until he was back in the Cessna, heading home to Hartford, new license in hand. Until then there was the chance someone would start asking uncomfortable questions.

He was irritated with himself for forgetting to bring something to read. He occupied the time by people watching. It was a universal rule in DMVs across America, the ratio of "down on their luck" people to those more fortunate ran about three to one. There was a guy about Bill's age, wearing a very old Aerosmith concert tee shirt, raggedy jeans, and Chuck Taylor's, trying to get his license reinstated. Another woman with way too much makeup on was wearing tiny, tiny shorts and very high heels, her shoulders draped with a fake fur coat. Bill didn't know what her business at the DMV was, but was certain as soon as it was concluded she was heading for her next trick. There was a young immigrant family, the dad in a wife-beater tee shirt, khakis, and work boots, and the mom in a small top and tight fitting jeans. Two young boys and a little girl were in tow, all with clothes that were too big. Mom and Dad had earned enough money to get the registration for their '99 Ford Windstar straightened out. But the lapsed registration probably hadn't stopped them from driving it, Bill assumed.

One thing was for sure, he was glad to be away from Laura right now. Not only was he furthering his plan, but he was also getting some much-needed breathing room. In the interim, she'd have gotten together with lover boy and forgotten all about Bill. Bitch. He wondered how long she would stay with him if he wasn't planning his dramatic exit.

Yes, that was something to consider. What if too many things went wrong with his plan? What would he do then? He hadn't thought about what he'd do if somehow he ran into too many glitches and had to abort the mission. He'd probably just go for a quick and quiet divorce. Given her situation, she would surely acquiesce to any reasonable demands.

But that was a moot point. The plan would not fail. Bill was thinking the next thing that Troy would need to do when he got back to Hartford was to secure an apartment, a base of operations. He'd need a place to keep all the supplies for the night he was to "die." The gun, the blood, the dummy, would all be stored there. And he now had an idea as to how he would collect the blood.

He was beginning to realize he didn't have a solid plan in the event things worked perfectly. What if he got all the money? He knew he wanted to live at the beach somewhere, keep a low profile, live a quiet life filled with umbrella drinks and birdies. But what beach? And would that be enough of a life? Was he ready to, basically, retire? Or would he need some kind of career? He hadn't thought that far ahead. He just knew he wanted the options that three million smackaroos would give him.

Previously he'd figured out he'd need a second new identity, the one he'd use to live out the rest of his days once he got the three million. But he assumed he'd take care of that after Bill was "dead" and he was living as Troy. He assumed there would be at least a few months after he "died" before Laura was awarded the money. Didn't there have to be a coroner's inquest in order for someone to be declared dead if there was no body? Sounded like something that would take a while.

In the shorter term, he needed to start thinking about a golf pro job. There were tons of courses in Myrtle Beach. How do you even look for an assistant pro job? Do they put ads in the paper, or on the Internet like everyone else? It couldn't be purely word of mouth, could it? That would make it harder. He made a note to himself that he'd do some Google searches when he got home and start investigating.

And he'd need at least some seed money. He didn't want to hit the Carolinas with no money whatsoever-- that would be dumb. He'd have to follow Laura's example and put together a little stash before his death. He smiled broadly to himself as he realized the best thing to do was open a savings account for one Troy Stevens. Oh, he'd overlooked something. Could he somehow find out what Troy Steven's Social Security number had been?

Finally, he heard the magic words.

"Stevens! Troy Stevens!"

He sauntered up to the counter, and was handed the shiny, laminated card. The card worth about three million bucks. The card that represented his future, his carefree life. The card that announced to the world he was now Troy Stevens of Cheyenne, Wyoming.

Chapter Twenty-Five

Sunday, February 8, 2009 – 2:00 p.m.

BILL SAT IN the living room of his furnished, one bedroom apartment, apartment number seventeen. The cloth cushions on the chair he was sitting in were beginning to fray, but it was comfortable enough. He wasn't expecting anything too fancy in this part of town, for this price. At least the chair didn't wobble. <u>When was the last time this place was painted? Probably when it was new, about twenty years ago. Okay, maybe not that long. But it's probably been years.</u>

He realized he was beaming from ear to ear. Idiotic for sure, considering he was alone. He couldn't help himself. The plan was working! He couldn't believe he'd actually come this far! Troy Stevens had a birth certificate, a driver's license, and a freaking apartment! Bill Ferguson would be "dead" soon and he'd be Troy Stevens within a few weeks.

The apartment had a kitchen he'd never cook in, curtains he would never open, and a bed he'd never sleep in. The cable television service wouldn't be turned on for a few days, but that hardly mattered.

The television was old and he wasn't planning on ever watching it. He'd be here a couple of hours a week, if that. He just needed a convenient, quiet, base of operations. He would sign up for utilities tomorrow, with the electric company and the phone company. He wanted voicemail. Since his driver's license said he was from Cheyenne, Wyoming, a place like a bank might ask for a utility bill as proof of residence. After the utilities were in Troy's name, he'd establish a bank account for him.

He'd paid sixteen hundred cash in advance for two months rent for this fifth floor unit at the Broad Street Apartments in the Frog Hollow section of Hartford. It was a relatively bad area of town, there was some crime, but nothing like it had been in the '90s. For Bill's purposes, it was okay that it had a bad reputation because the rent was low and he figured he could avoid being here at night. It was only a mile and a half from the Pearl Street offices of Greystone, so this place was very convenient from that standpoint.

While this was a cheap apartment, his expenses were starting to add up. He was paying cash for everything related to his plan so there wouldn't be any traceability. But it had been around three thousand dollars for the flights back and forth to Cheyenne, and now sixteen hundred for an apartment. And there were more expenses coming. He planned to buy an expensive life-sized dummy, as well as a gun. Eventually Troy was going to need a car. He didn't have a plan for how he would pay for an additional car yet. He'd had to pull a thousand out of the joint savings account to help pay for the apartment. There was plenty of money left in the account, twenty nine thousand more, but now there was a chance Laura would notice.

Maybe it was time to do a budget. He had planned out the activities for his escape plan, but had never added up all the expenses involved. He'd just kind of assumed he could absorb the expenses with his salary. And for the most part, that had been true so far. But he'd have to be a little less nonchalant if he didn't want to arouse suspicion.

Should he get a credit card for Troy, he wondered? He'd need one for just getting by in the world, wouldn't he? Troy wouldn't be working for a while and did he want to charge things for the plan on Troy's credit cards? He wasn't sure it mattered. If the police connected him with Troy, he was cooked anyway, wasn't he? Still, his instincts told him the less evidence the better. Troy might well need a credit card, but he wouldn't use it for buying things for the plan.

Thinking ahead, it seemed a good idea to pull a bunch of money out of savings the day he faked his murder. Then he'd have some traveling money. And it would hopefully add to the mystery. Help send the cops down the wrong path. Did he owe someone money? Was he in some kind of trouble? Surely the cops would assume the withdrawn money was connected to his apparent murder.

As he sat there, in the frayed chair, in the living room of his small and dingy apartment, for the first time it struck him that he was utterly and completely alone in this thing. He really couldn't confide in a single person. For the first time since he'd begun plotting, he longed for a partner, someone he could exchange ideas with, someone to act as a sounding board. But he knew that bringing someone else in at this point would be beyond stupid. All he could do was trust that he was creating a brighter future for himself, a carefree future where he would be the master of his own destiny.

Chapter Twenty-Six

Saturday, February 14, 2009 – 11:00 A.M.

PREMIUM VENTE LATTE in hand, Bill grabbed a table for two by the window of this unfamiliar coffee shop. He was lucky he got a table. The place was bustling with droopy-eyed college students, most of whom were wearing sweat pants and tee shirts under their winter coats. Many appeared to be trying to shake off the cobwebs of last night's parties with a large infusion of caffeine.

He had never been to this part of town before. Having new experiences and discovering new places were things he was really enjoying while implementing his plan. It had been many years since he'd seen a college crowd like this. It reminded him of his own college days, which in turn reminded him of golf. He should find a driving range with heated tees on the way back from this meeting. If he was going to work as an assistant pro somewhere, he needed to sharpen his game a bit. Tough to do in February, but not impossible.

While he waited, he thought about the events of the past week. Surprisingly, Laura had asked about the money he'd taken out of savings. He'd told her he used it to buy some new golf clubs; since there were great sales in February, he'd gotten a great deal. His response was met with a stony silence. It was as if he could hear her thinking, "this prick has no clue does he? No clue about anything." He met her silence with his own, suppressing the urge to blurt out anything about her affair or her stashing away thousands. It was almost like a social experiment now. It was fascinating to watch her operate while knowing what he knew. He knew that in her mind she was simply doing what she felt she had to do, nothing personal, very businesslike. Intellectually, he understood she was a damn good lawyer, but now he could feel it. She was capable of doing the job, regardless of anyone's feelings, including her own.

Bill picked up his copy of the *The Giver*, the weekly newspaper of Clara Barton College, one of the best nursing schools on the east coast. Turning to the classified section, he re-read his ad:

*

Easy job for a third year nursing student.
Earn five hundred dollars in the next
month. Call Troy
860–555–5555.

*

After he'd done some soul searching, he had to admit to himself that he was too much of a wimp to draw his own blood. Plus, if he screwed up, it might be dangerous. So why not get a hungry nursing student to do it? Easy money for someone. And he'd be a lot more comfortable. He hadn't given any particulars in the ad because he wasn't sure if this was legal.

Sheila had answered the ad. And had agreed to meet him here at the coffee shop just outside the campus. At this point, she was a few minutes late for their eleven o'clock meeting, but Bill didn't mind. It gave him more time to ogle the young coeds drifting in and out of the shop. The young coeds were twenty years his junior, he reminded himself. He felt a little like a dirty old man, as he smiled to himself.

There she was—a brunette wearing a red Clara Barton sweatshirt. She was nice looking, about five feet five, slender, and appeared to be Asian. Bill stood and waved, making his blue Mohegan Country Club golf cap visible above the crowd. They had agreed on those articles of clothing in order to recognize each other. Sheila smiled and pointed to the counter, indicating she wanted to get some coffee while she was near the front of the shop. Bill nodded and sat down, looking for something interesting in *The Giver* to occupy himself for the next few minutes.

Having secured her coffee, Sheila made her way over to the table. They shook hands, introducing themselves with first names only, Bill of course introducing himself as Troy.

"Okay, so what's the job?"

"I want you to draw my blood. One pint every week over the next four weeks. A hundred dollars a week, with a hundred dollar bonus when the job is complete."

"Doesn't sound too hard ... where?"

"I've got an apartment over in Frog Hollow."

Sheila didn't say anything, but she suddenly looked nervous. She had probably heard a lot of bad things about Frog Hollow. She probably wasn't from Hartford, and didn't know that Frog Hollow had been largely cleaned up. Bill had thought about how he'd handle this reaction.

"If you take the job, we can do it during the day. And you can bring whomever you want with you. Do you have the tools? Blood bags and stuff like that?"

He was trying to change the subject away from the potential dangers of going to a stranger's apartment in Frog Hollow to the mechanics of drawing blood. Bill needed to be patient now, she hadn't run away screaming, but she obviously needed some time to get her head around this odd request. He didn't want to push, so he decided to let her be the next one to speak, however long that took.

"I guess I can get that stuff. Once a week for four weeks? Then that's it?"

"No fuss, no muss. It'll probably take you about a half an hour a week. I'm hoping to get started on Wednesday."

"And I can bring a friend?"

"Absolutely."

He almost invited her to bring two friends if she wanted, and he was going to wink, but he caught himself. They didn't know each other, and the last thing he needed to be right now was creepy.

"Okay Troy, I'll take the job. I'll need the address. What time should I be there?"

They worked out a time in the afternoon based on her class schedule, and said quick goodbyes. Bill was quite pleased. His plan was really coming together. There were obviously a number of major hurdles left, but the plan was now well under way.

Chapter Twenty-Seven

Saturday, February 21, 2009 – 9:00 a.m.

FOR THE FIRST time since he rented the apartment two weeks earlier, Bill turned on the TV in the living room. Sipping the Starbucks latte he picked up on the way over, he switched the station to ESPN to catch up on the latest sports news. Ninety percent of the broadcast consisted of scores and reports about college basketball, which made sense with March Madness looming. It was an odd feeling sitting in the living room on a Saturday morning watching TV, as if this were part of his normal life. For only the second time he was sitting on the living room couch.

The first time had been the previous Wednesday, when Sheila had drawn a pint of his blood. She had arrived at the appointed time with all the necessary supplies, and with her boyfriend in tow. Bill was actually glad that she'd brought her boyfriend; it showed she had good sense. She didn't know Troy from Adam. For all Sheila knew, Troy could be the next Jeffrey Dahmer.

The boyfriend, Eddie, stood about six feet and had an athletic build. He seemed a little on edge. He didn't smile when they were introduced, and his eyes were constantly scanning the living room as if he were expecting someone to jump out from the hallway with an axe. So Bill tried to put him at ease. He engaged the younger man in conversation. What's your major, are you into sports, any part time jobs, etc. Once the needle was in Bill and the blood was being drawn, and no axe murderers appeared to be present in the apartment, Eddie relaxed.

As soon as the pint was drawn, Sheila and Eddie made their way out, confirming for the same time next week. Bill put the blood in the refrigerator and went back to the couch to relax, just as he would if his blood had been drawn by the Red Cross. But alas, something was missing. There were no cookies or coke or pizza! He'd correct that next week. It was probably a good idea to have some snacks available after the "draw," to replenish.

After about thirty minutes, Bill heard the expected knock on the door. He looked through the peephole just to be sure it was whom he was expecting. He felt he couldn't be too careful in this neighborhood. He opened the door.

"Delivery for Troy Stevens?"

"Yep, that's me."

"It's kind of a big box. I wanted to make sure somebody was home before I lugged it up the stairs. I'll go get it now."

"Okay."

Five minutes later, there was another knock on the door. The delivery guy was back, with a box that was as tall as he was.

"Sign here, please."

Bill accepted the clipboard and signed "Troy Stevens" in the highlighted box at the bottom of the delivery receipt. The delivery guy expertly ripped Bill's copy from underneath the top form and handed it to him.

"Have a nice day now."

"You, too."

Bill grabbed the box near its top and dragged it from the hallway into the apartment. Hmmm. He realized he wanted a utility knife to help him open up the box, but he hadn't brought any tools with him. He searched the kitchen and to his surprise found that the drawers were well stocked with silverware and kitchen gadgets. He hadn't expected that. Curious now, he continued to look around, opening the cabinets and finding a number of pots and pans. He even found a cookie sheet. He could cook a meal here if he'd been so inclined. Funny, that had never occurred to him since he had no plans to cook in the apartment. He finally pulled a steak knife out of the silverware drawer.

He laid the box on its side and used the knife to cut the masking tape holding the box together at the top. With the top of the box opened, he could see the top of Grapple Man's head. He thought of grabbing the head and pulling the dummy out of the box as if he were delivering a baby, but then thought better of it. Instead, he cut the corner of the box from top to bottom, using the steak knife as a saw. When he got to the bottom, the whole box kind of popped open, and there in all his glory, lay Grapple Man.

Bill started laughing. The whole thing was just so absurd. There was a life-like dummy in his living room, lying prone on his back, looking as if he was waiting for a hand up. And the dude was ripped! Quite muscular, with perfect abs. <u>I guess when you spend a grand on a dummy, you can expect one with a six-pack.</u>

He began to wonder if it wouldn't have been better to have Grapple Man delivered to the house instead of the apartment. He could have arranged a time for the dummy to be delivered when Laura wouldn't be home. Now he'd have to transport the dummy home and figure out a good time to sneak him into the house. But he had time to worry about that later. And this way, there was no chance that Laura would discover Grapple by accident.

Bill grabbed the fifty-five pound dummy under the arms and dragged him into the bedroom, leaving him right there on the floor. He wanted to be sure the dummy was out of sight when Sheila came to take his blood again on Wednesday. He wasn't really worried about Sheila in general, she needed the money and wouldn't blab about Bill's odd request. But throw a life-sized dummy into the mix and it might heighten her suspicions.

Okay, it was getting to be lunchtime. He'd have lunch downtown today, since Frog Hollow was so close to the business district. After lunch, there was an errand to run. The two-week mandatory waiting period was over. It was time to go and pick up the gun.

Chapter Twenty-Eight

Tuesday, February 24, 2009 – 7:00 p.m.

BAM! THE RECOIL surprised him a bit. Expecting it was one thing, feeling it was quite another. Was he really firing a handgun at a shooting range? Yet another adventure he never would have undertaken if not for his plan.

"Not bad for your first try. Fire a few more," said Terry, Bill's instructor.

While Terry spoke, Bill's eye remained focused on the white dot at the end of the Glock 17's sight. He fired three more rounds, squeezing the trigger slowly as he'd been taught. He hit the white target paper consistently, but in most cases the shots were landing low and left of the bull's-eye.

"Okay. Let's talk for a minute. You are definitely a good student. You are doing a really good job of keeping your wrist steady. But it looks like in order to do that, you're squeezing the handle of the gun a little too tight. So, that's making you miss low left. Try holding that right wrist steady, but when you fire, only squeeze the trigger finger."

When Bill had first been taught to play golf, the golf pro told him to hold the golf club like he was holding a bird. "Never stiffen anything in the golf swing," he had said. Bill was realizing some of those same principles probably applied to shooting a handgun. In golf it's okay to have a light grip when you address the ball because you will instinctively hold onto the club during the swing.

So he shot the next few rounds focusing on lightening his grip. The results were better, closer to the bull's-eye but now he was missing just to the right. Terry was smiling.

"Good stuff here, you are actually doing very well. Can you guess what might happen if your grip is a little too light?"

"Uh, you miss a little to the right?"

"Dude, nothing gets by you, does it?" Terry joked.

"But in all seriousness, you are overcompensating a little now, the grip is a little too loose. So, it's a balance. With more practice, you get better and better, just like anything else. For your first time, you are doing very well."

Bill continued to practice, trying to find the magical amount of grip pressure that would yield bull's-eye after bull's-eye. But of course, not having any previous training, he couldn't sustain the steady wrist for the whole half-hour session. So he began missing for new reasons.

Terry let Bill continue, tweaking and making minor corrections with every round. When time was up, Bill's right arm and wrist were tired. As someone who worked out, he was a bit surprised. Like many activities, shooting apparently required its own set of muscles.

"Okay, thanks, this was fun."

"Same time next week?"

"Yes sir!"

"Okay then, same time next week," said Terry, as the two men shook hands.

"Great job, Troy."

Bill waived to Terry as he was leaving.

Leaving the shooting range, he steered the car toward a house he knew was empty. Laura was on another "business trip." Well, there probably was some business involved, he guessed, but he also had no doubt she was with lover boy.

He guessed things would have been much different had she been able to bear children. They tried to get pregnant for a couple of years early in the marriage but were unsuccessful. Eventually they both went for testing. After many tests, Laura was diagnosed with Luteinized Unruptured Follicle Syndrome (LUFS), otherwise known as "trapped egg syndrome." Bill had never fully understood what it was, but apparently the ovarian follicle produced eggs normally, yet never released them into the ovary. And unfortunately in Laura's case, the treatment for LUFS didn't work. Eventually the couple accepted the fact they weren't destined to become parents. Neither had any particular interest in adopting. After the grueling process of being diagnosed with LUFS and the failed treatments, they decided to just focus on their respective careers.

Bill understood that had they been successful in having children, things would be much different. Instead of weekends filled with work, golf, R-rated movies and fancy dinners, they'd be driving kids around to swim meets, soccer tournaments, and birthday parties. The children would have become the focal point of their lives. He guessed that while he and Laura might have had less time for each other, they probably would have been closer.

<u>Moot point. Targeting March 13th as D-Day. Blood work should be done, but have several more things to put in place before then. Company thing tomorrow.</u>

Chapter Twenty-Nine

Wednesday, February 25, 2009 – 10:00 a.m.

HENRY JOHNSON. THAT would do just fine. An uncomplicated name, one that should be easy to remember. Now, it was time to call Smiley Wilkinson down in Tech Support. Smiley had helped Bill on several projects throughout the years when Bill was involved with automating and computerizing some old company processes. Smiley was always, well, smiling; hence the nickname. He was very popular and well-respected at Greystone because of his experience and demeanor. Unlike many tech gurus, he was very patient with non-techies and computer neophytes.

"Smiley? Smiley Wilkinson? Is it really you?"

"Bill Ferguson! Hadn't heard from you in so long I thought you quit!"

"Never happen, Smiley. I'll probably never leave until they are rolling me out of here on a gurney."

"Sounds like the Bill I remember. Anyway, what can I do for you?"

"Well, we've got a new employee up here, but I don't see his email address in the system. Probably just HR, slowness, you know? Can you help me out and get his account set up now?"

"Hmmm. We've never set up an email account before without the paperwork from HR, but I don't see why we can't do it."

"That would be awesome. We've got him slated to go to a bunch of meetings, documents to send him, etc. So if he didn't have to wait any longer that would be great."

"Okay, Bill. What's the guy's name?"

"Henry Johnson."

"Writing it down. You want me to send you an email with the temp password when I'm done?"

"That would be great. Then I'll let Henry know and we'll get him going. And I've got a call into HR about why it's taking so long to in-process him."

"Okay, sounds good, Bill."

"Thanks a lot, Smiley—I appreciate you helping me out. You da man!"

"Thanks, Bill. You da man, too. Talk to you later."

Bill knew that Smiley and his team were way too busy to follow up with HR for the official paperwork that was not on its way. So the new Henry Johnson email account would probably remain on the system for years before anyone realized there was no employee named Henry Johnson.

Bill logged into the email system as himself and added the new email address to a distribution list for large claims investigations. There were about fifty people already on the list, so no one would notice the addition of one more name. His new friend Henry was going to be Bill's way of keeping track of his own case after he'd disappeared.

The idea of disappearing was much easier for Bill than it would be for most. Bill's parents had been in their early forties when they had Bill. And both had been smokers. Vibrant and healthy for most of their lives, in their seventies a lifetime of smoking caught up with each of them. Bill's dad went first, about four years ago. His mom followed the following year.

It was the second marriage for both Andrew and Tonya Ferguson. Andrew had been involved in a roller coaster ride of a union that had produced three children before a very nasty divorce. The divorce was so nasty that Bill had only met his half-brother and two half-sisters on two separate occasions. Andrew Ferguson and his first wife, Natalie, could not stand to be in the same room together for more than about thirty seconds. Each had accused the other of multiple affairs, and there had been many separations and reconciliations before the end.

Tonya's first marriage had been to a man twenty years her senior. Joe McGinley was a successful and dashing businessman, and his worldly ways had very much impressed twenty-five year old Tonya Robinson. Naturally, her parents weren't very excited by the May–December love affair, but it really was true love. Against all odds, the marriage worked for ten solid years before Joe had a fatal heart attack at the age of fifty-six. No children resulted from the union, however. Joe always felt he was a bit too old, and Tonya wasn't one to pressure her husband into children he didn't want.

The bottom line was that other than Laura, Bill had no family to speak of. Friends, neighbors and co-workers would be shocked, concerned, and surprised by his disappearance. But no one would be organizing searches for him, holding candlelight vigils, or making emotional appeals into a camera for his safe return. He assumed that Laura wouldn't really give a shit. And as the months passed people would forget, and the memory of Bill Ferguson would quickly fade.

Chapter Thirty

Friday, March 6, 2009 – 4:55 a.m.

IT WAS A crime of opportunity. He'd gotten the idea when he had a stomach issue the week before. It had been a rough night, and at four-thirty a.m. he called it quits on trying to go back to sleep. He took a quick shower, got in his car, and headed for that donut shop down the street that was open twenty-four hours. He couldn't remember the name of it, just that it wasn't one of the big chains. The important thing was they had decent coffee. And really good donuts.

When he pulled into the parking lot at about five a.m., he noticed a man rolling a flat cart stacked with crates of something or other into an entrance in the back of the store. Every minute or so, the delivery man wheeled his cart to the back of a panel van, loaded up the cart with more crates, and disappeared back into the store. He did it a total of four times that Bill saw. Then he went in carrying only a clipboard. Obviously the delivery ticket, he needed to have it signed by someone in the store. All the while, the van was running. Why bother shutting off the van, Bill asked himself? No one was really around at that hour except the donut shop employees and one or two customers in the store.

Bill knew he wanted to use a similar van as part of his plan. He'd been thinking of buying one, but if he "borrowed" one that would be much more efficient, financially speaking. He couldn't tell what was in the crates. Was this a delivery that was made every morning? If so, this might not be too difficult.

The next morning he woke at four-fifteen, this time with the aid of his alarm clock. He took a shower and headed for the donut shop. He had no designs on any donuts this time. He parked across the street and watched. Sure enough, just like clockwork, the panel van pulled around the back of the donut shop at five a.m. So apparently there was a daily delivery of some kind every morning at five a.m.

Bill noticed the driver had the same routine, four trips from the truck to the store pulling crates, and then a final trip into the store for the delivery ticket. Bill recorded the amount of time the driver spent in the store during each round trip. He was in the store for about thirty seconds each time. Plenty of time to jump in a van and drive off with it, if someone was in the right position.

What was the right position? Somewhere right near the back of the store. Right behind those dumpsters over there. He could hide in the shadows, and when the driver disappeared into the store the first time, he would strike. Ideally, the van would be "borrowed" right at the beginning of the thirty second window, so the van would be half way down the street before the driver realized what was happening. He could leave his car at the "park and ride" about a half mile away. It would be inconspicuous there.

So Bill, acting as Troy, went that night and rented a storage unit large enough to hold two cars at the self storage place with twenty-four hour access. It was located about five miles away from the donut shop. He wanted plenty of space for the van, and its contents. And plenty of space to load the van with his own provisions, when the time came. Also, he wanted to do something about the advertising on the van. Currently, the words Soffler Foods and a phone number were printed on each side. Bill would want to paint over the sides or hide the advertising with decals or something. Don't they make magnetic decals for the sides of trucks? Did they have generic ones? Ah, it would be easier just to paint over it. It didn't need to be fancy. It just needed to not say "Soffler Foods" for a couple of hours on the night of the thirteenth. The larger storage unit would give him enough room to maneuver.

With the storage unit rented and a plan worked out, he'd gotten up at four this morning. He'd showered, dressed warmly, and driven his car to the park and ride near the donut shop. He'd left himself plenty of time, almost too much, to walk from the park and ride to the donut shop. His car had been the only car in the park and ride, but that didn't matter. His car was in an inconspicuous spot and he'd retrieve it later in the morning. No one would ever make the connection between a car parked in that lot and a missing panel van.

At four fifty-five, he was in position behind the dumpsters. He was sweating despite the forty-degree temperature. His heart was pounding. He'd been in position for fifteen minutes already. The driver was an agonizing five minutes late this morning.

Bill decided he was too nervous to "go" on the driver's first trip into the store. He'd grab the van on the driver's second round trip. The driver got out of the van, walked around to the back, opened it, and pulled his cart down and placed in on the ground. Grabbing crates two at a time, he stacked them on the cart. When he had roughly ten crates stacked on the cart, he started rolling the cart to the store.

After thirty-four seconds he reappeared, and started his ritual again. This was it. The crates were loaded onto the cart and the cart rolled away. It disappeared into the store. Time to go! But Bill hesitated. One second, two seconds, five seconds, ten seconds. He didn't move.

<u>Too late now! You fucking pussy! What the hell are you doing? You are a choker. Big time choker. You think you are going to be able to pull off faking your own death when you can't even jump in a van and drive it away? What the hell is wrong with you?</u>

Bill was still berating himself when the driver started his third round trip by loading up the cart once again. Bill decided he needed to gather himself; he'd wait until the fourth round trip. He focused on his breathing, consciously trying to slow it down, forcing himself to take deep breaths. He told himself, when the time comes, don't think, just act.

The driver reappeared after the third round trip. Last chance! The loading of the crates onto the cart seemed to take an eternity this time. But when that cart and the man pulling it disappeared into the store, Bill reacted. He sprung out of his hiding spot and sprinted the thirty feet to the van. What made life even easier was the driver's habit of leaving the driver's side door open. Bill was able to pull himself into the van without making noise opening the door. Bill didn't bother closing up the back of the van. Too much time and too much noise. As long as he didn't leave a trail of foodstuffs all the way to the self-storage place, who cared if a few things spilled out of the back of the van as he sped away? Certainly not him.

Bill threw the van into drive and punched the gas pedal. As the van lurched forward, he tossed the steering wheel to the right and headed for the donut shop exit. He was half way down the street when he looked out the rear view mirror and saw a shocked man with a delivery cart standing at the back of the donut shop. <u>Sorry sucker, don't you know you shouldn't leave the van running like that?</u>

Making a bee-line for the self-storage facility, Bill laughed uncontrollably. How insane was this? But what a thrill! He felt incredibly alive. He was practically high right now. He couldn't remember the last time his heart was pounding like this. But he needed to get hold of himself again, he wasn't quite finished.

As he drove toward the self-storage unit, he suddenly became paranoid. He was so close to pulling this off. It was only five-fifteen and there was very light traffic on the street where the facility was. But what if someone recognized the truck? What if someone saw it, and noticed the Soffler Foods truck was not where it was supposed to be? There was probably a bored cop sitting in a parking lot within a mile of here. He'd be all over this as soon as the call went out to look for a stolen Soffler Foods panel truck.

Bill pulled the van up to the storage unit entrance and nervously punched in his code. There was no one around. He had instinctively chosen a unit at the back of the facility, and right now he was very happy about that. Once he drove around the first group of units and headed toward the back, no one would be able to see the van from the street.

He opened his unit and pulled the truck inside. He turned off the engine, but left the keys in it. Why carry around the keys? He locked the unit back up and made his way on foot to the front of the storage facility. Walking toward a diner two blocks away, he was happy not to see any cops. He felt very vulnerable right then. He had no cover story for what he was doing there.

But he made it to the diner and ate a hearty breakfast. He then called a taxi to take him to the park and ride to retrieve his car. It was just about seven a.m. now, time to get to work. But he felt like he'd done more before seven a.m. than most people did all day.

Chapter Thirty-One

Monday, March 9, 2009 – 9:15 a.m.

"OKAY, TELL ME what you see."

"Well, a couple of things. The first thing I noticed as I walked up here was, of course, par four, dogleg left. Next, I see the tee box is actually pointing straight at those tall trees on the left. So, someone who's not paying attention might line himself up with the tee box and smack the ball right into the woods. And there is no way you are going to clear them. The next thing is the big bunker on the right at the end of the dogleg. From the middle of the bunker you are only about one hundred and thirty out, but it's not a great angle with the pin on the right today. Ideally, you'd be on the left side of the fairway with a pin like this, but then you're flirting with those trees. So for me, I'm going to play my three wood so I don't reach the bunker, and try to hit a draw off the bunker to the middle of the fairway. The fairway is sloped from right to left also, so that should help me get to the middle. With this setup, it might not be a birdie hole today."

"Pretty impressive. You must have noticed the pin placement from the fourth tee, because you can't see the pin from here."

Grinning, Bill reached into his bag for his three wood. Step by step he progressed through his normal pre-shot routine, taking his grip, setting his feet, waggling, etc. After a deep breath, he got the left shoulder moving, and everything after that was automatic. The result was a gorgeous drive, with a pro style, five-yard draw off the bunker to the middle of the fairway.

Don Delamar was impressed. Through four holes, his potential assistant pro was one under par, and sitting pretty in the fifth fairway. As the head pro at the Driftwood Club, he'd interviewed dozens of job applicants. Don liked to conduct the first half of his interviews this way, a mix of golf and conversation. He felt he got a better feel for the person than he would if he just verified his handicap, followed by a formal interview. No question, this guy could really play golf. After both players secured their pars on the fifth hole, they hopped into their golf cart.

"Good playing so far. Refresh me, how come you're doing this now? Being an assistant pro, I mean. Most guys that try this are twenty-five or younger."

Don had asked this question when he'd talked to Troy on the phone. And he remembered the answer he'd been given. But over the years Don had found that if he asked the same question on a different day, he might get a different answer. And that was a deal breaker in most cases. He wasn't in the business of hiring saints, but his assistant pros had to be relatively trustworthy.

"Just tired of the rat race. Bored with the daily grind. And now that my dad has passed on and left me a bunch of money, I can relax a little. Not saying I'd relax on this job, but it's not about the money anymore. You know what I mean? I can spend my days doing something I really enjoy."

They pulled up to the tee at a picturesque downhill par three. It measured 175 yards but played shorter because of the elevated tee. To get to the right hand side of the green, where the pin was positioned today, one had to carry the ball the entire way over a pond. There was dry land on the left, but the course architect had strategically placed two sand bunkers on that side. One bunker was just short of the green, the other even with the middle of the green. The bunkers collected the balls of those chicken-hearted souls who bailed out, either consciously or subconsciously.

Bill pulled out his seven iron and took dead aim at the pin. He went through his normal routine, but was feeling a little off kilter. He'd never been a great liar, and had become anxious while bullshitting about Troy's past. He chunked his shot into the pond, took a drop in a designated drop area, and proceeded to flub his pitch shot from the drop area. By the time it was all over, he'd recorded an aggravating double bogey on his scorecard.

Luckily for Bill, Don didn't make the connection between the disastrous hole and the conversation that preceded. Bill settled himself down, playing the rest of the round in two over par for a respectable round of seventy-five. He needed to get better at explaining his past. It needed to be second nature if his plan was to succeed. He'd have to start rehearsing, as absurd as that sounded.

After a quick lunch in the clubhouse, it was time for the second part of the interview. The two jumped into a cart and headed to the practice tee. They drove the cart to the right hand side of the range where a young slender man was hitting balls. The guy was fairly tall, six foot, one inch. Don bounded out of the cart and headed toward the young man. Bill followed.

Don introduced Troy to the young man. "Troy, I'd like you to meet Kenny here. He's been having a little trouble with his swing and we thought it would be good if you took a look."

"Okay. No problem. Kenny, looks like you've already had a chance to warm up, so why don't you take out your seven iron and hit about five balls."

Kenny nodded, and complied with the request. After a couple of swings Bill saw that Kenny's shots were all pulled straight and left of their intended direction. In his view Kenny was going 'over-the-top,' a premature move of the shoulders and a fairly common amateur problem. Bill explained his diagnosis to Kenny, with Don listening close by. He gave Kenny some drills to work on, which should correct the problem. Kenny did a few of the drills and then started crushing the ball.

Bill was a little perplexed. He knew he was on the right track with the drills; he'd had the same problem himself as a junior golfer. But how could the problem be corrected so quickly? Had he missed his calling as a golf instructor?

"Okay, good job, Troy. Now, diagnose this issue."

He watched as Kenny suddenly started slicing the ball wildly. The kind of shots that can break the screen doors of houses too close to the course. <u>What the hell? Oh, Duh. This guy's not an amateur. They are testing my teaching ability. He's slicing on purpose so he and Don can evaluate my advice.</u>

Bill showed Kenny a few drills that could be used to combat a slice. The big one being practice hitting shots with your feet together. "This drill keeps you from swaying too much, and helps promote good balance and timing," Troy explained.

After the 'lesson' was over, Don spoke. "So, how long did it take you to figure out that Kenny was a pro?"

Bill chuckled. "Well, after I cured his fake over-the-top move so fast, I didn't know what was happening. But then when he started slicing like that, I knew something was up."

"Troy Stevens, meet Kenny Lumpkin, the other assistant pro here at the club."

Kenny and Bill shook hands warmly.

"Okay Troy, so far, so good. Let's go back to the office and talk about some of the other duties of an assistant pro around here. And we'll also need to talk money." Back in the office, Bill was formally offered the job, and accepted it. The salary was only a meager twenty thousand per year, but he could get a cheap apartment and make it work. It wouldn't be forever, after all. Someday, he'd be sitting on a beach working on the perfect tan and would look back on his assistant pro days and laugh.

Chapter Thirty-Two

Thursday, March 12, 2009 – 11:30 p.m.

BILL MARCHED ON through the pitch-black night. He was fifteen minutes into his forty-five minute hike. The whole thing was aggravating. It was chilly, but at least it wasn't raining. But he hadn't been able to figure out how else to get the pickup truck to the quarry and then get himself back home without getting someone else involved. So he had to walk the three miles back to a main road. Luckily, there was an all-night diner not too far from the intersection of the main road and the road he was on. At least he could eat a piece of pie while he waited for a cab to take him home from Sally's Diner.

As far as he could tell, there wasn't a living soul along this stretch of road at this time of night. It was completely deserted. And that seemed kind of strange considering he was within three miles of a densely populated area. The desolation was both eerie and comforting. Eerie because if someone was nearby and wanted to mess with him, there was nowhere to run other than the very dark forest. Every rustle of a leaf in the woods caused the hair on the back of his neck to stand on end. Then he'd realize it was just a squirrel, or just a deer. Still, he was on edge, his senses heightened. He was alert on a level he had rarely experienced before he undertook his grand scheme.

On the other hand, the feeling of being all alone in this part of the world was comforting because it meant that for tomorrow night, his big night, he had picked the perfect location. There would be no witnesses to his movements, his actions. He would be able to quickly and quietly dispense with the panel truck and all its contents. And the mystery of what happened to Bill Ferguson would begin.

Earlier in the week Bill had painted over the Soffler Foods advertising on the panel truck. It had taken him much longer than he had anticipated. It had needed three coats of paint to completely cover the ads. Not a fun job in the confines of the storage unit. No air, no windows. It had been just Bill, five gallons of white auto paint, and an aging panel truck. But it was a necessary step. He couldn't take the chance someone would recognize the truck on his big night.

By about ten-thirty p.m. Bill had driven the pickup truck over to the Frog Hollow apartment and loaded all the items he would need into the trunk. He had filled the duffel bag with all the necessary gear, loaded the Glock and had thrown it into the bag. Earlier in the week he'd bought the divers belts and weights from a store that sold scuba gear. He had loaded the belts with the weights and stuffed them into the bag. Once he'd gotten everything together and into the pickup truck, he had driven it to the storage unit and transferred everything into the panel van. After that was done, it had been time to position the pickup near the quarry's edge.

Grapple Man had been moved to the basement of the house late Tuesday night so no curious neighbors would notice. The whole week of prep had been made much easier by the fact that Laura was out of town on a big case. She was gone for the entire week. Even so, there had been a lot of late nights this week, and Bill was ready for this phase of the operation to be over. The second phase, of course, would be securing yet another identity and actually getting all the money.

He planned on sneaking out of the office in the morning for a half hour in order to meet a professional cleaning crew at the Frog Hollow apartment. It was something he felt compelled to do, but he couldn't explain why. He'd tried to talk himself out of it several times. There really was no justification for it, other than the removal of his fingerprints. And if things got to the point where his Frog Hollow apartment was being dusted for prints, that would mean his plan had unraveled. Needless to say, he had better be long gone at that point.

Between working and prepping for his big night, he'd been very busy this week. As he trudged along in the darkness, it just now dawned on him that tomorrow would be his very last day as Bill Ferguson! How strange was that? Come Saturday, he'd be asking everyone he meets to call him Troy. It would take some getting used to.

He had to be "careful" at work tomorrow. It was to be his last day at Greystone, but no one else knew that. He'd have to force himself to behave as if it was just another Friday, which would be followed by just another Monday, from a work perspective. No goodbyes. No farewell lunch. No regrets.

Chapter Thirty-Three

Friday, March 13, 2009 – 11:30 a.m.

BILL GOT BACK from Frog Hollow just in time for his lunch with Jennifer. The cleaners had been late and he'd had no choice but to wait for them. He wanted that apartment in pristine condition before he disappeared. He'd paid two months' rent, and now would just simply not renew and leave no forwarding address. Troy Stevens got very little mail as it was.

This lunch was going to be odd. He knew he'd probably never see Jennifer again, but he couldn't say that, not even hint at it. He had grown very fond of her over the years. She had been such a trooper during the whole demotion debacle. In many cases, loyalty falters as confidence in the boss wanes. Will it be good for my career to stay aligned with this person? Should I switch to a boss with more "upside?" But Jennifer never flinched.

Bill and Jennifer jumped into Bill's BMW and headed for the Wicked Onion. It was a quick trip in the car. Bill tried to think of fun things they could talk about over lunch. He wanted to create almost a script to follow. Below the surface, he had a growing feeling of sadness, but he couldn't allow that feeling to show through. He would miss Jennifer. And other than his golf buddies from the club and a few co-workers, he wasn't sure anyone else in the world would really miss him.

The master plan wasn't just a fun idea anymore. It had taken on a life of its own. It was unstoppable; it had momentum. There was no choice but to follow through. The problem today was that he had not fully considered how it would feel to kill off Bill Ferguson. He had been so consumed with the planning, the scheming, the execution of the plan. No real thought had been given to his feelings in this regard. His focus had been solely on the end game, getting the three million dollars and living on a beach somewhere. Now, with just hours left of his current existence, it was starting to hit home just how fundamental the changes in his life would be. It wasn't like he was moving to another city and could still keep in touch with everyone through Facebook. As a matter of fact, it was just the opposite. Once he became Troy Stevens, and eventually the person to follow, he would continually live with a vague fear of running into someone from his past life. A chance encounter with an old chum or co-worker could very well be disastrous. What if someone he knew came to play golf at Driftwood Club? Thankfully, that wasn't very likely since it was a private club. But suddenly, he was second-guessing his choice of Myrtle Beach. Too damn popular! But it was too late to worry about it now. It was something to think about for the next phase. He'd better shy away from vacation hot spots when picking his final destination.

"Why so quiet? Is everything all right?" The question from Jennifer jolted Bill back into the present.

"Oh, yeah, sorry, just day dreaming. And really hungry, too. I skipped breakfast this morning." And that was true. It was very late when he'd gotten home from his adventures the night before. He'd slept in, and gotten up at the last minute for work.

Bill found a parking spot at a meter about a block from the restaurant. Having recently practiced, he deftly parallel parked. Jennifer was impressed. Bill threw a few quarters into the meter and the pair headed for the restaurant. As Bill sat across from Jennifer, he realized he was seeing her in a way he really hadn't before. She looked pretty damn good. Had she lost weight? He didn't think so. She'd probably always looked this good and he'd just never noticed before. And that was mostly a good thing, he figured. He was her married boss after all. But she looked great to him today and he had always admired her personality.

How ironic. After years of working together, Bill was just now noticing Jennifer "in that way," and he was about to become single and would no longer be her boss. Maybe it was just a classic case of a guy wanting someone he couldn't have. Because making any kind of a move in Jennifer's direction right now would be ludicrous, of course. Things might be different if he was simply getting divorced.

Bill started off doing a good job of keeping the conversation light but Jennifer took it a bit deeper than he wanted when she talked about her most recently failed relationship. She seemed pretty disappointed. She thought this latest guy had a chance to be Mr. Right. Luckily they hadn't been seeing each other for that long, so it wasn't the end of the world. For Bill it felt like she was pouring salt on an open wound. She was looking great and she was available. There wasn't a damn thing he could do about it.

While driving back from lunch, Bill wondered what he should do for the rest of the day. He would keep work to a minimum, but what about this evening? Oh crap! He hadn't accounted for his car. He'd have to go home, drop off the car, and take a cab over to the storage unit in order to pick up the panel van. Otherwise he would wind up leaving the Beamer at the storage unit, and that would be a disaster. Bill Ferguson and Troy Stevens would be linked instantly. Since he didn't need to pick up the panel van until around eleven forty-five per his schedule, he'd have gobs of time to take care of this gaffe. He just needed to figure out the best way. Timing was the key; he wanted to leave his car at home, yet entertain himself for the rest of the evening. He decided to go home and have dinner, and then "sneak" out of the neighborhood around 9:00 pm and catch a cab to the storage unit. No one would notice him leaving the neighborhood on foot at that hour.

Chapter Thirty-Four

Saturday, March 14, 2009 – 3:00 a.m.

IT WAS ONLY two hours into his drive south and he was missing his 3-Series BMW badly. It wasn't that the Chevy was a bad truck; the ride was just fine. But this 1995 model had none of the bells and whistles he had grown accustomed to. He had been spoiled by his in-dash navigation system, satellite radio, and the active steering technology that adjusted the steering responsiveness for different speeds. It was a middle of the night reminder that he had chosen to live a spartan lifestyle for the next months while awaiting his big payoff. So he better suck it up regarding the little conveniences he'd been taking for granted. This was just the beginning.

    He pulled off the highway at a large rest area to get some coffee. His plan was to drive for six hours, get a motel room, sleep for three hours, then drive the remaining seven hours to Myrtle Beach. But he was fading already. He'd had a long week with not much sleep, and now the adrenaline that had carried him through the fake murder was wearing off. The one amenity the pickup truck had was a CD player, but he hadn't thought to buy any CDs for the long drive. Hence, the trip at this point was pure drudgery. He scanned the FM radio stations for songs he liked. Eventually he would lock onto a station, but it usually didn't take too long before that one was out of range and it was time to begin searching for the next one. It was a pain. He'd have to combat his fatigue and boredom with frequent stops and lots of caffeine. And while he was tired, he didn't have the stomach for deviating from his plan and finding a place to sleep right now. Laura wasn't scheduled to come back until Sunday, but he wanted to be as far from Hartford as possible, as soon as possible, in case she came home a day early.

In addition to the CD player, the other good thing about the pickup truck was that he'd been able to buy it for two thousand in cash. And he had about that amount with him for incidentals as he headed for his new, temporary life in South Carolina. He'd secured a Frog Hollow-style apartment in North Myrtle, mostly over the phone. He just needed to actually see the place, make sure it wasn't a complete wreck, and put down his security deposit. He'd shore up that deal on Saturday evening, rest on Sunday, and start his new job on Monday.

He'd lived poor before, in college and the early days of Bedrock. But he assumed it would be much harder to do it now that he'd grown accustomed to affluence. It was one thing to pop in once a week to Frog Hollow to have his blood drawn. It was another thing altogether to live in an apartment like that full time. Damn! He should have bought a new laptop or a flat screen TV, or both, when he still had access to Bill Ferguson's credit cards. Then again, a purchase like that might arouse more suspicion. People would speculate that he could still be alive if a recently bought laptop could not be located. He would just have to acquire those things when he could. He was starting over again, in every way.

He'd been driving for five and a half hours and was losing his battle to stay awake. He'd actually dozed off for a second on two different occasions. It was never a good feeling to find yourself suddenly awake when behind the wheel. Just north of Baltimore, he decided it was close enough to his six-hour target. Steering the truck off I-95 at the White Marsh, Maryland exit, he headed for the cheapest motel he could find. He paid cash for an extremely basic room, threw on some sweat pants and a tee shirt, and was asleep before his head hit the pillow.

The next thing he heard was the beeping of the alarm as his eyelids struggled to open. It was the alarm on his watch, which he'd placed on the dresser across the room so he'd have to get out of bed in order to turn it off. Sitting up and placing his feet on the floor, he rubbed the sleep from his eyes. He felt like he could sleep for another six hours. But as he awoke, he started to feel really good.

Refreshed. He made his way over to the dresser to turn off the alarm. Holy crap! It was twelve p.m.! The alarm had been going off for hours and he'd slept right through it. No wonder he felt good, he'd had a solid six hours of sleep.

No way he could make it to the apartment complex office and pay the security deposit in time. They closed at five p.m. on Saturday. And he had another eight hours of driving. The office was open for a few hours on Sunday afternoon, so he'd have to do it then. In the meantime, he'd stay in a motel in Myrtle this evening. Not great, since he was on a budget now. Incidentals like this, that he wouldn't have thought twice about just last week, now mattered. His meager assistant pro salary was already influencing his decisions and he hadn't even started the job yet!

Hungry, he checked out of the motel and headed for a convenience store a few blocks away. He decided to see how far he could go on an energy bar and a bottle of water. He got those two items for two dollars and fifty cents. It was all about saving money now. He'd try to do better for dinner. He wanted to call the apartment complex in Myrtle to let them know he would be coming tomorrow, not today, but he had no cell phone. Argh! He'd tried so hard to think of everything in his planning, but was now realizing he had done almost no prep for this part of the operation. He decided to buy a phone card at least, so he could make calls at a pay phone until Troy could get a cell phone. He'd need to establish an address and get a credit card, he assumed, before getting a cell phone. So that would take a week or two.

The rest of the drive to Myrtle was much easier than the driving he'd done in the middle of the night. The energy he'd gained while sleeping was further fueled by brilliant sunshine. He could feel spring elbowing Old Man Winter out of the way, especially as he drove south. At about three p.m. he stopped to stretch his legs, get some gas, hit the head, and buy a diet soda. He bought some cheap sunglasses for eight dollars. As luck would have it, this rest stop did have a pay phone, so he made his call to the apartment complex. He didn't want to lose that apartment.

At six pm he decided to stop for a proper dinner in Fayetteville, NC. It was time to splurge a little; a minor celebration was in order. He followed his nose to a brew pub in town. After no breakfast and a minuscule lunch, he was ravenous. The joint was packed; it was obviously a hot spot on Saturday evening. He grabbed the last stool at the end of the bar and enjoyed a nice local ale and gourmet cheeseburger that tasted like it came from heaven. He had a second pint for dessert, and then hit the road for his final leg to Myrtle Beach.

Chapter Thirty-Five

Sunday, March 15, 2009 – 3:00 p.m.

DETECTIVE DMITRI JONES turned his unmarked cruiser left onto Mapletree Drive. About ninety minutes before, he'd gotten the call about a possible homicide. His experience had taught him it was best, for him, if he didn't rush to the scene. He would just wind up waiting for the techs to do their work, and he'd be trying his best not to get in their way. So instead of pacing around a crime scene, where he'd be antsy and wanting to jump in, he took his time. He finished his meal, or took that shower, or even finished making love to his wife before heading out.

He already had mixed emotions about this case and he hadn't even reached the scene yet. He'd really been enjoying watching his son Darren play soccer that afternoon. Darren was twelve, and was a midfielder on a really good travel team. The call came about ten minutes into the game. Dmitri was loath to leave the game. The weather was decent for March, his son was doing well, and it was a good, competitive game. But it went with the territory for his job. Occasionally, he got a call. So he waited until halftime, then ran home to change his clothes and make a sandwich before going to the scene.

So, the bad news was it was Sunday. The good news was it was the afternoon. So many of these calls came between dusk and dawn. It was nice to be able to start working a case during the daylight hours. His alertness stemmed from the fact that he was actually awake and not from the usual post-midnight coffee and adrenaline-induced rush.

He would be working this case solo for the next couple of days until his partner Brad Davis got back from Disney World. It was spring break for Davis's kids and they had been planning this trip for a full year. He liked Brad, they got along and usually saw things from different angles, so they were a good team. But working a case alone wasn't always the worst thing in the world. He could make his own decisions without conferring with someone and making sure they were "on the same page."

Dmitri guided the cruiser very deliberately down the street. He had been trained to observe everything. Especially people. People hanging out near a crime scene. Sometimes, perpetrators got additional kicks by watching the police roll in and process a crime scene. Part of their rush, he supposed. As he got closer to the Ferguson house, he could see the patrol cars, the yellow tape acting as a fence around the front yard, and roughly two-dozen spectators.

He drove the cruiser right up to the house and showed his badge to a patrolman he didn't recognize. The yellow tape was lifted and he drove his car underneath it, then eased the cruiser in behind a patrol car in the Ferguson's driveway. As he got out of the car he made a point of quickly assessing each person hovering around the scene. He noticed no one who looked particularly suspicious, but he tried to make a mental note of all the people. Every once in a while he'd later connect a mug shot with a face he remembered from the scene. In a couple of those cases it was someone from the neighborhood who someone else knew.

He popped out of the car and nodded to the patrolman who had let him through. He then walked up to the front door and entered the house. A tech, was dusting the front parlor for prints called out, "Joe! Detective Jones is here." Within a few seconds Joe Spencer, the senior crime scene technician working that day appeared in the parlor.

Detective Jones glared at Spencer with utter disdain. Narrowing his eyes and furrowing his brow, he created the nastiest scowl he could come up with. It was a look he had used to terrify fellow cops and suspects alike. He addressed Spencer.

"You again? Christ, they'll let anybody work a crime scene, won't they?"

"Oh really? And where did they find you, old man? Did they run out of detectives who are actually alive?"

Dmitri clenched his fists and pulled his right one back, ready to smash Spencer in the face. But he couldn't hold the scowl any longer. He unclenched his fists, and broke into a wide smile. Spencer, ten years Dmitri's junior, laughed. He had processed many of Jones's crime scenes and they had developed a rapport over the years. Each respected the other's work.

"Okay, enough with the pleasantries. Go do something productive, will you?"

"The techs are close to being finished. We'll be out of the way in a few minutes."

Just then, a patrolman entered the foyer. "Detective? I'm Officer Harrigan. I was the first on the scene and oversaw the securing of the premises."

"Okay. What have we got?"

"The wife called this in. She's in the living room with a couple of patrolmen. She seems genuinely shaken."

"What happened?"

"When the 911 call came in, she said she had just gotten home and her husband was missing. She said there was lots and lots of blood and she needed help. When I got here she told me the same thing."

"Where is all the blood?"

"It's a crazy scene. Lots of blood, but no body. Looks like the victim might have been shot in the home office and then dragged out the back door. Two distinct sets of bloody footprints, suggesting two perps. There is a tire mark in the grass near the back door, right where it looks like the body was dragged."

"Why do you think the body was dragged out the back?"

"There is a blood trail leading from the office all the way out the back door. It's a wide smear of blood, as if something quite bloody was dragged."

"Anything else?"

"Yes. There is a bullet hole in the wall. Looks like a nine-millimeter slug. And we found a second casing in front of the desk. We have not found a gun."

"So, it appears to you that the victim was shot in the home office, then dragged out back by two guys to a waiting vehicle?"

"That's sure how it looks."

"Okay. Make sure the wife stays put. I want to look around a little before I talk to her."

"No problem. I think she's too stunned to go anywhere."

"Which way to the home office?"

"It's just off to the right. Oh, and no signs of forced entry either. If the guy was killed or abducted, he probably knew the perps."

"Thanks for your analysis officer." He really hadn't wanted to sound condescending, but he knew he did.

"Wait, one more question—is anything missing?"

"Not that we know of. The wife hasn't noticed anything, but she's kind of in shock."

"Okay, thanks."

Dmitri had been to many crime scenes over the years, but he didn't recall ever seeing this much blood. He stood in the doorway of the home office, taking in the scene. There was a desk across the room. The chair at the desk had a lot of blood on it. Just above the chair was a bullet hole in the wall. There was blood on the wall behind the chair. Something about this scene seemed very strange, but he couldn't put his finger on it.

He moved to the right so he could see behind the desk. There was a great deal of blood puddled on the floor underneath the chair. Especially to the right of the chair. Perhaps the victim fell in that direction? He didn't know exactly how much blood was in this office. But it was enough. In his experience, no one lost this much blood and lived very long afterward.

Dmitri looked more closely at the blood on the wall, but especially on the floor. The blood patterns didn't look like anything he had ever seen before. Usually there is some kind of uniformity, if one knows what he is looking for. But here, he noticed a mixture of passive bloodstains, suggesting dripping, and projected stains, suggesting a splattering. He didn't ever remember seeing the two types of stains combined like that.

"Joe!"

A few seconds later, Joe appeared, as if out of thin air. "Yes, sir."

"Make sure the camera guys take lots and lots of pictures of this blood splatter. I want lots of pictures, from every conceivable angle. Capiche?"

"Got it."

"Also, has anybody been through the desk, or any of the files in the office?"

"No, sir. In order to get back there we'd have to clean up the blood on the floor. And we didn't want to do that without your okay."

"Good thinking. And after you get the pictures, have someone start cleaning this up. I want to go through the desk sooner rather than later."

After his examination of the office, Dmitri headed down the hallway where the body had supposedly been dragged. He took his time, making sure not to step in any of the blood, and examining the blood as he walked. It was definitely smeared, just as Harrigan had said. After a couple of minutes, he passed through the mudroom and then out into the backyard. It was a nice big backyard, with lots of old, tall trees. Someone in the neighborhood was burning a fire in the fireplace. He could smell it.

He followed the blood trail for several feet and then it stopped. As luck would have it, there happened to be a bare patch of dirt just to the right of that spot. A bare spot just large enough for a tire track. He made a mental note to make sure that the techs had taken a picture of the track. He couldn't imagine them missing this, but it could be his butt in a sling if he didn't make sure.

He went back into the mudroom. Joe was waiting.

"The office is ready now."

"Wow, that was quick."

"We aim to please."

"If that were true, you wouldn't be here. Where are all the twenty-five year old hot babe techs, anyway?"

"They heard you were coming and quickly lost interest in the case."

"Oh, you're a comedian now? Please spare us and stick to being a mediocre tech guy, will you?"

Joe had no comeback for that.

Dmitri walked to the home office and sat down at the desk. He tried to imagine what the victim went through. He must have been shot in an artery to spill that much blood. Or his jugular vein. Yeah, that made sense. He's sitting at the desk, having some kind of a meeting in the office that goes bad.

Then one or both perps whip out a Glock and shoot him. One shot lands in the jugular vein, bam, blood everywhere. So the guys drag him out to a vehicle out back. But why? Why not just let him die right here? Did they want to try to keep him alive for some reason? He'd have someone check the hospitals in case the perps took him for medical attention. One thing was apparent; he was shot on purpose. Nobody fires two shots by accident.

The whole thing seemed a little strange. Ferguson lets two guys into the house, brings them into the office, then he sits down behind the desk, yet they remain standing. Maybe he wanted to check something on his computer? And why would they have a vehicle out back if he let them in? A second vehicle? Or somehow they had a key and didn't need to break in? That almost made more sense. They let themselves in, then surprised him in the office.

So, what would the preliminary focus of the investigation be? Who, and why? What was Ferguson into? Some insurance fraud scheme gone wrong? Or something else? But before he went down that road, he had to rule out Mrs. Ferguson first.

He began his examination of the desk. Weird. Not a thing appeared to be out of place on top of the desk. Apparently, no arm flailed and rearranged the objects on the desk. If Ferguson held his hands up to his face in a defensive fashion when he was being shot, then fell to his right after being shot, then okay, he might not knock anything off the desk.

Dmitri opened the middle desk drawer. The first thing he saw was a big brown envelope. Hmmm. No markings on the envelope. He opened it up. Pictures. Very interesting pictures. Pictures that would make it impossible to rule out Mrs. Ferguson any time soon. He'd spend a few more minutes going through the papers in the desk, then maybe a few more minutes going through the filing cabinet. Then it would be time to take Mrs. Ferguson downtown for a good long talk.

Chapter Thirty-Six

Monday, March 16, 2009 – 5:00 p.m.

BILL WAS PLUM tuckered. While he'd kept himself in decent shape over the years, he wasn't used to being on his feet all day long. But his first day as an assistant golf pro had gone very well. He'd learned the ins and outs of working in the pro shop and he'd given two lessons. And he'd really enjoyed the day. He couldn't believe it was five p.m. already. It was really a joy to work at something that didn't have anything to do with the insurance business.

It was only the second day, but he was enjoying the apartment so far. Although he did need to sign up for cable and buy a flat screen, soon. He'd secured the apartment just after noon on Sunday, then headed for Walmart for some clothes. While at Walmart, a paperback mystery title caught his eye and he grabbed the six-dollar book. It would serve to fill his current entertainment void. Bill couldn't remember the last time he'd sat down on a Sunday and read a novel. The concept was, well, novel. He'd purchased a twelve pack of beer, and alternated between drinking a beer, reading the novel, and dozing off. It was exquisite.

He was astonished by how relaxed he felt. It was one of those deals where he didn't realize how stressed out he had become until he got a chance to just sit. No issues, no responsibilities. The only thing he had to do was show up at the golf club. And how tough was that? It was as if a mountain of worry had been lifted from his shoulders. No doubt, his complicated preparations had added to his stress during the preceding weeks. But that stress damage probably paled in comparison to the damage he would have felt if he had confronted his wife and gotten a conventional divorce. Months and months of heartaches and headaches. Lawyers and loneliness, each scheduled around a job he could no longer stand. And worse, Laura was a lawyer and knew the best lawyers. In the end, he had divorced Laura all right. Just not the usual way. And now he would become rich because of it.

The biggest challenge so far was he still had to consciously remember to respond to the name Troy. Because he was so focused on it now, it was easy. The danger would be in a few weeks. He recalled the days just after Greystone had bought Bedrock and he'd had to move offices. For the first two weeks he'd make it a point to remember to drive to the new office. But as soon as he got comfortable with going to the new place, he forgot. That third

Monday he'd been thinking about his latest work project while he was driving and found that he had absentmindedly driven to the old building. He did it once more the week after that. No big deal in that scenario. But not responding to your name could lead to questions. And he didn't want any questions.

"Hey Troy, before you leave, we want to take your picture for the website. It will just take a second. As I'm sure you've seen, we have a little blurb about each of the pros on the site."

<u>Crap!</u> Bill wanted to decline, but he was quickly learning that Don Delamar usually got his way. Refusing the picture would only arouse suspicion. Besides, what were the chances someone from his past life would happen upon the Driftwood Club website and recognize an anonymous assistant pro named Troy Stevens as Bill Ferguson? Slim to none, he figured. The picture would be up on the site later in the week. There was nothing he could really do about it.

In the apartment that night, something occurred to Bill. Maybe the picture was a good thing. Eventually, after he disappeared with the money, the Troy Stevens persona would probably be discovered. Once he'd stolen the money the authorities would have to go looking for it, and the theft would be under the name of Bill Ferguson. If the connection was made between Bill Ferguson and Troy Stevens, the pictures would look the same.

That was fine. Because the permanent replacement for Bill Ferguson would be the persona that followed. That third identity is the one that would wind up with all the money. It was that new person who would need to look different.

So in order to be better able to disguise himself later, he needed to maintain his current weight the whole time he was Troy Stevens. Then in his next life, he figured he could trim down twenty or even thirty pounds, if he really put his mind to it, in an effort to alter his appearance. While golf wasn't super strenuous, he'd have to be mindful of not losing weight. He was after all, switching from being a desk jockey to someone who was on his feet most of the day.

Chapter Thirty-Seven

Wednesday, March 18, 2009 – 9:00 a.m.

"HOW WAS THE trip, partner?"

"Oh, it was good. The kids had a blast. The wife, too."

"But not you?"

"Well, I guess a few days of Mickey is enough for me, you know what I mean? Not sure I needed a whole week of that stuff."

"I get that. It's easy to suffer from sensory overload in Orlando."

"Yeah that's it. Sensory overload. Well put. Maybe I can go on disability now, kind of like if I had traumatic stress disorder."

Dmitri Jones laughed out loud, something he rarely did.

"Good to have you back, partner."

"Thanks. Apparently I'm back in time to help catch a piece of the 'who-dun-it' of the decade."

"Well, it's certainly a mystery right now."

"Here's where we are," Dmitri continued. "A woman comes home to find a lot of blood in the home office of the house. And I mean a lot of blood. Her husband, an insurance executive, is gone, and it appears that someone was shot in the office and dragged out the back of the house to a waiting vehicle. Probably him, since it's his blood everywhere. It looks like there were two perps. Two sets of blood stained footprints all over the office and down the hallway where the body was dragged. If there was a body. Bullet hole in the wall, same ammo used in a 9mm Glock. Nothing missing from the house according to the wife. No signs of forced entry either. Neighbors saw and heard nothing, naturally. A big house with a big yard, it would take a lot for them to hear a commotion."

Dmitri paused to take a sip of water, then continued.

"While searching the desk in the office, we find pictures of the wife with another dude. She's been having an affair and apparently the husband got suspicious and hired a PI. So we find the pictures in the desk. We grilled her for six hours and she never budged. Plus, we verified her alibi. She was away all week working a case—she's a lawyer."

"The footprints, they were men?"

"Yes, and I see where you are going. We haven't ruled out her involvement entirely. And there is a lot of life insurance money involved. A lot. Three million smackaroos."

"Whoa. I guess the guy got a company discount?"

Dmitri chuckled. Brad's droll sense of humor was one of the reasons Dmitri liked working with him.

"You said 'if there was a body,' as if there might not be one."

"Well, I talked to some of the folks he works with yesterday. His secretary, his current boss, his former boss. The guy recently got demoted, but before that he was sort of a rock star. Or at least as close as someone can come to a rock star as an insurance guy. So, like I said, recently demoted, but no enemies to speak of at work. His secretary is pretty torn up."

"Do you think something is going on there?"

"She denied it. No reason to think there was anything at this point."

Dmitri continued, "Anyway, we've got a lot more digging to do obviously, but the guy was pretty darn clean. His biggest vice was golf. Worked hours on end, didn't drink much, didn't smoke. Worked out almost every day. Haven't found anybody who would want to hurt the guy. It's early yet, I understand that."

"Okay. Why am I getting the feeling you don't think it's the wife? From what you've told me so far, she should be the number one suspect. A boyfriend. A huge insurance policy. No one else wants to hurt the guy …"

"It was the interview mostly. You know me, I can usually tell if someone is lying. I think she's telling the truth. I've been fooled a few times though. We'll just go where the evidence leads us. If she is lying, and she hired someone to take out the husband, we'll figure it out. Honest people usually make poor criminals. If she did that, I'm sure she made a mistake along the way."

"Okay. What are you thinking then? What's the next move?"

"We have a few more people to talk to at his work. And Greystone is going to turn over all his recent emails as well. Maybe there is something there. Some insurance fraud angle we aren't aware of yet. Also, we're going to drop by his country club and talk to his golf buddies. If he was doing something untoward they would probably be the first to know. Maybe there are gambling issues or something along those lines."

"That's usually what solves these things. Knocking on doors until you knock on the right one. Anything else?"

"Yeah. This is going to sound weird. But something was strange with the blood splatter in the home office."

"Strange?"

"Yeah, it just didn't look right. It was a really odd mixture of passive and projected stains."

"So?"

"Well, how many times have you seen passive stains at a scene involving a gun shot?"

"None that I can recall. So, what does it mean?"

"I have no idea. But if we don't turn up something in the canvassing, it might be worth calling in an expert."

Lost in thought, Davis didn't say anything.

Dmitri continued, "It may not mean anything, I admit I'm no expert. But if you consider what we have so far, the guy doesn't seem to have any enemies, his wife doesn't appear to be involved. Throw in a lot of insurance money … Oh, and don't forget, there isn't a body yet …"

"You're saying this could have been staged?"

"Stranger things have happened."

"But why? If he staged it, wouldn't the wife get the money?" Davis paused for second, "They could be in cahoots I guess …"

"I'm just throwing it out there. This is a crazy case, and will probably have a crazy explanation in the end. We've just got to work the evidence and see where it leads us. Oh and one other thing. When my buddy Stapleton heard about Ferguson going missing, he called me. It was his firm that took the pictures of the wife. I'm just telling you this in the interest of full disclosure. I don't see how it's a conflict of any kind at this point."

"I agree. Just a coincidence. But I'd let the captain know, just to cover your ass."

"The captain knows. So what do you say pal? Want to head over to Greystone? Then we can head over to the country club after that."

"Sounds good. I'm really looking forward to a day without any princesses."

They both chuckled.

Chapter Thirty-Eight

Saturday, March 21, 2009 – 5:00 p.m.

IT HAD BEEN kind of a bad week for Laura Ferguson. Not only had she come home to a bloody mess just the Sunday before, but she had been interrogated by the police for six hours the same afternoon and evening. She knew something terrible had happened to her husband. Seeing all that blood in the home office had nearly caused her to pass out. But she'd managed to get it together enough to call 911. She had sat in the living room in a state of shock for she didn't know how long. She barely remembered the police arriving. Then all of a sudden the police had asked her to go downtown. Routine stuff they had said. But they were lying. Laura could barely get her head around the fact that something terrible had happened, but suddenly she was being treated as a suspect. The cops had placed her alone in a small, stark room. An interrogation room. She had waited and waited.

Finally, a detective Jones had walked in. He had asked her the nature of their marital relationship. She had been confused. She needed to get home and call some people. Bill had no family to speak of, but there were friends. She needed to call her sister. His company needed to be informed. But wait, it's Saturday, can't call them today.

Ma'am, I know this is difficult for you, but try to focus. The sooner you answer my questions, the sooner you can go home. How were you and your husband getting along? Did he have any enemies? Do you know of anyone who might want to harm him? Did you kill your husband, Mrs. Ferguson? Was it a crime of passion? He was in the way at this point, wasn't he? Wasn't he the only thing standing between you and your lover? Would you submit to a polygraph, Mrs. Ferguson? Detective Jones and a Detective Henry took turns asking questions. Henry was much nicer. Good cop, bad cop garbage.

Eventually they had shown her the pictures. Pictures of her and Preston. Bill had been smarter than she'd thought. He'd caught on. He'd hired a private eye. How long had he known? The pictures had been in his desk in the home office. But his knowledge of the affair couldn't have anything to do with all the blood, could it? It didn't make sense. Any of it.

They had badgered her and questioned her for hours. But she had been steadfast, she'd told the truth. Yes, she was having an affair. Yes, she was planning on leaving Bill. But no, she didn't kill him. She'd been gone all weekend, how could she have killed him? She'd never even hurt a flea in her entire life.

After six hours, she had finally exploded. Can't you simpletons get it through your thick skulls that I didn't kill my husband? I wasn't home, and I didn't kill him! I had no motive to kill him. It wasn't that long ago that I loved him very much. Now let me out of here right now, or else I want to call my lawyer! I'm an attorney, I know my rights!

They had to let her go but she wasn't off the list yet. There could still be a powerful motive. Money. Based on some paperwork found in the home office, it appeared that Bill had a substantial amount of life insurance. Detective Jones kept that nugget to himself for now. He could confirm that the policy was still valid during the coming week. Plus, for the most part, he believed her. If she was telling the truth about where she'd been all weekend, then she did have an alibi. A really good one. Of course, that didn't rule out the possibility that she'd hired someone to kill him. But it seemed unlikely. If that had happened, he should be able to figure it out during the course of the investigation.

As if the discovery of the bloody office and the subsequent interrogation weren't enough, the police hadn't let Laura back into the house until Monday evening. They kept the house sealed off all of Monday and searched the whole house looking for possible clues. Every conceivable surface was dusted for prints and scanned for additional blood evidence. The home office was completely torn apart in an effort to find any documents that might be relevant. When she was finally allowed back in, Laura came home to a house that could have been declared a federal disaster area. She cried relentlessly that night.

By Monday morning she had consulted with the best defense lawyer in town. She hadn't given him a retainer, but he was on board in case the police decided to continue to pursue her as a suspect. On Tuesday, a local television news reporter called. On Wednesday, someone from *The Hartford Courant* called. She told them, on the advice of her attorney, that she had no comment. There would be no emotional pleas for the return of her missing husband seen on the evening news.

But for the moment Laura was safe. She and Preston had been making these Saturday evening sorties once a month for about a year now. Since Preston was pretty well known in Hartford, the lovers would go to nearby towns, usually at least thirty miles away. Laura would travel under the guise of a girls' night out, a girls' weekend, or a business trip that spilled into a working Saturday. The first few times they drove separately, but they soon tired of that routine. They started meeting in neutral parking lots and traveling together. Much more fun that way.

This weekend they decided to go further away, for obvious reasons. They drove southeast until they hit the coast and then northeast along it until they reached the quaint resort town of Narragansett, Rhode Island. They wanted to go to a place where there would be no chance anyone would recognize or bother them. They planned to stay until Tuesday. Take the extra couple of days and recuperate. She called Detective Jones and told him where she was and gave him her cell phone number in case he needed to reach her. He was surprised and appreciative.

She wasn't in love with Bill anymore, yet the whole ordeal was extremely disconcerting. The thought that she'd lost Bill to some kind of an unexpected and violent end was stunning. What could he have gotten himself into? She had no idea. Maybe he'd been doing something untoward at work. Anyway, he was surely gone now, and she needed to decide the best way to move forward.

Chapter Thirty-Nine

Saturday, March 28, 2009 – 9:00 p.m.

LAURA LIFTED HER glass of chardonnay as she and Preston waited for their appetizer, mussels in lemon and garlic sauce. It was a late dinner at their new favorite restaurant in their new favorite town. They had discovered both Ocean Blue and Narragansett the weekend before when looking for a place where they could act as a couple, yet be out of sight of any prying eyes.

"How is the wine?"

"It's delicious."

"How are you feeling?"

"Better than last week. Getting over the shock, I guess."

Preston didn't respond. Not because he wasn't sympathetic, but because he had no idea what to say. What do you say to someone whose husband may have been brutally murdered just two weeks before? True, she didn't love him anymore, but still, he couldn't imagine it, and didn't pretend to be able to.

"Have you heard anything about the investigation? You know, anything that hasn't been announced in the news?"

"Well, I've heard some rumors. Sounds like the police are stuck. Nobody knows what happened, or if someone does, he or she isn't talking. Bill really didn't have any enemies, as I'm sure you know."

They were interrupted by the arrival of the mussels. It was a welcome interruption, as both were famished. After they'd taken the edge off their hunger, Preston continued. "The lead guy, Dmitri Jones, is asking questions about blood splatter and such. He wants to dig deeper into the idea, and don't shoot the messenger now, he thinks maybe Bill set this up himself."

Laura nearly choked on the mussel she was eating. "What? That's ridiculous! There were a lot of things wrong with Bill, but he wasn't capable of something like that!"

"Honey, try to keep it down."

Laura shrugged as if to say, "too late now."

They didn't speak for a while. Preston understood that Laura was still very much on edge and he wanted to give her emotional space. The nearly finished bowl of mussels, as well as the bread basket, was taken away. Laura spoke. "What do you think?"

Preston looked at her quizzically, his expression asking, "Think about what, dear?"

"What do you think? Do you think it's possible he did all this on his own?"

As an assistant district attorney, Preston felt like he needed to be very careful here. Laura wasn't privy to all the details of the investigation for a reason. Not that a civilian attorney ever would be, even a defense attorney wouldn't get everything. But Laura was still technically a suspect. Preston knew she was innocent, but it wasn't to his advantage, professionally or romantically, to reveal everything he'd seen in Jones' reports.

"I think I understand Jones's approach. With not much to go on, he's going to want to explore all possibilities. Even as crazy as that particular theory sounds." Preston paused for a moment. "Did you know Bill had gotten demoted recently?"

"No. No I didn't." Laura looked disappointed. It was a real life example of just how far apart they had really drifted.

Their dinners arrived. Preston had ordered halibut; Laura was set to dine on snow crab legs. Again, no one spoke for a while, but it wasn't an awkward silence. For Laura it was an, *I'm exhausted and I want to digest what you just said*, kind of silence. Plus, the food and wine were both very good. They didn't speak about the case for the rest of the evening.

After sleeping in and missing breakfast at the bed and breakfast, the couple went out for an early lunch at a restaurant overlooking the water, then spent the afternoon perusing the shops along the pier. Laura got her nails done while Preston bought a Grisham novel and grabbed a spot on the end of a bench on the boardwalk. The ocean view more than made up for the nippy forty-six degree temperature. The combination of the cool breeze and salt air energized him.

At about five p.m., they started the journey back. Laura had been very quiet throughout the day. Once they were on the highway, she spoke. "You know, I've been thinking about something."

"Okay. What's on your mind?"

"Do you think we are going to wind up together? You know, permanently?"

"Of course I do. You know that. We've talked about this. I thought we were just waiting for the right time to divorce what's-his-face." Preston deliberately threw the "we" in there, to emphasize that he thought they were a team at this point.

"Okay. Just making sure."

"Why do you ask? What are you worried about?"

"Nothing really. But I've been thinking about what you said last night. About Bill setting up the whole thing."

"Uh huh." At this point, Preston had no idea where this was going.

"Well, either way, he's gone right? I mean, even if he set this up himself, which I still don't believe, he's gone. He's not coming back."

"Yeah. That sounds right."

"Well, Dear God, what I'm about to say better not leave this car. But I'm thinking we'd be better off, how should I put this, if he was gone gone, instead of fake gone. Does that make sense?"

"Uh, I'm not sure. I think I know what you mean by gone gone and fake gone, but why would we be better off. In the case of gone gone, I mean?"

Laura was quiet for a few seconds while she thought about the way she wanted to phrase her next sentence. "Because if he's gone gone, you know, all the way gone, then he could eventually be declared dead. Correct?" Preston finally saw the light, and began nodding his head.

"And if he's all the way gone, then there might be a certain monetary advantage to that scenario. Possibly."

"Yes, precisely. Possibly, of course, given that scenario that we just mentioned."

"Uh huh."

Neither spoke for thirty seconds as they rolled down the highway. Preston noticed the speedometer was pushing eighty miles an hour. Over the years he'd experienced a phenomenon where his foot got heavier as his heart rate increased. It happened subconsciously. He backed off the gas pedal immediately. A number of years before he'd been driving while on the phone with a girlfriend. They'd gotten into an argument, and the next thing Preston knew was he was getting pulled over and got a hefty speeding ticket out of the deal. And he hated getting speeding tickets.

Laura was the next to speak. "One last thing regarding our last topic. If there was anything an ADA could possibly do to help things along in terms of scenario A, that might be, you know, advantageous. Possibly. Given the monetary angle."

"Uh huh."

Chapter Forty

Tuesday, March 31, 2009 – 9:55 a.m.

DMITRI AND BRAD Davis arrived for the Ferguson briefing five minutes early. Captain Miles Keegan was a no-nonsense boss, which was an advantage in some ways. Things were usually done efficiently. And it was better if you weren't late for a meeting, if at all possible. At ten o'clock sharp, Keegan's door swung open.

"Gentlemen," he said, gesturing the partners into his office.

"Okay men, where do we stand?"

"Well, nowhere, sir."

Dmitri knew that Keegan didn't want bad news to be sugarcoated. He had learned over the years to give his boss the opposite, almost playing the role of doomsayer. Then the truth wouldn't sound so bad.

"Nowhere?"

"Nowhere, in the sense that we really don't have any suspects right now. The guy just wasn't into anything that would explain a violent death. At least not that we've found so far. He wasn't into gambling or drugs, he didn't cheat on his wife that we've found. No financial problems either. He had been recently demoted at work, but there was nothing there that would explain anything like what happened."

Keegan nodded. He knew all this from the daily reports, but felt the in-person briefing was a good idea. He got a better feel for what his detectives were really thinking. Sometimes body language hinted at thoughts and feelings that weren't in the reports.

"Okay, Meech. What is your plan?"

Captain Keegan called Dmitri "Meech," claiming Dmitri was too hard to pronounce. He made up nicknames for everyone in the department. The nicknames never stuck. Keegan was the only one who used them. But he didn't care; he seemed to think the nicknames were funny.

"Well, I've been wondering about something. The blood splatter seems ... odd. And given the fact we haven't found a body ... something seems fishy here."

"What, exactly, is your concern detective?"

"It's the blood splatter pattern sir. It's just, well, strange. I've never seen anything like it."

"So, what, are you a blood splatter expert now, Meech?"

"No, not an expert. Just a cop who's been around a few crime scenes-- trained to sift through evidence, draw conclusions, follow leads. You know, that kind of shit."

"Okay, let's drop the sarcasm, Meech. That never gets anybody anywhere. I understand that you are concerned, and I respect that, but the chief, after reading the reports, feels the preponderance of the evidence points to foul play. How could it be anything else?"

"Honestly, I'm not being sarcastic now. But if I knew exactly what was wrong this early in the investigation then I wouldn't need to investigate. In the past when something didn't add up at a crime scene, there was usually a reason for it."

"And you're saying the blood splatter doesn't add up? It was all Ferguson's blood, was it not?"

"Yes."

"Okay. And would you also agree that with that much blood loss, he wasn't long for this world?"

"I suppose."

"You suppose? What's the alternative, Meech? That he somehow staged all this? Gathered up four pints of his own blood and created this crime scene?"

"In my experience, people are capable of all kinds of crazy things."

"What, because his wife was cheating on him? This guy sold insurance, right?"

"Well, he was an insurance executive. From what we've learned so far he is, or was, a pretty sharp guy."

"Okay, Meech. Say he did all that. Say, somehow, he got a bunch of his own blood and faked this thing. Why? Why would someone do that? Unless he was trying to screw over the wife by having her take a murder wrap? It just doesn't make any sense."

"I don't know why. Yet. But she was cheating on him."

"But was there really that kind of animus, that kind of anger?"

"Honestly? There didn't appear to be. But why leave that stone unturned?"

"Well, the word from on high is, based on what they've seen of the evidence, that they want us focusing on the foul-play angle. Period. If, while pursuing that angle, you come up with evidence that suggests the guy is alive, then so be it. But you better bring anything like that to me first."

"Shouldn't we at least bring in a blood splatter guy? Someone who can explain a little better how the crime scene went down?"

"No. At least not yet. Not after the meeting I had yesterday. The brass will never pay for that. Not now anyway. Maybe down the road, if in a few months we still haven't turned up anything else. In the meantime, I suggest you guys go back to the beginning. Work it like you just caught the case. Re-interview everyone if you have to."

"Okay." Dmitri shrugged. "But it's damn frustrating. Why would they limit us like this?" Because you are way too much of a freaking wimp to stand up to them, Dmitri wanted to say.

"I don't know. So they can stand in front of a microphone at six p.m. and say they are doing everything they can to catch the killer? It doesn't really matter. This is a job, we have bosses, we answer to them. If you look at it that way, you won't drive yourself crazy chasing ghosts on this one."

Dmitri left the meeting thoroughly irritated. His detective's sixth sense was screaming at him that that crime scene wasn't right. What was extra aggravating was he kind of knew what was wrong. The blood ... something didn't add up. But he had an idea on how he could work that side of the case with his bosses being none the wiser.

Chapter Forty-One

Wednesday, April 1, 2009 – 7:30 p.m.

"HEY JOHN!"

"DMITRI, my boy. What's shaking?"

"Other than your jelly belly?"

"Ha! Touché. Got time for a beer after basketball tonight?"

"Sure do. You gonna head over to the Dog's Breath afterwards with the rest of the guys?"

"Actually, I was hoping to run something by you privately."

"Oh yeah? What's up?"

"It's about the case. How about we head over to that wing joint in Newington after b-ball?"

"Works for me."

John Stapleton and Dmitri Jones had been friends since high school. Dmitri had been the fullback on the same high school football team where John had played right guard. Lots of running plays went to the right side, with John hammering the defensive tackle in front of him, and Dmitri wiping out the first linebacker that came into his view. A mutual respect for each other's blocking skills blossomed into a close friendship off the field.

During the past twenty-some odd years the closeness of their friendship had ebbed and flowed depending on a variety of factors. The two bonded once again during the last few years over Wednesday night pick-up basketball at the YMCA. Plus, their chosen professions ran parallel to each other. They knew many of the same people, be they cops, lawyers, perps or snitches.

At about nine forty-five the thirsty and sweaty ball players grabbed a semi-private corner booth at the Wing Joint. It was about half-full, a decent crowd for a Wednesday night. They did have the best wings in town, one of the reasons that Dmitri suggested the place. He loved his wings and had scouted out all the places in Hartford until he had settled on the Wing Joint as the place he liked the best. And he was not in the minority in that opinion.

They put in their order for wings and a pitcher of Sam Adams. Both shared the opinion it was better to pay for a beer they loved than to go for something less expensive that they merely liked. As middle age beckoned, quality had become more important than quantity when it came to alcohol.

After the first glasses were poured and half consumed, John got the ball rolling. "All right, what's up?"

"Well, it's about the Ferguson case, of course."

"Of course."

"I just don't have any good leads right now. I've got a theory, but the brass has blocked me there."

"Politics?"

"Who knows? It's the strangest case I've ever worked. I've got one good idea but the captain, well, I'm sure it's really his bosses, won't let me pursue it. I guess it's par for the course on this one."

"Okay, so how can I help?"

"We'll get to that in a minute. First let's go over what you know, then I can fill you in."

This kind of exchange had happened a few times between the two friends. John had learned to just play along because it usually got very interesting for him if he did.

"Okay. Other than our business transaction, I only really know what I read in the paper. He's missing, and it appears to be foul play. The news hasn't said too much. I assumed you guys told them not to."

"Yeah, well, we haven't told them much. We didn't want any kooks calling up claiming credit. And sometimes it's better to keep details close to the vest, as you know. You can nail someone if he starts talking about things only the perps would know. Anyway, I've been working on this for two weeks now, and I can't find a soul who had anything against the man. Even his wife, who was cheating on him, really didn't hate him. I just can't

A DEVIOUS PLAN 233

find a motive. For someone else to have done it, that is."

The light bulb went off in John's head. "But maybe there was incentive for him to set this up himself?"

John went silent as he began thinking. It wasn't until then Dmitri noticed that, at some point, the wings had arrived. He dug in. John saw Dmitri eating and began munching on wings himself, but he didn't taste them, he was too deep in thought.

John spoke. "I just can't come up with a reason to go to all that trouble. Yeah, his wife was cheating on him. But why not just get a divorce? What's the advantage to faking a death like that? If he did it to get back at his wife … he didn't strike me as that bitter. But maybe his feelings changed since I saw him last …"

"It is strange. But there are three million reasons sitting out there that might be an incentive."

"Ah, the insurance angle. But wouldn't the money go to her? Unless they are in it together … but based on what those pictures showed, it didn't seem like they'd be much of a team anymore. That would be one elaborate plan, to hire me to 'catch' his wife having an affair and then pretend to get killed to get back at her. I don't see it."

"I know man, all the pieces don't add up yet. But I have a feeling if I pursued the 'he did it himself' angle, something would shake out. I've got a copy of the file in my trunk if you're interested. I would guess Greystone Insurance would be mighty interested in saving three million dollars."

"I would imagine. Hell, I'll bite. Why not? No harm in looking into it a little."

"And I get that you wouldn't have a real client in this case, at least not right off. But if you do a little digging along the 'he did it himself' line, who knows what you'll come up with? And of course, you'll keep me abreast of any significant updates," Dmitri added with a broad smile and a wink.

"Of course my friend. Of course."

Chapter Forty-Two

Thursday, April 2, 2009 – 3:00 p.m.

ANDY HAD BEEN reading the fascinating Ferguson murder/disappearance file since late morning. Engrossed, he'd almost forgotten to eat lunch. John Stapleton had given him the case, with the understanding that he was only to spend a week on it. There was no actual client in this case yet, but John was willing to go out of pocket in the short term. There was potentially a big payoff in the end. Andy's job was to do some digging and try to figure out if Ferguson had staged the bloody murder scene. In which case, Ferguson would still be alive and hiding somewhere.

Andy of course knew a little of the history. He'd taken the pictures of Mrs. Ferguson with her lover in Boston. He knew she'd cheated on Mr. Ferguson. John had explained that maybe Ferguson had done this to get back at his wife. And maybe somehow three million dollars in life insurance came into play. What a crazy turn of events!

Andy had never had access to a police file like this before. He was struck by the graphic pictures of the blood--lots of pictures taken from many different angles, mostly in the home office. Close-ups of the shell casings. A close-up of a bullet hole in the wall. There were many pictures of the layout of the house and the bloody footprints tracked through it. The crime scene notes stated there were two distinct sets of footprints, a fact fully supported by the pictures. Even if he wasn't looking at a real murder scene, the matter of fact way the pictures told the story was very grim.

Along with the initial crime scene report was documentation regarding the subsequent investigation. Ferguson had no known relatives other than Laura. So far, the cops had been unable to identify any suspects. They could not find anyone who wanted to harm Bill Ferguson. They found no evidence that he was involved in anything untoward. No gambling issues. No drinking or drug issues. No financial issues. If the guy was addicted to anything, he might have been addicted to golf.

Andy was stunned by the sheer volume of blood at the scene. Wow. No way Ferguson survived unless he faked it somehow. But the police had confirmed it was his blood. Maybe he collected it somehow and saved it for the "big day?" It might be worth going to that kind of trouble for three million bucks. But how he faked it, if he did, wasn't really Andy's concern. Andy's job was to assume he had faked it and try to find the guy. For some reason the cops weren't going down that road.

Andy considered his assignment. It might be hard to do anything in a week. It wasn't necessarily that easy to find someone who didn't want to be found. It often took time. Usually the person had a good plan and stuck to it early on. However, as time went by he'd become more confident and start making mistakes. The most common error was contacting a relative but Ferguson didn't have any relatives other than Laura. It was time to review things with John. Andy made his way to John's office with the Ferguson file in hand.

"So, what do you think?" John asked Andy after he sat down.

"Crazy case. Lots of blood. It's hard to believe the guy survived that scene."

"I know. But the devil is always in the details. Detective Jones thinks the blood pattern might suggest the scene was staged. He wanted to bring in a blood splatter expert but the department said no. He was frustrated by that; he thinks it's worth exploring that angle. That's why he came to us."

"Even if it looks that way, it really doesn't make any sense, does it?"

"You'll drive yourself crazy if you ask why, how, etc. There are a lot more questions than answers with this case right now. So let's just focus on assuming it was staged. The question then is where did he go?"

"But weren't there two sets of footprints? The body was probably dragged off somewhere, wasn't it?"

"Ah, ah, ah. That's exactly what I'm talking about. The guy was a successful insurance executive, a pretty smart dude. If he did stage it, maybe he hired some help. We can always get those kinds of answers when we talk to him," John said with a smile.

"Any idea where to start?"

"I did have one thought. The bullets and casings found at the scene were from a Glock 17. A nine-millimeter. But there's no mention of hunting or guns of any kind in this guy's background. Maybe at some point recently he became a gun guy."

"I get you. If he staged it, he must have at least bought a Glock along the way."

"Right. But we don't have the resources to track down Glock sales. But let me ask you something. What would you do if you had just bought a gun but didn't know what to do with it?"

"Well, I'd probably go practice. Maybe even take some lessons," Andy said with a grin.

"Exactly. It's worth a shot anyway. Take his picture around to some local gun and shooting clubs. See if anybody has seen him around. Maybe it will turn up something. If he's been practicing, it might be a piece to the puzzle."

A DEVIOUS PLAN

"I'm on it, boss."

"Okay. You can start on that next week. In the meantime I've got some pictures for you to take. There is a Mr. Swanson over in Granby who hasn't been a very good boy lately."

Chapter Forty-Three

Thursday, April 8, 2009 – 7:30 p.m.

ANDY SAT IN the car outside the West Hartford Gun Club. He couldn't believe it. He just couldn't believe it. It had only cost fifty dollars, and he'd done it. A critical piece of the Ferguson puzzle had been found. He'd been to a different shooting club every night this week. After three misses, he had started to think that this tack was a waste of time.

He'd approached the gun club guys just the way John Stapleton had taught him when asking for information. First, just come out and ask. If you ask straight out, sometimes people tell you what you want to know without you having to pay for the information. He'd shown the guy at the front counter the picture of Ferguson and asked him if he recognized Ferguson. The guy said maybe he did, he wasn't sure. Which really meant, I do recognize him, but I'll only tell you if I have a little incentive. So, Andy showed him the picture again, this time producing a twenty as well. This time the guy said, on second look, the person in the picture did look very familiar, and he thought he'd probably seen him at the gun club before but he couldn't be one hundred percent sure. Andy pulled back the twenty and showed a fifty. The guy said it was all coming back to him now; the man in the picture was a customer. Troy something or other, he couldn't remember the last name. He'd have to look that up. Troy? Yep, Troy. He was certain of it, but for the last name, he'd have to look in the computer. Andy said, okay, look in the computer. He was quite surprised the guy was calling Bill Ferguson Troy, but kept a good poker face. The guy said, well I really shouldn't, those records are confidential. He was fishing for more cash. Andy was at his limit; he wasn't paying anymore. That's it, boss. Fifty is as far as I go. If you can't help me for that, then I've got to take my business elsewhere.

Andy turned to leave. Turning to leave wasn't as hard to do as it sounded. Andy really didn't have any more cash.

The guy spoke. "His name is Troy Stevens. Came here for three or four shooting lessons, then one other time just to practice. At least that I saw." Andy thanked him, handed him the fifty, and left.

Troy Stevens. So Ferguson got himself a gun and was learning to shoot under an alias. Wow, that really changed the game. Was he living some kind of exciting double life? But why? Maybe he was into something that wound up getting him killed. Of course, the alias and the gun didn't prove that he got killed, did they?

After Andy got home, he picked up the phone to call Stapleton. Then he stopped. The task was to find out whether or not Ferguson was still alive. Probably best to hold off on letting the boss know what was happening until he had a better feel for the outcome. He'd sleep on this information and try to come up with a game plan. No doubt Stapleton would love to know this tidbit, but he'd also want to know how Andy planned to attack the situation. At the moment Andy had no idea.

He got a beer from the fridge and sat down on the sofa. The plan for going forward would have to be based on what Ferguson might do if he had staged the "killing." It was a what-if game. What if he was running around under the alias Troy Stevens and then faked his own death? What would he do next? Would he still be using the name Troy Stevens? Where would he go? What would he do? But, one thing at a time. Tonight he would be satisfied with finding out about the alias. He thought the best thing to do now was to have a couple of beers, turn on the boob tube, or in this case the boob flat screen, and just chill out. He wouldn't think anything more about the Ferguson case this evening.

Andy awoke at four a.m. with a start. It was like he was struck by a lightning bolt. Golf. The guy's only real hobby was golf. If he skipped town, maybe he was doing something with that. He had read Ferguson was quite the golfer.

Andy didn't really know much about golf; he had never played. Two drunken trips to the driving range in college had proved to be hilarious, but that was the extent of his golf experience. He tried a Google search, "Troy Stevens golf," but it returned no results. What to do? Andy remembered he had a friend who played golf in college. He'd call his friend later in the morning, it was obviously much too early now. He rolled over and went back to sleep.

At ten a.m., Andy called his friend, Josh Barry, the former college golfer. He got no answer, but left a message. Since he'd been working the Ferguson case in the evenings, he wasn't going to the office until later in the day. That was one thing that was cool about the PI business, the hours were odd, but also flexible. The latest season of *Dexter* had just arrived from Netflix. He decided he'd watch a few episodes and then hit the gym on the way to work.

At about six p.m., Andy's phone rang. It was Josh.

"Hello?"

"What's up man? Long time no hear."

"Well, I've got a quick question."

"Okay. But first, I want to know if you're still dating that hosebag Melissa."

"Oh man, no, we split months ago. Has it been that long? And she wasn't a hosebag. She was smoking hot and you know it."

"I know, I know. Makes me feel better to say that because I couldn't have her."

"Well, you can have her now. Want her phone number?"

"Naw. I've got my own thing going at the moment."

"Since when have you ever been monogamous?"

"Uh, since about three months ago."

"Oh yeah? This sounds serious. You falling in love or some shit?"

"I think I'm going to invoke the Fifth Amendment on that one. The jury is still out on that anyway."

"Oh Christ, can't stay away from the lawyer talk even when you're talking about chicks, can you?"

"Oops. I try hard not to be a lawyer when I'm not billing hours at the firm. Anyway, what was your question?"

"Well, I'm working what you might call a missing persons case. The guy is a big golfer and I think that he might be working at a golf course somewhere."

"Ah. What do you mean, working? If he's working as a golf pro he could be easy to find. If he's working cleaning golf carts, good luck."

"Don't know. The golf angle is all I've got to go on right now."

"Okay. Try www.pga.com. I think they have a way to look up golf pros by name."

"Ha! I knew I called the right asshole for this."

"Well, no problem I guess. But you ought to buy me a beer for my expertise. It's cheap, normally my time goes for one hundred fifty an hour."

"Holy crap! You lawyers are real crooks, I'll tell ya."

"Hey, it's not like I get all that. That's just what the firm charges our clients for my time."

"I see, anyway, yeah man, I'll buy you a beer. How about next Friday? We'll do a happy hour like old times."

"Oh hell no! I've got to work on Saturday. Happy hour, yes. Like old times? No can do."

Andy chuckled, "Okay, okay, I really can't drink like that either any more. I'll touch base next week."

"Later, man."

"Later."

Andy was typing in the URL for www.pga.com almost before he hung up with Josh. After about thirty seconds, the search returned with about twenty-five names. The eighth one on the list was

Troy Stevens, Associate Assistant Professional. The golf course listed was the Driftwood Club in Myrtle Beach, SC. And the picture right next to Troy Stevens' name was that of Bill Ferguson.

Holy crap, holy crap, holy crap! The son of a bitch is still alive! He did do this all by himself! How awesome was that! Andy had a new personal hero. It was Friday night, about six-thirty p.m. John Stapleton had gone home to his family about an hour earlier, so Andy didn't have to lie about going to another gun club as he left the office. He wasn't ready to tell Stapleton he actually had a huge, huge lead in the Ferguson case. He wanted to construct a game plan first.

Chapter Forty-Four

Friday, April 17, 2009 – 8:00 p.m.

TIRED AND SWEATY, Bill opened the door to his apartment. He was excited, he'd shot a sixty-nine, the first time he'd been under par since taking the job at Driftwood. Really, the first time he'd been under par since college. When he opened the door, he was immediately hit with a strong smell of coffee. <u>Did I forget to turn off the coffee pot this morning? Crap! Of course, now that I'm trying to conserve funds, I'm going to need a new coffee pot!</u> He had given up his morning Starbucks routine in favor of the cheaper alternative of brewing his own. The kitchen was only a few steps from the front door of the apartment, off to the right. Glancing into the kitchen, he was quite surprised. Sitting in the coffee maker was a fresh pot of brewed coffee.

Then he looked down the hallway into his living room. He saw a pair of sneakers and tube socks attached to thin legs. Working his way up from the floor, Bill saw the legs were attached to a young, thin guy, with a gun in his lap. The young guy was sitting in Bill's easy chair. He was drinking a cup of coffee, Bill assumed. Just staring at him, drinking coffee. Bill didn't move. Most people would have been terrified, but Bill was too stunned to feel anything.

Andy spoke. "Bill, come in, please sit down. Or should I call you Troy? Nice coffee by the way."

Bill didn't respond. In shock, he moved slowly, taking a seat on the couch.

"Listen, I don't want you to be too alarmed. I'm not here to hurt you. This gun is to make sure you don't try to hurt me. But obviously, I know that you are Bill Ferguson. And I know you aren't dead. So, let's talk." Andy continued, "Basically, I figured out that you weren't dead, and I tracked you down here. I'm not going to tell you how, maybe someday over a beer, but for now … I just know. That's all that counts. And I'm the only one, for the moment. We can keep it that way if you want, but I'll get to that in a minute."

Bill sat on the couch in stunned silence. How had this dude found him so quickly?

"The only reason I can see for you going to all this trouble is, it must be about the insurance money. Correct?" Andy didn't wait for Bill to reply. "Cool man. I've never seen anything like this. You are my hero. After what that bitch did to you, I don't blame you. Anyway, it has to be about the insurance money. No other reason, correct? So, I'm cutting myself in."

Bill's brain was beginning to function again, and he found himself getting very angry. But he was able to choke back the anger. He really wasn't in a position to argue.

Andy was over his own nervousness and having fun now. He continued, "I really don't need to know how you plan on getting the money. And I figure I'll be able to find out when it's coming on my own. So it's simple. You cut me in, I don't tell the cops or the insurance company you are still alive. My boss, John Stapleton, doesn't know either. Yet. The whole thing is kind of win-win, don't you think?"

Andy knew he was getting close to really pissing Bill off. And he actually was pissed off enough to finally speak.

"So, who the fuck are you? How did you get in here?"

Andy considered the questions carefully. "In terms of getting in here, it's a piece of cake. This place is easier to get into than a whorehouse is for a millionaire. I can understand you being kind of upset, but you need to watch yourself. The detective in charge of this case thought you might still be alive. But his bosses called off the dogs. That's how I wound up getting involved. One word from me and all hell is going to break loose in Connecticut." Next Andy asked, "So, fifty-fifty partners—right?"

"Whatever. Give me some kind of name will you? So I don't just wind up referring to you as asswipe."

"Call me Johnny. And watch the attitude. I'll be in touch." And with that, Andy waltzed out of the apartment.

Bill was angry, irritated, nervous, and a little scared all at the same time. Had he really just agreed to give away one and a half million dollars? Money that he didn't even have yet? <u>Take a deep breath. Calm down. I didn't exactly agree to give the money away. I was blackmailed. At gunpoint. Not the time to disagree.</u>

Bill wanted to process what had just happened, but right now he was too shaken. He dumped out the coffee—what a waste, and grabbed a beer. Scotch was really what he wanted, but luxuries like that would have to wait.

Then, he noticed he had a message on his voice mail. The discount flat screen he had ordered from <u>woot.com</u> had arrived; the apartment complex office had accepted delivery for him. The TV was down in the office and he could pick it up whenever there was someone there. It was too late this evening, the folks who worked in the office had already gone home. He'd have to pick it up in the morning. But at least it was good news.

Chapter Forty-Five

Saturday, April 18, 2009 – 10:50 a.m.

RODNEY WAS A loser. He was thirty-one and only on rare occasions had he held a steady job. Those occasions usually corresponded to the equally rare occasions when he had a girlfriend. A steady job meant he would be able to take her out to fancy dinners at the the Ponderosa. Rodney was white, five foot ten, two hundred and fifty pounds and he drank cheap beer by the gallon. At any given time, on any given day, there was a good chance it was happy hour at Rodney's house. Currently, he was working part time as a bouncer at a local nightclub. He was lucky because it was almost always a tame crowd, and truth be told, he couldn't bounce too many people. He was big, but he was big from fat, not muscle. It was a great place for him to work. He could sleep in, eat, drink and then go to work in the evening. And when he got there, as a bouncer, he was a minor celebrity.

Rodney was a thief. That was how he got by, mostly. The bouncing job was fun, but he buttered his bread with the proceeds from stolen items. He was lucky, because so far he'd never gotten caught.

He'd break into houses, steal the valuables, and sell them to bad guys who bought stolen items for ten cents on the dollar and resold them. But he spread his thieving around. He'd never hit the same neighborhood twice until many months had passed. If there was a rash of burglaries in a particular neighborhood, it would never be Rodney.

Rodney was an opportunist. He would listen to the patrons at the bar and pick up tidbits. Who was going on vacation.? How long they would be gone? Who just got a fancy new home theater system? Who appeared to have money? When people were drinking they were happy, they let their guard down. He'd strike up a conversation and make "friends." Then he would take advantage.

Sometimes, like earlier this morning, he would just watch. This particular apartment complex had multiple buildings and the kind of stairs that were exposed to the outside. There were sets of four apartments on each level. From his current vantage point, Rodney had the best view of Building C. As luck would have it, he saw a normal size guy leave Building C, go over to the apartment complex office, and return carrying a flat screen TV. Bingo! Usually people who had flat screens like that had other "useful" stuff. Stuff he could sell. At any rate, he could make a quick buck off that flat screen but he needed to know what apartment the guy was in. So he hopped out of his car and he followed him.

Rodney had to hustle to make up the distance, but the guy was slowed by carrying the bulky box. He followed him into the building, then up the stairs, making sure to maintain a respectable distance. No point in spooking him into dropping the flat screen! The guy stopped at an apartment on the second level. As he put the flat screen down to open his apartment door, Rodney pretended to ignore him and kept climbing to the third level. But of course, in the process, he saw the apartment number. After he heard the door click closed on the level below, he bounded back down the stairs and out to his car.

He watched as a few minutes later, the guy got into an old Chevy pickup and left. Rodney was quite hungry, so he went for some breakfast. If the pickup wasn't there when he came back, he would strike. He headed to his favorite diner. One of the girls who frequented the bar was a waitress there. She would hook him up with some extra pancakes.

Rodney finished breakfast and returned. There was no sign of the pickup. It was time to make his move. He grabbed his pistol and put it in his ankle holster. He had never had occasion to use it, and never really intended to use it but when you make part of your living sneaking into other people's houses, it was best to be prepared. Now packing, he semi-waddled across the parking lot and up the stairs to the second level where the flat screen apartment was. He quickly looked around and saw no one. He expertly picked the lock and gained entrance.

Much to his disappointment, the apartment was very sparse. There was barely any furniture. Only the pure basics, an old TV on an older TV cabinet, a small coffee table, an easy chair, a couch. A cheap carpet covered half the living room floor. There was a dinette and two chairs, presumably where Mr. Flatscreen ate his meals. Rodney saw no pictures on the walls, nothing on the bookshelf, no mementos of any kind. There was a laptop that had to be at least three years old sitting on a desk in the corner. Worthless. Rodney figured if the guy had bought that laptop recently, it must have come from a pawnshop. Mr. Flatscreen appeared to be poor, just like him. But, he was inside, he might as well have a look around. If he didn't find anything else he'd just grab the flat screen and be on his way.

He checked the kitchen drawers and cabinets. Nothing. Barely even any utensils or pots and pans. Lots of people hid valuables in the kitchen, but not this guy. The one drawer in the desk with the laptop didn't contain anything except a slip of paper with what looked like an email address. It looked like this guy didn't have any valuables at all. This was not going to be the payday he expected. Well, one room left to check. The bedroom.

Finally! In the top drawer of the nightstand next to the bed, Rodney found roughly two hundred dollars in cash. <u>Okay!</u> Suddenly, this venture had become worth his while. He started to bend down to check under the bed when he heard a noise. Was it the front door?

<u>Shit! Someone else was in the apartment!</u> Okay. He decided to move quietly to the bathroom that was off the bedroom. It was best to avoid any confrontation if possible. Maybe Mr. Flatscreen was just stopping home for a minute and would leave quickly. Rodney could grab the TV and go after he left. He drew the gun from its holster and stationed himself in the bathroom, sitting on the toilet seat.

Chapter Forty-Six

Saturday, April 18, 2009 – 10:55 a.m.

ADNY SAT IN his car in the parking lot of Ferguson's North Myrtle apartment complex. While in his estimation his confrontation with Ferguson just the night before had gone quite well, he wanted to see if he could find some additional information. He'd been so focused on the conversation he was going to have with Bill, he didn't think to sweep the apartment when he'd had the chance. So he was back to properly search the place while he knew Ferguson would be at work. The beauty of coming right back this morning was Ferguson wouldn't have had time to install better locks or other security measures.

His plan to make coffee last night to distract Ferguson seemed to have worked. Ferguson had been a bit confused by the coffee, and it had disarmed him, sort of. It seemed better to throw another element into the game, instead of having Ferguson discover only Andy right away, sitting in the man's easy chair.

There wasn't much in the apartment, was there? He didn't even remember seeing a TV, come to think of it. Had there been a laptop on the kitchen table? He was tempted to beat himself up for not being too observant, but he didn't want to be too hard on himself. It's not every evening you sneak into someone's apartment and then blackmail them. Anyway, he was back to do the sweep now.

Upon his arrival in Myrtle on Thursday evening, Andy had easily located the Driftwood Golf Club, and waited in his car for Ferguson to leave. Luckily, there had been enough cars in the parking lot that Andy, sitting in his car, wasn't conspicuous. It seemed they served dinner and such even after the golf course itself was closed. Once Ferguson had closed up the pro shop, Andy had followed him to this apartment complex and had gotten the apartment number from the mailbox at the base of the stairs. Ferguson's apartment was on the second floor.

He was set to make his next move when he noticed a heavy set guy headed up the stairs to the second floor of Building C, right where Ferguson lived. Oh well, he'd give it five more minutes to make sure that guy was safely in whatever apartment he was going to. And then he'd head up.

Now that he'd blackmailed Ferguson, there was no going back. He was in for a pound. Or maybe one and half million dollars worth of pounds. He'd asked Stapleton for a couple of days off to make this trip, so his boss would be none the wiser. He could just continue to tell him that he was hitting dead ends at the gun clubs. It was a good idea, it was worth a shot, but it hadn't worked. And then someday, when Ferguson got paid, Andy would be there to cash in. Thanks Ferguson, for doing all the work. And Andy in turn, would disappear. Hell, maybe he'd even ask Ferguson for tips on how to do that, he chuckled to himself.

Where would he go? What would he do? He really liked being a PI, maybe he'd just work freelance somewhere, take on work he wanted. If he was smart with the money, he wouldn't have to work. He could invest it. He'd have choices. That would be fun.

Okay. Time to roll. He wanted to get in there and take his time. Maybe there was something in the apartment that would help him. Something to give him additional leverage. He'd learned in his few short years as a PI that information was never a bad thing. Even if it didn't apply to that specific situation, there was always insight to be gained. Insight into how and why people did things. What made people tick. As he gained experience, he was realizing that life was a game, and in order to win you had to be able to match wits with the other players. Andy had caught Ferguson by surprise, but once Ferguson had a chance to regroup, he might counter strategize about how to cut Andy out of the loop. So if Andy could find something, it would be to his benefit.

He got out of the car, and headed back to Ferguson's apartment.

Chapter Forty-Seven

Saturday, April 18, 2009 – 11:00 a.m.

ANDY PICKED THE lock on Ferguson's apartment just as he had the previous afternoon. He went inside. He noticed there was no aroma of fresh brewed coffee wafting through the apartment. He smiled to himself. That move had been both strange and funny. The place felt even more barren in broad daylight. But, it made sense. Ferguson had left his old life completely behind. He was starting from scratch, and not on an insurance executive's salary either. Plus, Andy wasn't looking for material things, he was looking for information. A complete search was in order, and he figured he had plenty of time. On a Saturday, a golf pro was going to be working a very long day, Andy assumed.

He began a systematic search. The kitchen was the first room one came to when entering the apartment, so he started there. He opened every drawer and cabinet but found nothing except a few utensils and a couple of pots and pans. Obviously, Ferguson was no Bobby Flay. He opened the oven, nothing there. The microwave was empty. The fridge contained only a half-gallon of milk, a two-liter bottle of Pepsi, a few beers, the requisite ingredients for making a salad and some sandwich meat. A few condiments as well. The freezer had a couple of full ice trays as well as a couple of microwavable meals. Andy determined that Ferguson was hiding no secrets in the kitchen.

After relieving himself in the bathroom off the hall, he moved on to the living room. The desk with the laptop seemed a logical place to start. The laptop was powered off. Andy found the button to power it on and pressed it. The laptop, which appeared to be a bit old, began the boot process. In the meantime, he opened the only drawer in the desk. He saw a slip of paper.

Bang! The door to the back bedroom flew open. Andy grabbed the slip of paper and jammed it in his pocket. The hair stood up on the back of his neck. A hefty guy with a gun emerged from the hallway.

Rodney had tried to be patient, but it had been a full ten minutes. This obviously wasn't going to be a quick, I forgot my sunglasses, stop by Mr. Flatscreen. This was something else. It had sounded like someone was searching the place. Another burglar? What were the chances? At any rate, he couldn't take it anymore. He had to find out what was up.

Rodney spoke first. "Who the fuck are you?"

Andy had the same question, but had to tread carefully. The other guy had the gun. Andy had left his own gun in the trunk of his car. Dumb!

"I'm a friend of Bill's."

"Bullshit! If you're his friend, then why are you searching the place?" Rodney had the gun trained right at Andy's chest.

"I left something behind when I was over here last night."

"Dude, you better come clean, or I'm going to blow your head off. Nobody searches like you've been searching if they left a cell phone behind. Something like that would be a two second search."

The first BANG! was a delivery truck backfiring out in the parking lot near Building C. It was loud, like a shotgun going off. The thing was, that BANG caused Rodney to flinch. And he flinched while he was pointing a loaded gun at Andy's chest. So the second BANG! was the gun going off. Andy crumpled to the floor, and rolled to a prone position on his back on the living room carpet.

Rodney strode over to Andy, who was laying there with a look of complete shock on his face. His face was turning white, and blood was pooling up on his chest where he'd been shot. His expression was asking, *Did that really just happen?* He was reaching up with his right hand, trying to communicate something, but couldn't get any words out. He was gasping for air. Rodney hadn't meant to shoot him, at least not yet. But now he felt he had no choice. He lifted the gun, pointing it directly at Andy's forehead. Andy's eyes widened and his face showed the horror he was feeling inside. Rodney pulled the trigger once more and put Andy out of his misery. Rodney immediately called his friend Jasper. Jasper answered the phone on the first ring.

"Yo, what's up?"

"I need some help."

"Yeah, what's going on? I'm kind of busy this afternoon at work."

"This can't wait. Remember that thing I helped you with a couple of years ago? The problem with the ugly guy?"

"Yeah, I remember."

"Well, this is just like that. I need help right now."

"Okay, let me finish up one thing and I'm on my way."

"Okay man. This is huge. I'm not sure what I would do if you weren't coming."

Rodney gave Jasper the directions to the apartment complex before hanging up. Then he helped himself to a couple of the beers that were in the refrigerator while he waited. He turned on the old TV and watched part of a baseball game. But it was hard to watch low def TV after having had high def for a while. There was nothing to do but wait. He just really hoped that Mr. Flatscreen didn't show up. If he did, Rodney would have to smoke him, too.

Jasper showed up just after one o'clock.

He took one look at Andy and declared, "Damn dude, you really did have a problem."

The two hoodlums worked together to roll Andy's body up in the carpet he was lying on. Then, making sure no one was watching them, they loaded the carpet into the back of Jasper's van. Rodney went back for the flat screen, but noticed some blood on the floor. He cleaned up the blood with paper towels, then hustled back to the van, completely forgetting the flat screen. It was about two o'clock. They agreed they'd wait until well after dark to dump the body. Jasper went back to work for a few hours, while Rodney went home and called in sick to his bouncer job. It would be much too late to deal with the body after the bar closed. Jasper said he knew just where to dump it, but it was a long drive, about an hour and a half. They agreed that Jasper would pick up Rodney at his house at ten p.m. and then dispose of the body. Rodney went home, and realized, oh shit, I forgot the flat screen! Well, at least I've got the two hundred bucks. Still, it had been a hell of a day so far. Rodney found that he had half a bottle of Jim Beam in the cupboard. He attacked it, and passed out at about four p.m.

Rodney was awakened at ten-twenty p.m. by the ring of his cell phone, which sounded like a freight train roaring through his front yard. He had a splitting headache and could barely open his eyes. It took all his energy to reach over, grab the phone, and answer it.

"Hello?"

"What the fuck man! I've been banging on your door and ringing your doorbell for fifteen fucking minutes! You got us into this fucking mess! Now get your ass out here!"

"Okay, okay, stop yelling will you? I'll be right out." He desperately wanted to take a shower first, but that was out of the question given Jasper's level of agitation. He threw on some clean clothes and headed out to the van.

Jasper took one look at him and just started shaking his head. "Dude, I usually don't care about people drinking, but was this really the time?"

Rodney was too hung over to answer.

They headed west out Route 501. Jasper announced they were going to the state park near Lake Norton; he knew some access roads that were seldom used. They would dump the body near there. Along the way they made a quick stop for fast food and Rodney started to feel a little better.

When they got to the state park it was midnight and it was pitch black. Jasper guided the van along a bumpy and twisting access road near the park.

Given its state of disrepair, Rodney assumed the road was little used. He wondered why Jasper was so familiar with this area, but thought better of asking. Jasper pulled the van off into the woods about fifty yards and parked it, lights off, of course.

They both jumped out, and Jasper opened up the back of the van. Sitting on top of the rug with the body were two spade shovels. Without saying a word, each took a shovel and starting digging. It took about a half hour to get the shallow grave dug out enough to take the whole carpet, which was about eight feet long. Each grabbed an end of the carpet, and unceremoniously dumped it, with Andy's body wrapped inside, into the hole. Then it took another fifteen minutes to cover the hole with dirt and spread the excess dirt around randomly. They then covered the dirt with leaves and twigs and such, in an attempt to conceal the dirt's freshness.

It was about one a.m. when they piled into the van, dirty, sweaty, and irritated. Rodney felt especially gross, and still a bit hungover. But he also felt relieved. The only words spoken between the two the whole way home were Jasper's words when he dropped Rodney off.

"We're even now, chief."

Rodney got out of the van without saying a word. There was no need to respond.

Chapter Forty-Eight

Saturday, April 18, 2009 – 9:00 p.m.

AS BILL WAS driving home after a long day at the golf course and a slow dinner out, he realized it was going to be another lonely Saturday night. He'd been in Myrtle Beach a month and hadn't really made any friends. Mostly because he was scared. Friends ask questions. Friends want to know about your past, where you came from. He envisioned uncomfortable situations with people sitting around having drinks, shooting the breeze, and they'd want to know, so, why aren't you married? Any girlfriend right now? Really, your dad left you a lot of money? That's why you are a golf pro now? So you'll be buying a nice house eventually, right? I know a great real estate agent, want her number? Bill thought it would be nice to have someone to hang out with, but didn't want to answer all the inevitable questions. Not yet. He needed to think about and rehearse some good answers. And why do that now? Life as Troy Stevens was only temporary.

Another source of friends is hobbies. And Bill didn't really have any. He had turned his one hobby into a job, and the pros were discouraged from fraternizing too much with the members. The other assistant pro, Kenny, was twenty-five. Don Delamar had been in Myrtle for many years and had a wide circle of friends. Meanwhile, Bill just wanted to get through this Troy Stevens phase so he could go on to the next phase, which would be his real new life.

<u>Hmmm. Time to start thinking about the next persona. Start planning that. Who will I be next?</u>

He parked the pickup truck and headed for his apartment. As he entered, something didn't feel quite right. But he couldn't put his finger on it. At least there was no smell of coffee, thankfully. He walked down the hallway into the living room. It felt like something was missing. But what? The flat screen was still there in its box.

<u>Hey, is the computer on? I could have sworn I turned that off this morning …</u>

He shrugged and went to get a beer out of the fridge. There were six Sam Adams Boston Lagers. <u>Weren't there eight of them in there this morning?</u> He shrugged again and went to sit in the easy chair. He turned on the TV. Wait, the walk over to the easy chair had felt wrong. Then he finally noticed it. The carpet was missing.

<u>What the hell? Someone was in here, again! Had to be the asshole Johnny, which couldn't be his real name. But why would he take the carpet? Who</u>

A DEVIOUS PLAN 269

breaks in, drinks two beers, and steals a carpet for crying out loud?

Bill was steaming. He wondered where he could find this guy. "Johnny" had said he worked for John Stapleton, hadn't he? His instincts were telling him that this deal he had just been forced into making with Johnny would never work out. Even if he went along with Johnny's blackmail scheme, something was bound to go wrong. The guy was obviously crazy, and could easily fuck the whole thing up. Was this worth a trip to Connecticut, he wondered? He might need to get rid of this Johnny character. The question was, was he really ready to kill someone? Bill wasn't sure he could kill anyone, even if it was to save one and a half million dollars.

Well, let's sleep on this first. You're upset because he keeps breaking in here. Let's just see what happens. If you still feel this way two weeks from now, then we can think about it.

One thing was for sure, he was not going to call the cops. That would make no sense, even if the carpet had been pure Persian. Calling the cops to investigate would only serve to open himself up to the same questions he didn't want from potential friends.

Another thing was for sure. He needed to install better locks, immediately. What time did Home Depot open on Sunday? He'd buy something on the way to work, then he could install it on Sunday night. Or maybe he could have the superintendent do it for him. Yes, the super could do it while Bill was at work. That's what he'd do, he'd get up early, hit Home Depot when they opened, then swing by the office on this way to work and have the superintendent install the new lock. Then he'd feel safer. And hopefully be safer.

As the beer kicked in, and he now had a security plan, his thoughts turned back to his loneliness. His isolation. In all his grand planning, he hadn't thought about that aspect of things. He actually missed the social aspect of work. He missed golfing with his friends at the club. He wondered what Jennifer was up to. Boy would she be a sight for sore eyes right about now. And the thought was only slightly sexual in nature. He really would just enjoy her company.

The good news was Bill had rediscovered how much fun reading could be. Between low definition television, a slow computer, and no friends, reading was now his chief source of entertainment. He was working on his fourth novel since he'd moved to the apartment. That might change a bit once he got the flat screen hooked up, but his goal was to keep reading. He'd missed out on a lot of good books in his previous life.

He read for an hour and then set the alarm for seven a.m. Home Depot opened at eight a.m. on

Sunday; he'd have to get there right when they opened in order to drop off the lock and make it to the golf course by nine a.m.

Bill woke up the next morning at six fifty-five without the alarm. He showered, dressed, and gobbled down a quick bowl of cereal. He was ready to leave when he realized, Fuck! His cash was missing. Johnny, no doubt about it. Two hundred bucks, gone. A drop in the bucket in his old life, but now it hurt. At least he still had a couple hundred in his checking account. He wasn't making much, but he wasn't spending anything either. He was on the road by seven-thirty.

He was looking forward to working today. He was confident the office would handle his request to install the new lock, and he was scheduled to teach several lessons. He'd helped a few people and was starting to develop a following. Anyway, he'd left a little early for Home Depot because Starbucks was calling his name. It had been a month and he had a craving the size of the Grand Canyon.

After buying the most bad-ass deadbolt lock he could find, he was heading back to the apartment complex when he had a thought regarding Johnny. After a good night's sleep he acknowledged the obvious. Charging up to Hartford to find Johnny, and then shoot him, was insane. He would simply have to stay a step ahead of him, and be gone by the time that nut job arrived again in Myrtle with his hand out. Perhaps he could move the week before the money arrived. Then Johnny wouldn't know where he lived. He could quit the golf course job also, or somehow make sure he wasn't followed when he left the course. Or take that week off. That would be better than quitting in case something went wrong. Johnny would arrive in Myrtle to collect "his half" of the money and Bill would be nowhere to be found. And possibly already on to his next life. With that in mind, it was time to start planning. He'd need another identity lined up. And he'd really need to think about the mechanics of transferring the money from Laura's account to a neutral account and then on to the final account.

Chapter Forty-Nine

Wednesday, April 22, 2009 – 9:30 p.m.

DMITRI AND JOHN grabbed a table at Wing Joint, just as they had three weeks before. This time though, it was John who requested the post basketball meeting.

As John poured them each a mug from the pitcher of Sam Adams, Dmitri spoke. "Okay, what's up? Got something on the Ferguson case?"

"I can't really say that. But something has come up."

"Oh yeah?"

"I had assigned my guy Andy to look into the Ferguson thing, but he's gone missing. I filed a missing persons report this morning. He told me he was taking a little trip over the weekend, and he was supposed to be back at work yesterday. But he hasn't shown up, hasn't called, and isn't answering his phone or email. It's very atypical."

"No chance he's just still on vacation?"

"Well, there's always a chance. But I double-checked the email he sent, it was clear; he should have been back yesterday. And if he extended, no big deal, but that should be cleared up with a phone call. And he's not answering."

"Any idea where he was headed?"

"Unfortunately, none."

"Well the missing persons folks are pretty good. They can track his movements if he used a debit or credit card."

"I wouldn't count on that. I think he had pretty bad credit and mostly used cash. But maybe …"

"Had he made any progress on the Ferguson case? Any proof the guy is still alive?"

"He told me he hadn't found anything. He was working the gun angle mostly."

The wings arrived and both dug in while intermittently taking sips of beer. After a few minutes Dmitri spoke. "Well, I'm sorry John, I know you like that kid. Hopefully this is just some kind of mix up."

"Yeah, I hope so, too."

"I just can't help but think, man, I don't like coincidences. He was working the Ferguson case part time and then he disappears?"

"I hear you. But I can't imagine that he figured something out and then lied to me about it. He was no angel, but I can't see why he would do that. He'd done a great job up until now."

Both went back to attacking their wings. They passed on a second pitcher of beer and each got a glass of water instead. Both men were getting full.

Dmitri spoke one last time, "I know one of the missing persons guys pretty well. I'll talk to him about this and have him keep me up to date. Damn. I can't go to my bosses, because they'd have my head. Maybe my job if I told them what Andy was up to but I can keep tabs in an informal way."

"Okay, thanks man. Nothing to do but wait I guess."

"The wings are on me tonight, brother."

As Dmitri drove home, he wondered if there was more he could do. But he couldn't think of anything. If he acted too concerned about an apparently random missing persons case, his bosses would want to know why. They might figure out he had orchestrated the involvement of the Stapleton Detective Agency. If they found out he had given them a copy of the Ferguson file, he'd be facing disciplinary action, if not outright termination. So his inquiries into the disappearance of Andy Jacobsen had better be fairly discreet. Still the disappearance only served to heighten his initial suspicions that when it came to the case of Bill Ferguson, something was amiss.

Chapter Fifty

Friday, April 24, 2009 – 9:00 p.m.

BILL GRABBED A beer from the fridge and sat down in front of his outdated laptop. It was slow to process the sophisticated graphics it was receiving from the Web. But it worked. Eventually. He just had to be patient. Buying a better machine at this juncture didn't make sense. Acquiring his next identity was going to cost money, one way or another. Even if it meant a couple of flights back and forth to Cheyenne once again. So a new laptop was not in the cards.

He logged into the Greystone web page using the Henry Johnson account. He wanted to see if there was any development in his case. Johnson got plenty of email, but nothing related to Ferguson. He hadn't expected anything as it had only been a little more than a month since he disappeared. But still, it was disappointing. It was really hitting home that any real news might not be coming for a while. Meanwhile, he was in this self-created limbo. He thoroughly enjoyed being at the golf course every day. But outside the confines of Driftwood, he felt isolated. He needed to develop some hobbies to fill the non-work hours. Maybe he'd do something off the wall, like take a cooking class. He had been surviving on mostly prepackaged convenience foods, which weren't especially healthy or tasty.

He deleted all the emails in the Johnson inbox. He decided he would check for new emails once a week, on Friday evenings. More often than that would be fruitless. Less often, he might miss something important. And he resigned himself to the idea that it might be many months before anything happened.

He started typing an email to Jennifer, but thought better of it. If he was going to contact her, it made more sense to do it later, when he was closer to getting all the money. Besides, the police were probably still investigating his case and if he contacted her now he would be putting her in a terrible position. And putting himself in a terrible position. He'd possibly be giving away the Henry Johnson account, not to mention it would be proof that he hadn't been brutally murdered. So, he couldn't afford to contact her now. The email address was his only lifeline as to what was happening with his case.

He was wondering what he should do about another potential problem; he'd lost five pounds. He didn't want to lose any more. He wanted to remain as close to two hundred as possible in order to make it easier to disguise himself later on. It was a strange concept, the idea of trying to keep weight on. It had proven harder than he anticipated since he wasn't sitting at a desk all day. He needed to balance eating foods that help you gain weight against maintaining some modicum of a healthy diet. He could probably keep the weight on by eating fast food every meal, and he could probably swing that financially, but that would wreak havoc on his digestive system. Maybe the cooking class wasn't such a weird idea after all.

Chapter Fifty-One

Tuesday, May 5, 2009 – 8:00 p.m.

IN THE END, Bill decided he'd create his next ID the same way he had created the Troy Stevens persona. Originally he'd wanted to make it easier on himself. His idea had been to seek out the help of some kind of identity broker. Someone whom he could simply pay to provide all the necessary identification, but then he thought better of that idea. He didn't have the thousands and thousands he imagined a service like that would cost. Besides which, he had no guides who could help him safely navigate that terrain, and if he did find such a broker, he'd have no idea whom he was dealing with until it was too late-- a shyster or a cop.

When he sat down and thought about it, his conclusion was that going the broker route would be very expensive and fraught with peril. So he decided he would do it the old-fashioned way, get a real birth certificate and create a new person on his own. He'd done it once before, he could do it again. This time, he could save himself a lot of time and money by simply flying commercial flights as Troy Stevens. The Stevens ID was a throwaway. He wasn't worried about it being discovered, which it certainly could be once the money was missing. It didn't matter what Troy Stevens did as long as there were no clues left regarding his next ID.

The tricky part this time would be finding an identity to use. The Troy Stevens name had come to him easily. More research would be needed this time. Ultimately, he was after the names of infants who had been born and then died in 1969. So, he started Googling. He looked for towns in New York State that would have established newspapers going back forty years or more. The idea was the name he needed was hidden somewhere on microfilm among the death notices from forty years ago.

It quickly became apparent that none of the newspapers he found using Google made their old microfilm copies available online. The furthest he could go back online was about ten years, depending on which newspaper's website he was navigating. But he did discover that the microfilm for *The Albany Evening Star*, going back to 1913, was housed in the public library in Albany, New York. As far as Bill was concerned, Albany was as good as any other town to start with. It seemed like making a road to trip to New York's state capitol was the best approach he could devise.

He checked commercial flights and it wasn't too expensive to fly from Myrtle to Albany. The trip from Myrtle to Cheyenne was a bit steeper, and

A DEVIOUS PLAN 281

he'd have to do it twice--once for the learner's permit and once for the driver's license. He'd have to save his pennies to pull it off. Or maybe it was time for Troy to get a credit card and use that to pay for flights. He could make the minimum payments until he was done being Troy Stevens. Probably a good idea to have a credit card for unexpected expenses anyway. That pickup truck in the parking lot wasn't getting any newer.

At any rate, he had made a decision. He had a plan now and that felt good. He could handle the round trip to Albany out-of-pocket, and in the meantime he'd go for a credit card for the Cheyenne trips. As interesting as it had been to fly with Adam, commercial flights would prove to be a lot faster and cheaper than hiring a private pilot. Mondays and Tuesdays were his days off from work. He'd fly out as early as possible on a Monday morning and fly back on Tuesday evening. Find his new name on Monday, then secure the birth certificate on Tuesday.

He reviewed the requirements for getting an official copy of a birth certificate in New York. You had to be either the person named on the birth certificate, or one of the person's parents. Anyone else had to show an order from a New York State Court. And the person obtaining the copy was supposed to show some sort of government issued photo ID. Or, you could provide two documents showing a name and address, for instance a utility bill or a telephone bill, or a letter from a government agency. Bill wondered if he could figure out how to get, or make, some of the documents in question in order to obtain the birth certificate. He just had a bad feeling about trying the misdirection strategy he'd used to get Troy's birth certificate.

He wanted to wait at least two weeks to fly in order to get the best rate. Looking at the calendar, the Monday three weeks from now would be Memorial Day. The golf course might be busy, he might not get that Monday off. So he booked his flight for Monday, June 1st, four weeks away in order get the best rate on the flight. But he'd have to fly back on Wednesday evening, not Tuesday. The Monday morning flights didn't get to Albany until late morning or even early afternoon, as there were always connecting flights. The Sunday evening flights left Myrtle around eight p.m., which was too early. In June he might be at the golf course until eight p.m. He'd never make it. So he decided he better take the extra day since he wouldn't have a full day on Monday. He just needed to let Don know. He didn't think it would be a problem since he hadn't asked for any time off yet.

So, he'd have a month to think about how he wanted to approach the Department of Vital Records this time. He was too young to pass for the

A DEVIOUS PLAN

father of someone who would have been forty years old. So he'd have to go for a different angle. Maybe he would create a document that looked like it was an official court order from a New York State court. How often would the folks at Vital Records get any requests like that? Would a teller get them often enough to spot a fake? Why would they? Were there that many people trying to fake court orders at the Department of Vital Records?

Chapter Fifty-Two

Monday, June 1, 2009 – 1:00 p.m.

WITH THE PLANE safely on the ground, Bill waited impatiently in his seat. Didn't these people know he had a lot to do in a short period of time? That fat guy is moving so slowly. He can barely get out of his own way. It had been dumb to take the window seat for the leg from Charlotte to Albany. Now he was trapped. Oh well, nothing he could do about it. He'd simply have to wait a few minutes to get his carry-on bag from the overhead compartment.

This trip had pointedly reminded him of one of the reasons he was going to all this trouble, instead of just getting a divorce. He hated flying coach. He wanted the money to travel first class. Or in a pinch, he'd settle for business class. Champagne. Good food. A chair you could actually sleep in. He could do it all with three million bucks.

Finally, it was time to move. Bill grabbed his antiquated laptop from its position under the seat in front of him and then located his overnight bag. He hustled down to the car rental area, and for the first time, used his Troy Stevens Visa card. It was fun to use a credit card after many months of not having one.

He jumped into his rental car and headed for the Albany Public Library. The directions he had printed before leaving on the trip sat on the passenger seat next to him. He was a little hungry, but was too excited to stop for food. He'd go for a big dinner tonight. Time was short and there was work to do. The snack he'd had on the plane would just have to hold him over for now. He had a credit card; maybe he'd really treat himself. Yes, he'd go for some fine dining once he got the name.

He was thankful it was only a twenty-minute drive from the airport to the library. The library was open until nine p.m. He would be able to search all afternoon and then as long as he could hold on before the hunger took over. He hoped it would be a productive afternoon. He had secured an inexpensive hotel room in the downtown area as well. He'd probably have to call them and arrange for a late check-in.

There was an office of the New York Department of Vital Records a few blocks from the library but he wouldn't be able to go directly there after securing the name. He would need a chance to fill in the name on the fake court order document he'd created on his laptop. He was impressed with his handiwork. The document looked real. After he filled in the name, he'd find a place like Kinko's and print it. Then he would sign the "judge's" name and stamp it with the official-looking custom seal he had ordered online. It had set him back fifty bucks, and hinted at being an official New York State seal. It was adorned with the letters NY inlaid across the top, the scales of justice in the middle, and oak leaves along the sides. A total fake, but someone who didn't know what the real one looked like would be hard pressed to reject the form and the stamp. At a glance, it would be very official looking. So, he was banking on a bureaucratic teller not looking too closely at it.

After the time it took to rent the car and the drive downtown, Bill arrived at the library about one forty-five p.m. He left the laptop and his overnight bag in the trunk. Not having been to a public library in many years, he asked for help from the front desk. They showed him the reels of microfilm for *The Albany Evening Star* and demonstrated how to use the microfilm reader. He hadn't used one in almost twenty years, when he was in college. By two-fifteen p.m. his search was in full swing.

By four-fifteen he was bored to tears. It had been kind of fun at first, learning how to use microfilm again as he had well before the millennium. But after two hours he'd scanned through all of approximately two hundred death notices for January 1969. Everyone he came across had been a loving grandmother, a devoted husband, a cherished wife. Most had died peacefully after a long bout with something or other. He hadn't come across any teenagers, much less infants. This was like looking for a needle in haystack.

He stayed the course for two more hours. It was an arduous task. By about six-fifteen p.m., he couldn't take it anymore. Hunger was making him distracted and he was frustrated. He was getting the sense that people who lost infants didn't bother with death notices in newspapers. It was time to check into the hotel and get some dinner. He'd see how he felt after that, maybe he'd come back to the library tonight, or maybe he wouldn't. One thing was for sure; he needed to think of a new approach.

It was a short drive to the hotel. He checked in, got his room key, unloaded his bag and the laptop and then went back down to the lobby. There was a steakhouse right across the street, so he jogged over once there was a lull in the traffic. It was interesting being in the middle of a city again. His current life was quite suburban.

He had decided in the morning he wouldn't reward himself with a nice meal until he'd secured his next new name, but this was a nice place and he was famished. He ordered salad, striped bass, vegetables and wine. He rarely drank wine, but for some reason he was in the mood tonight. Even though he was relatively full after dinner, he decided to go for dessert. He ordered chocolate cake and a third glass of wine. It was an unspoken declaration that he was done working for the night. Besides, he wasn't driving. Luckily, wine went a lot better with cake than beer did. He would forgo his beloved coffee for this particular meal.

And suddenly, while waiting for his wine and cake, Bill smiled. He sighed a big sigh of relief. It was like the weight of the world had been lifted from his shoulders. He knew what to try next.

Chapter Fifty-Three

Tuesday, June 2, 2009 – 9:00 a.m.

BILL ENTERED THE Albany Public Library at two minutes after nine, one minute after they unlocked the doors. He had slept very well, despite being excited about his new approach to finding the name. He'd been extra tired from having traveled a fair distance by air. Just one of his quirks, he supposed.

He went back and pulled the microfilm roll that had the copies of *The Albany Evening Star* from January 1969. But instead of scouring death notices, he had another idea. He went to the metro section for each day, and looked for articles regarding fatal car accidents. In hour number three, in the papers for the month of March, he found what he was looking for--sort of. There was an article about a family that had been wiped out, including a six-month-old boy. But there was a problem. The boy's name was Rufus Mallington. And the other kids in that family were a bit older, and the names not much better sounding.

Rufus Mallington? No. He could not become Rufus Mallington. Okay, if it got to be the end of the day and he didn't find anything else then … maybe. He could always legally change the name. How funny would that be? Create a fake identity and then immediately go for a name change. And maybe that would be beneficial in some way. An act of misdirection that might help him. At any rate, it was noon. Bill left the library for a quick lunch and when he came back he had until nine p.m. to find something better.

With something in his belly, and buoyed by his earlier success with his new approach, Bill was able to attack the rest of 1969 with vigor. But by six p.m. he hadn't come across any other family tragedies. He had just gotten through all the metro sections for September and he was starting to get hungry and thirsty. Keep going? He was averaging a month an hour. He could make it through of all '69 if he kept plugging away. If the library closed before he found another name, he would simply have to go with Rufus Mallington. He couldn't afford another trip to Albany to search through another year. Not with two trips to Cheyenne coming. He decided to take a ten-minute break, find a quick snack, and then get back to work.

He found it at eight-forty p.m.. On December 23rd, 1969, sadly, there was a Christmas tragedy. A local family traveling to see relatives was wiped out by a tractor-trailer just as they reached the interstate. There had been five members of the Goodman family. Steve and Molly were raising three children, Philip, nine, Audrey, five, and Miles, just six months old. Very sad. The baby's name was Miles. Miles Goodman. He could live with that.

Ravenous now, he headed straight for the nearest pub. He could see one down the street a few blocks, so he opted to walk. As he got closer, he could see it was an Irish pub, O'Malley's. That would do. He ordered Shepherd's Pie and Guinness. Once he had something in his belly, the long day started to catch up with him. Beginning to get drowsy, his thoughts turned to Wednesday's activities.

The research was done. Now it came down to execution. He needed to add the Miles Goodman name to his court-ordered document, save it to his flash drive, have it printed, and then stamp it. He could take care of all that in the morning. There was a copy center about a block from his hotel; he could print the updated document there and then be off to the Office of Vital Records.

He arrived at Vital Records just after ten o'clock on Wednesday morning. The whole thing was wonderfully anti-climactic. The clerk barely looked at his forged court order, merely checking the name of the authorized person, Troy Stevens, against his Troy Stevens driver's license. By ten-thirty a.m., he had an official copy of Miles Goodman's birth certificate.

Now he would employ the same charade as before. He'd fly to Cheyenne, get his Miles Goodman learner's permit, then fly back two weeks later and get his Miles Goodman driver's license. And he'd be well on his way to becoming Miles Goodman.

For the flight back to Myrtle, Bill was feeling his oats. Maybe he'd start a business someday. He could help people disappear. He was getting good at this. He had skills. In the meantime, he decided to use his credit card and splurge for a business class upgrade for the flight home. It didn't cost too much, and didn't mean too much for a short domestic flight. Mostly it was just a little extra legroom, which was nice. In his mind, he'd earned an upgrade, even if he really couldn't afford it, and, it would be a lot more fun if he had someone to upgrade with. A partner in crime. It was a cruel irony that he was now single, but could not approach the one woman he was interested in, and who also happened to be single--Jennifer.

As Bill relaxed in his chair, the upgraded one that reclined further than its coach equivalent, he began thinking about the future. He guessed he had several months to go before the money would get to Laura. He'd be able to track the progress through the Johnson email account. There was more planning to do but at the moment he couldn't think anymore. His body was melded to the comfortable seat and his eyes refused to remain open. He drifted into a deep slumber as the jet droned away, high above the earth.

Chapter Fifty-Four

Monday, August 10, 2009 – 2:00 p.m.

BILL REALIZED HE had a serious problem a couple of weeks before when he was doing some online banking. It was a Friday morning and his paycheck from Driftwood had gone directly into his checking account; even golf courses offered direct deposit these days. So, he wanted to transfer a little of his paycheck to his savings account. While making the transfer, he noticed there was a one thousand dollar limit, per day, on electronic transfers between bank accounts. Okay. Sounded reasonable. A safeguard against fraud. He thought he remembered a similar limit with the bank he'd used in Hartford. He didn't give it that much thought at the time.

But later that day he'd almost crashed his car on the way home from work when it occurred to him what the daily transfer limit would mean to his plan. Suddenly, he realized his plan to get the money was deeply flawed. Deeply flawed as in, "No way in hell this is going to work." His assumption had been he could use Laura's account name and password to transfer the money to an account he controlled, but with a one thousand dollar limit on transfers that would be impossible. He'd have to transfer one thousand dollars every day for over eight years and three months to get all three million. And of course, he'd probably only get two or three thousand before Laura realized something was wrong and finally updated her password after all these years.

At first it felt is if all was lost. It felt like he was destined to be golf pro Troy Stevens for the rest of his days. And not only was he not going to get the money, but he'd have no way to stop that nut Johnny from turning him in. His plan with regards to Johnny had been to simply disappear with all the money before Johnny realized what was happening. By the time Johnny realized the insurance company had paid off, and it was time to collect "his" half, Miles Goodman would be enjoying an umbrella drink on some far away beach. And Johnny would be looking for a ghost. But now what?

One fun idea under that scenario was to tell Johnny to extort the money from Laura! Johnny had found Bill, and he would keep that tidbit quiet for a percentage of the take. Otherwise, if it's proven that Bill is alive, the insurance company would certainly come looking for their money. Even better, then Bill could swing a three-way deal, because he could always threaten to turn himself in, and nobody would get anything.

But eventually he stopped feeling sorry for himself and cranked up Google. He learned that most large bank transfers are done in person at the bank in the form of a wire transfer. He knew that Laura would most likely put the money in one of their joint accounts before moving it to other investment vehicles and accounts. He'd have a small window of time to grab the money right after it had been paid to Laura. His name would still be on those accounts. Laura would be so focused on having him declared dead, she wouldn't think about taking his name off the accounts. That was a detail that could be taken care of in due time. And Bill still had his Bill Ferguson driver's license and credit cards. Plan B began to germinate in his mind.

Monday was his day off, and he spent the afternoon Googling. In the end, he thought he'd come up with a very solid plan. Absolutely crazy, of course, but utter lunacy was the new normal for Bill at this point. Now he knew how he was going to pull off this final stage of the operation. The plan was so ridiculous and fun that he was almost laughing out loud, despite being alone. One thing was for sure--Miles Goodman was going to need a passport.

Chapter Fifty-Five

Saturday, September 19, 2009 – 8:00 p.m.

PRESTON AND LAURA were dining once again at Ocean Blue on Narragansett on a Saturday night. By now they had "their" waiter, Miguel, who knew what they liked and what they didn't. He suggested wine for them, had acquired a feel for which of the specials they would like, and knew just when to approach them and when to give them their space.

Preston noted that Laura was very quiet. And when she was quiet, there was often trouble brewing. He was a little burnt out from an intense case that had gone his way, barely. It had been a knockdown drag-out affair from the git-go. Three months of all-out war. Motion after motion, reluctant witnesses, and an ornery judge. Hence, he had been hoping for a mindless getaway this weekend. So for the moment, his plan was simply to enjoy the glass of cabernet sauvignon in front of him. Normally he would gently probe, ask her if everything was okay, try to find out what was on her mind. But tonight he wasn't feeling that sensitive. He was hoping whatever it was could wait until the morning.

But of course, it couldn't. Laura spoke. "You know, it's been six months now."

Preston racked his brain, six months, six months since what? Oh shit. Don't let on you didn't remember this was roughly the six month anniversary since Bill disappeared. He needed to say something, without putting his foot in his mouth. "Has it really?"

"Yes. Do you remember what we talked about in the beginning?"

"Yes."

He was partly bluffing, but he was pretty sure she was talking about how it would be better if Bill was dead. Even if he wasn't.

"Well, it's been six months now. And of course, no sign of him."

"Yes."

Preston could tell she was getting a little frustrated. He could hear her thinking, are you daft? Do I have to spell it out for you? But for some reason, he felt like being a little cagey. He knew very well after her last statement where she was going, but he felt like being a contrarian. Probably because he was spent, mentally. He wanted her to lead this discussion.

"So, what do you think we should do?" Now, he was a little irritated. She was a lawyer, and a good one. She knew as well as he did what the next step should probably be. Say what it is that you want, woman! "I don't think we should do anything. As you said, it's only been six months." He knew that would piss her off. But at that moment, he didn't care. Laura, of course, was angling for his support. Preston was supposed to say yes, six months had been long enough to do something about the fact that Bill was probably dead but he wasn't in the mood tonight. And the look on Laura's face suggested he might want to position himself to be able to quickly duck, because there could very well be a hot bowl of soup coming his way in the immediate future.

"Do you still love me?"

Low blow! But he wasn't going to give in. Now it was a battle of wits, and he wasn't going down without a fight. "What do you think?"

She paused. "I don't know what to think right now."

"Oh really? That's interesting." He said this to make sure it was clear that he thought he was now the wounded party. How dare she question his love for her? And the gloves came off. "Is it that you are hoping he is still alive?"

"What in the world are you talking about?"

"Are you hoping he'll turn up? Is that your exit strategy?"

"Exit strategy? Have you lost your mind?"

"Then why else wouldn't you want him declared dead?"

"Who said I didn't want him declared dead?"

"If you want him declared dead, then why wait? Don't you want to be with me?"

"Oh, for Christ's sake."

Tears were running down Laura's cheeks now, declaring her the victor. Miguel was in a quandary. The dinners were ready, but he knew that now wasn't the time to serve them. But the food wouldn't be nearly as good if it sat under the warmers for too long.

Preston spoke. "Listen, you just caught me off guard. In the back of my mind, I was thinking the one-year mark would be when to go for a coroner's inquest. Six months seems a little quick to me, that's all." He reached out and grabbed her right hand with his left. "Would you like me to make some calls?"

She half smiled, while wiping the tears from her cheek. The smile told Preston that looking into a coroner's inquest was exactly what she wanted.

Miguel saw the gesture and swooped in with the dinners. They were still very tasty.

Chapter Fifty-Six

Friday, September 25, 2009 – 10:00 p.m.

BILL DID A triple take. Was there really an email related to the Ferguson case? Could it be there was finally something happening? He was afraid to open it. This could be it. Sheepishly, he clicked on the bold subject line that read, "Ferguson Inquest."

He devoured the email as if he was a starving man who had happened upon a smorgasbord. He read it again to make sure he hadn't misinterpreted. Then he read it a third time. There was no doubt about it. There was to be a coroner's inquest on October fifth at ten a.m. A coroner's inquest to decide whether or not he was dead.

He laughed out loud. He couldn't stop laughing. How freaking cool was this? This insane, crazy plan was actually working. And oh, how he wanted to attend the inquest. He could create a disguise and just sit in the back, couldn't he? Maybe he could get away with that. But he didn't think he'd be able to refrain from laughing. He felt a little bit like Tom Sawyer.

Okay. Time to think. Assuming he was declared dead on October fifth, it would take roughly three weeks for all the i's to be dotted and t's to be crossed and the money to be paid. That would be approximately the week of October twenty-fifth. So, he had roughly a month to work out all the details and logistics of how to move the money and where he would go. Yes, where to go? Things were slowing down at the golf course. Golf courses always were less busy after Labor Day. So he'd have more time for planning because he'd be working less.

He'd done some research already. First, he'd need some help getting the money out of Laura's bank account into his own, probably an offshore account. An account in the Caymans or a Swiss account. He'd read online that you could set up a Swiss account in the Caymans. And it might be better to have a Swiss account for three million bucks. The Swiss had really good security. But the money wouldn't be in that account for very long anyway. A sort of a shell game is what he had planned. He'd move the money a few times before it wound up in a Miles Goodman account. If the plan worked, they'd never be able to find him by following the money. It would be untraceable.

As for the help he'd need, Jennifer was the logical choice. She was really the only woman in the world he felt he could trust at this point. The only person, for that matter. Plus, if she was willing to help, maybe that would be a sign. A sign that they could eventually wind up together. Regardless, once he became Miles, he'd have to have a story for his past ready to go. Living in isolation like he had been wouldn't work long term. Plus, he was too young to go without the company of women for the rest of his life.

He decided to start checking the Johnson email account every day. In case there were developments. In case the inquest got rescheduled. He needed to get the results of the inquest and find out when the money was to be paid.

It was ten p.m., normally the time he thought about heading to bed. But he was too jazzed up. The adrenaline was flowing. No way he could go to sleep right now. His mind was racing; he needed to get organized. <u>Okay. Take a deep breath. Slow yourself down a little bit. Prioritize.</u> He had a month to figure out exactly how to pilfer the money and get himself to a new location as Miles Goodman. What were the most important things to do? Surely, it would be critical to get the banking plan squared away. What accounts would he need? He'd probably need a quick trip to the Caymans in the next few weeks in order to have that first bank account already in place.

Timing would be critical. He'd have to swoop in and take the money before Laura invested it somewhere. And he'd have to move the money at least twice before anyone realized it was gone in order not to get caught. So a good plan would be critical, as would its execution.

Part of the banking plan would have to include an accomplice. So at some point in the next month, Bill would have to contact Jennifer. But how? Email? In person? He needed to think about that. And when to contact her. He'd want to give her a little time to process his request, but not enough time that she might feel guilty and wind up turning him in.

The account in the Caymans would be created as Troy. Obviously. He started researching flights. The prices weren't that bad. He'd fly on a Monday, fly back on a Wednesday. Give himself all of Tuesday to set up an account. Plus, hell, he'd never been to the Caymans. If he had time, he could have an umbrella drink by the beach. Party a little. Maybe he'd try to get laid, but he wasn't sure he remembered how. And how do you pick up chicks when you're forty years old anyway? He'd been married so long he had no idea what to do. He had no game. Time to start thinking about getting a game, he guessed.

Chapter Fifty-Seven

Monday, October 5, 2009 – 10:00 a.m.

FRANK COULD HARDLY believe his good fortune. He had never seen this much cash in his life. The standard white letter envelope he held in his right hand felt heavy and quite substantial. He peeked inside again. Nothing but beautiful green bills. He thumbed the bills; all were of the fifty-dollar denomination.

How to spend the money? That was easy. He'd pay off a few bills and then take his wife Delores on a trip to the Caribbean. Maybe he'd also do something for the grandchildren. Perhaps he'd buy them one of those fancy new swing sets that's a full-on jungle gym. He'd have to look into that.

Preston Malloy had originally offered the County Coroner five grand, but Frank had been able to negotiate it up to ten. He didn't know exactly how much was involved in the bigger picture, but he figured there must be a lot at stake for Malloy to request an expedited inquest. Especially when he was offering a cash incentive to make it happen. The reason was obvious even though it hadn't been stated. This had to be about life insurance.

Ferguson's wife reached out somehow and convinced the ADA that her husband was dead and she could sure use the insurance money. Malloy must be getting his own payoff from her in order to go to work on her behalf in this manner. Frank was pretty sure of this; Malloy had made it clear that for ten thousand, it would be a lot better if Bill Ferguson was declared dead.

He glanced at his watch. It was time, ten a.m. Malloy had made the arrangements for the use of the adjacent courtroom. These kinds of proceedings were relatively rare in Hartford County, so there wasn't a standard procedure. As Frank was bracing to rise out of the regal judge's chair, he took one more look around the chambers adjacent to courtroom number seven. It was a much nicer space than his own office. Mahogany bookshelves on three walls framed the mahogany desk. A large portrait of President Lincoln hung on the wall behind him. The decor was very austere, and he thought about the gravity of the issues that were normally decided in this room. He pictured judges scolding lawyers who had gotten out of line, lawyers arguing motions of critical import, and decisions rendered that were critical to the fate of those involved.

But Frank saw this particular inquest as more of a formality. The evidence was overwhelming. Despite the fact that there was no body, with the amount of blood lost it was easy to deduce that Bill Ferguson was dead. Plus, there was no evidence that Ferguson was alive. He had simply disappeared. No credit card activity, no cell phone use. Nothing. It was a classic case of a missing person one could safely presume had passed away.

Frank reviewed the list of witnesses one more time before he entered the courtroom. He planned on calling Mrs. Ferguson, Detective Dmitri Jones, Dr. Anthony Welman, who was another doctor from the coroner's office, and Jennifer Weaver, the executive assistant to Bill Ferguson.

He would ask each one relevant questions regarding the evidence. There was no concept of cross-examination in a coroner's inquest. The evidence was presented to the six jurors by the witnesses answering the coroner's questions, often in reference to crucial documentation such as photographs. Once the evidence was presented, the jury would deliberate and rule as to whether or not the missing person was in fact to be considered dead.

Frank opened the chamber door and entered the courtroom at five minutes past ten. He noticed the jurors were duly seated in the jury box, and all four witnesses were present. There were only about a half dozen other people in the courtroom, none of whom he recognized. While the inquest was technically open to the public, no billboard had been rented to announce the date and time. The disappearance of an unknown insurance executive had initially made the local news, but the story didn't have legs. It had been drowned out by the noise of the latest murders, armed robberies, and gasoline price spikes. Notably absent from the courtroom was Preston Malloy, the man who had made all the arrangements. Oh well, no time to dwell on that now, there was business to attend to.

Frank called Mrs. Ferguson first. They discussed her discovery of the tremendous amount of blood in the home office, and the fact she'd been out of town all weekend prior to discovering the blood. She noted that nothing of Bill's was missing from the house except his wallet. His car was in the driveway, all his clothes were in the closet, there were no missing suitcases, and, of course, she had not heard from Bill. He had vanished almost into thin air, save for the blood.

The next witness was Dmitri Jones. Frank would spend the majority of the time with Detective Jones. They discussed the bloody crime scene, as well as the footprints and smear marks leading from the home office out to the backyard. The jury saw those pictures, along with the photos of the foreign tire track at the end of the bloody trail. The pictures of the bullet fragments and bullet hole in the wall were shared, along with the information that the slug was most likely from a Glock 17 9mm.

Detective Jones confirmed that roughly four pints of blood, all of it Bill Ferguson's, was found in the home office.

Frank made sure not to ask questions that would allow room for any doubt that the jury was looking at a bloody murder scene. And that was easy to do by just sticking with the physical evidence. So, the fact that Bill had no enemies to speak of, and was not involved in any activities that would normally get one killed in such a brutal way, was not discussed. Mrs. Ferguson's infidelity was not discussed. In Frank's mind, it possibly went to why Ferguson was killed, but was not relevant to whether or not he was dead.

The testimony of Dr. Welman was fairly short. Frank wanted the jury to hear from a doctor that no one would survive the amount of blood loss suffered by Bill Ferguson without immediate medical attention. Which Ferguson could not have received, because there was no record of him receiving treatment of any kind at any of the area hospitals on the weekend in question. Thank you doctor, that will be all. Frank saw no need to get into what types of injuries would cause someone to bleed to death as Mr. Ferguson apparently had. What did it matter? Someone losing four pints of blood was someone losing four pints of blood, period. He'd been shot, he bled out, good night nurse.

The final witness, Jennifer Weaver, was on the stand for an equally short stint. First, Frank had her review the fact that she had been Bill Ferguson's executive assistant for a number of years. Then there were really only two questions. Have you heard from him since the weekend he disappeared? And to the best of your knowledge, has any other colleague of his heard from him? No and no. Thank you, that will be all.

With that, Frank felt he had done his job and turned it over to the jury. Based on the way he'd presented things, it would be very, very difficult for a jury to render any ruling except the desired one. From a medical standpoint, the case was pretty simple after all. Four pints of the man's blood had been found in the home office and that was more than sufficient to cause his death.

The jury came back in about a half hour. It probably really only took them ten minutes, but most juries are conscientious and don't want to rush to a judgment or even give the appearance of such. So they go over the evidence a few times, looking for holes, problems, flaws in the arguments. But in this case, there was only one harsh and obvious conclusion to be drawn.

Chapter Fifty-Eight

Tuesday, October 27, 2009 – 10:00 a.m.

THE NEXT FEW days would decide whether or not this had all been worth it. Would the months of planning, scheming, and self-imposed exile pay off? Had it been a good choice to trade in being a member of a country club for working at one? Had it made sense to substitute a Folgers lifestyle for his beloved Starbucks? Would he have the chance to trade in his Chevy pickup for a Lamborghini? By the end of the week Bill would know the answers to those questions.

It was time to execute the final few steps of his master plan. Could he pull this off? He had no backup plan. Failure was not an option. Because finally, the eagle had landed. The money had arrived.

He had been monitoring Laura's checking account every day since the coroner's inquest had come to the conclusion that he was six feet under. It was actually still their joint checking account. So now it was time to move. Time to claim the bounty he had worked so hard for.

There was no plan regarding his current job. In lieu of a better idea, he decided he would just call in sick for the next few days. Sorry, I can't make it in. I've got a fever, the runs, whatever. It was late October, things were really slowing down at the golf course. It wouldn't be a big deal if he missed a few days. He'd just reschedule the handful of lessons he had lined up. This way, if something went terribly wrong in Connecticut, at least he'd have a job and an apartment here in Myrtle. If he got the money, would he call and quit? Over the phone? Or just disappear? Would it matter? How could it possibly matter?

Okay. Now things were going to get a little weird. This next move was a huge gamble. But he felt he had to try to give Jennifer some kind of a heads up that he was going to be asking for her help. No way could he just show up on her doorstep, not under the circumstances.

Of course, trying to give her some kind of forewarning might lead to his downfall. If she decided she didn't want any part of this, the authorities could be waiting for him when he arrived. But he felt he needed to take the chance. He needed someone to pose as Laura in order to actually get the money. If Jennifer turned him in, then so be it. He doubted she would. So he had to take this shot.

A DEVIOUS PLAN

Bill logged into the Greystone website as Henry Johnson. After accessing the Johnson email account, he pushed the "New Message" button. And then he struggled. What to write? How could he tell her it was him, without being blunt, and without sounding really creepy? Eventually he typed this:

*

> Meet me at the Wicked Onion Wednesday at 6:00 p.m. I'll buy you a chicken Caesar salad.
> –B.
> P.S. If you check, you'll find there is no Henry Johnson.

*

At two p.m. he got the following response:

*

> If this is who I think it is you are insane. Meet me at my apartment Wednesday at 7:00 p.m.

*

And that was it. He went online and booked a plane for Hartford for the next morning. Luckily, Jennifer was in the online White Pages, so he was able to look up her address that way, without another email exchange. It was probably a lot smarter to meet at her apartment instead of a public place.

Chapter Fifty-Nine

Wednesday, October 28, 2009 – 7:00 p.m.

BILL WAS STANDING outside Jennifer Weaver's apartment at precisely seven p.m. He reached to grab the doorknocker but just as he did, the door burst open. Jennifer, with an incredulous look on her face, motioned for him to come in.

With Bill safely inside, they stared at each other for a second.

Jennifer spoke first, irritated for having to do so. "This is the part where you start explaining."

"Right. I'm sure you're ... curious."

"You think?"

"Well, for starters, I'm still alive."

Bill recognized her expression as saying, if I had a frying pan in my hand right now, I'd brain you with it.

"Okay, Okay. She was cheating on me. So this is payback. I faked my death and I'm going after the insurance money."

"Oh. Well, that's good. Because for a second there, I thought you were going to say something crazy."

"I know, I know, when you just say it out loud like that, it sounds nuts. It started as a crazy idea that just took on a life of its own."

"So, now the sixty-four thousand dollar question: Why are you here?"

"I need some help. You know, actually getting the money."

Jennifer nodded sarcastically, as if she fully understood.

"So let me get this straight. You faked your own death in order steal the insurance money. And apparently, you did the first part right. They believed you. I went to court, and a bunch of people got together and decided you were dead. Plus, I read it in an email I got the next day. Now, silly me, I of course believed the email, and cried and cried. But we can talk about that later."

<u>Fuck. This is going a lot worse than I hoped.</u>

Jennifer continued. "Anyway, after all that, now, you need help getting the money? What, you didn't plan that part? Seems like kind of an important part, don't you think? So, please explain," she said with mock politeness.

"I had a plan originally. And then I realized it wouldn't work."

"And why not?"

"It doesn't matter. The point is the money is in a joint account, with both mine and Laura's names on the account."

Jennifer paused, then the light bulb went off in her head. "Oh, I get it. I've seen her picture. You think I … Oh my God, you've got to be kidding …"

"Oh shit, Jennifer, I get it, this was a bad idea. It's just that I didn't know where else to turn. There really isn't anybody else I trust right now."

Jennifer didn't say anything for a few seconds.

"Let me think about this."

And they didn't speak for several minutes. Finally, Jennifer had a question.

"Okay. What if I went along with this insanity? What if I played the part? Suppose I went to the bank and pretended to be Laura Ferguson and you got the money? Then what? What happens to me then? You know as soon as the money is gone, they are going to figure out you took it. And they are going to question everyone you ever knew, including me. And I'm not a good liar. So if I, or we, do this … how much money is there, anyway?" Jennifer looked very nervous and

Bill realized she was right. "It's three million dollars. But you're right. I'm sorry. I'm sorry I put you in this position now. It's just that I've come so far with this thing … I'm right on the one-yard line. I just need someone to help me punch it in."

"Punch it in?"

"Into the end zone. Sorry, silly sports analogy. But you get the point?"

"Yes. I get the point."

They both fell silent. Bill felt that what happened next would be crucial. He was either going to have to commit fully to her right then and there, or walk away. He sensed she wouldn't be interested in a situation where she helped him get the money and then was left to weather the storm in Connecticut on her own. Even if he offered a generous payment.

<u>Fortune favors the bold. Just do it.</u>

Suddenly, Bill grabbed Jennifer and kissed her. She kissed him back. They shared a passionate kiss for a full minute before Jennifer pulled back. She pushed Bill away.

"Wait a minute, is this real?"

"I've always wanted to do that," Bill lied.

"This is confusing. What are you telling me? That if I help you, we'll be together?"

"Yes."

But the truth was Bill hadn't thought that far ahead. His plan had been so carefully crafted up to this point, except for actually getting the money. When he realized the hole in his plan, he had just assumed he could enlist Jennifer's help without thinking it through.

Jennifer sat down and began thinking. Bill moved toward her, wanting to keep the passion going. But she avoided his kiss with a turn of her head. She waved him off. After another minute she spoke. "Okay. So I help you get the money. Then what? We just disappear? What is the plan?"

<u>Good question. What is the plan?</u>

Jennifer continued, "I don't see how this will work. The two of us on the run somehow? Where will we go? How will we not get caught? This doesn't make any sense."

He didn't know what to say. He had another identity all lined for himself, but not for her.

"Bill, you know I care about you, but this isn't right. Not this way. I wish you had kissed me a long time ago."

"I couldn't."

"I know. This won't work. You should leave now."

And she disappeared into the bedroom. Bill stood there, with the taste of the kiss still on his lips. The kiss had ignited a flame inside him. He had never allowed himself to think of Jennifer in this way before, but now he wanted her. Suddenly, he wanted her badly. He wanted to follow her into the bedroom and finish what he had started.

But she was right; now wasn't the time. He had to complete his mission without her help, get the three million dollars, and vanish. He'd have to lay low for a while. Go to the mattresses, as the old-time mobsters would have said. When the time was right, he'd come back for Jennifer. Because now he didn't just want the money. He wanted the girl too.

Chapter Sixty

Thursday, October 29, 2009 – 8:00 p.m.

IN A YEAR filled with crazy stunts, this had to be one of the craziest. Bill Ferguson, who had been ruled dead by a jury just three weeks before, was now back in Connecticut, hiding out in the basement of his own house. This particular clandestine move hinged on the fact that Laura hardly ever came down into the storage room. He accepted that if she happened to come down here tonight, he was screwed.

Then again, what if she did come down? The best thing he could think of, if she came downstairs and found him, was try to talk her into a making a deal. Granted, she had the three million bucks already in her account. But Bill was holding a lot of cards. If he simply went to the FBI and turned himself in, no way she gets to keep the money. So that was the way he'd play it. But there was little chance it would come down to that.

Candy, an operative Bill had hired earlier in the day, had dropped him off two blocks from the house, just after dark, at his request. He was wearing what he considered to be a semi-disguise. A dark hooded sweatshirt with the hood pulled over his head, and a baseball cap underneath. Black khakis and black sneakers. He wasn't going for any particular look, other than to not look like Bill Ferguson. He then made his way to the neighbor's house that backed up to his own. He moved quietly through the neighbor's yard and hopped the fence into his own backyard.

He was also wearing a back pack that contained a change of clothes, sweatpants and a tee shirt to sleep in, and a few snacks in case he got hungry. He'd had the foresight to bring a book and a flashlight with him too, so he'd have something to do all evening.

Laura wasn't home yet, so he simply used his old key and went in through the back door into the mudroom. Immediately he was transported back to March, back to the last time he'd been here. There was definitely a touch of adrenaline flowing right now, but nothing like that night.

He remembered vividly his actions of March thirteen. The shooting of the blood filled bag. Dragging the blood covered dummy through the house and out the back door. Changing his shoes to make it look as if two "perps" were involved. Then the ditching of the panel van into the lake at the quarry.

But now the house looked normal. The bloodstains had been cleaned up. There was no trace of blood in the home office and the bullet hole had been repaired. What would it have been like to come home to that mess he left behind? Up until now, he hadn't thought too much about what he'd put Laura through. It must have been a nightmare. Oh well, she'd made her own bed.

He went back down into the storage room to get himself situated. He found his old sleeping bag on one of the shelves. The plastic tub with the extra pillows in it was right where it always had been. He found a foam pad he could put between the concrete storage room floor and the sleeping bag. He brought out the flashlight and the book and set them aside. If needed, he could use the bathroom in the finished part of the basement. He just had to make damn sure he remembered not to flush.

He'd brought a cell phone with him and set the alarm on it to wake him up at six a.m. He set it to vibrate and put it in his pocket. There probably wasn't a need to get up quite that early, but he wanted to make sure he was alert and ready when it was time to make his move. Timing would be critical.

He'd been smart enough to bring a few snacks. A couple of protein bars and a bottle of water. Just enough to get him through the night if he got hungry. He'd made sure to eat a full meal just before sneaking over here.

After being rebuffed by Jennifer, he'd been in scramble mode all day trying to find a substitute. And naturally, he couldn't think of anyone off the top of his head that looked like his wife and would be willing to pose as her at the bank while he took three million dollars out of her account. So, he made a few calls to local escort services. He described the kind of woman he was looking for. Luckily, Candy was available by early afternoon.

They met at Bill's hotel. She was a bit baffled when at first he didn't want to sleep with her. Instead, he wanted to hire her for a specific assignment. She was to be his employee for the next twenty-four hours. She would drop him off at his old house, and then be on standby early in the morning to pick him up. Then she would go with him to the bank to pose as Mrs. Ferguson. She was close enough in height and weight to pull it off. They agreed she would be paid five hundred dollars after the first drop off, and then five hundred more after they were done at the bank. Once that was all settled, Bill succumbed. He hadn't been with a woman for months and months, and Candy was ready, willing, and more than able.

At nine p.m., Laura came home. Bill's senses were on high alert. He was straining to hear every sound, every step. He listened intently for any indication that she might be coming down to the basement. And none came. It sounded as if she made several round trips around that first floor during the next ninety minutes. He could tell she was on one extended phone call while she bounced around the kitchen. He assumed the call was to lover boy.

Finally, things quieted down by about ten-thirty. By eleven, he hadn't heard any noise coming from the main level. It appeared she had gone upstairs and turned in for the night. Okay. He could breathe easier now and he was suddenly very tired. While at first he doubted he would be able to sleep at all, he had no doubt he'd be sleeping for several hours very soon. It was time for his tee shirt, his sweats, and the latest legal thriller from Mr. John Grisham.

Chapter Sixty-One

Friday, October 30, 2009 – 6:00 a.m.

BILL AWOKE TO his phone vibrating annoyingly in the pocket of his sweatpants. It was irritating but effective. He assumed the next couple of hours were going to be a struggle. Like most people, he was accustomed to taking a shower when he first woke up. And worse, he had no coffee. Naturally, he wasn't too excited about the prospect of having neither of those after crashing in a sleeping bag on the cold storage room floor. But after a few minutes his adrenaline kicked in and he wasn't feeling anywhere near as groggy as he thought he would.

Remembering not to flush, he used the basement bathroom. Then he straightened up his makeshift campsite, putting away the pillow, the sleeping bag, and the foam pad. Grabbing a folding chair, he opened up the novel to occupy his time while he waited for Laura to wake up. Ah! He remembered he had a protein bar left in the backpack. He dispensed with it quickly, and drank the bottle of water.

At five minutes past seven, he heard signs of life upstairs. Laura bopping around the kitchen.

Making coffee, no doubt. Her routine when they were together had been to come down to the kitchen to get her coffee, and then take it back upstairs and get in the shower. That's when he would strike.

He slowly crawled up the stairs. The top step would be a listening post, where he could hear her leave the kitchen and head upstairs to the top level. As he reached the top step, his heart was pounding and his mouth was dry. All it would take was for Laura to decide she needed something in the basement and he would be nailed. But she didn't. And finally, at about seven-fifteen, Laura's footsteps faded as she left the kitchen and headed upstairs.

Okay. Bill decided to wait until precisely seven-thirty to move. He wanted to make sure Laura was actually in the shower before he entered the kitchen. So he just sat there on the top step, waiting. It was the longest fifteen minutes of his life. There was nothing to do but watch the time. He could pull the book out of the backpack and read for a couple more minutes, but he felt too nervous so he just waited.

Finally, after what felt like an hour, it was seven-thirty. Standing up, Bill slung the backpack over his left shoulder and carefully turned the knob for the basement with his right hand. He pushed the door open. Thankfully, it didn't squeak. He heard nothing. Slowly, he took a few steps and emerged into the kitchen. It was confirmed, he was alone. After making his way to the bottom of the stairs that led to the top level, he listened for a few seconds. He could hear the water running. Yes! Laura was in the shower. Perfect. He went back into the kitchen; her purse was sitting on the island, as it had been every morning for the last umpteen years. He grabbed the purse, opened it up, and dug through the morass of lipsticks, receipts, coupons and keys until he finally found her wallet.

Opening it, he deftly removed her driver's license and a little used credit card. He put them in an outside pocket of the backpack. He figured it would be days before she realized they were missing. How often do you actually use your driver's license, anyway? She would probably realize the money was gone before she noticed the missing cards.

Next he sent Candy a text message with nothing but the numbers "777." It was a code he'd made up for the occasion to tell her it was time to come pick him up. Once the text was sent, he hustled out through the mudroom, out the back door, through the neighbor's yard, and up the street to the rendezvous point.

Candy, God bless her, was right on time. This was very exciting for her, by far the most interesting "date" she had ever had. Not only was she being very well paid, but also she found all the cloak and dagger stuff to be very intriguing. She wanted to know if Bill was a private eye, how does one become one? What does it pay? He told her he wasn't at liberty to discuss such things while he was working a case. His answer made no sense of course, but Candy seemed to accept it.

It was about seven forty-five, plenty of time for Candy to drive Bill back to the hotel where he could shower and change his clothes. After washing up, he put on the cheap suit, dress shirt, tie and shoes he'd bought at the Goodwill store. He wanted to look the part when moving three million dollars from the joint bank account to a numbered Swiss account.

At five minutes past nine, Bill Ferguson, acting as himself for the first time in an eon, with Candy the escort on his arm, strolled into the Worthington Bank and Trust in downtown Hartford. He asked to meet with a manager; they had a very large bank transfer to conduct. The bank manager invited them into her office. She had them fill out some forms and asked for their IDs.

"Bill Ferguson, don't I know you from somewhere?"

"Oh I don't think so, I've just got one of those faces."

"Hmmm. For some reason I think we've met."

The bank manager glanced at Candy, then glanced at Laura's driver's license photo, then

A DEVIOUS PLAN 329

glanced at Candy one more time. It was clear she was unsure, and Bill thought they might be in trouble. But just as in football, ultimately there was insufficient evidence to claim that Candy wasn't Laura. The two looked just enough alike.

So, after a few nerve racking minutes, the transfer was completed. And the bank manager gave them the whole spiel regarding how sorry she was to see their business go, if there is ever anything we can do for you in the future, please let us know…

And with that, Bill had Candy drive him to the airport. He paid her, thanked her profusely, and then Miles Goodman bought a one-way plane ticket to the tiny Pacific island of Padai.

Chapter Sixty-Two

Monday, November 2, 2009 – 2:00 p.m.

"PRESTON MALLOY."

"PRESTON? It's me. Something has happened."

"What is it, baby? You sound upset."

"It's the money. It's not in my account."

"Huh? What money?"

"The insurance money. It's not in my account."

"What do you mean? The three million dollars? How much is missing?"

"All of it. The account is showing a zero balance."

"Well, that doesn't make any sense. Did you call the bank? It's probably some kind of computer glitch."

"I haven't called yet. Maybe I should just go there and talk to them in person."

"Sounds like a good idea. Let me know what happens."

Two hours later, Preston's phone rang again. "Preston Malloy."

"Hey. I'm scared now. This is a disaster. First, I got to the bank and I couldn't find my driver's license anywhere. I showed the bank some of my credit cards, but they said that wasn't good enough. So I went home to get my passport. By the time I got back, that police detective Jones was here …"

"Wait a minute, the police are involved? Are you saying the money really isn't there?"

"Yes, that's what I'm saying. Apparently someone came to the bank and forged my signature and transferred the money somewhere else."

There was silence on the other end of the line.

"Preston?"

"Sorry, I'm just stunned. Someone actually came in and stole the money? That's incredible …"

"They showed me the wire transfer form. The signature was close, but it wasn't right. Luckily I've got enough other examples of my signature where they believe me …"

"So what now?"

"They want me to wait here; they've got me in an office in the back. They are trying to pull up some surveillance tapes or something. They want me to look at them. It would be great if you were here with me …"

"Sorry, baby, not a great idea. Why would an ADA suddenly show up at the bank with an interest in this situation? This early on? Remember, we agreed it's way too early to go public."

"I know, I know. You're right. I'm just scared right now. Someone is out there forging my signature. And my license is missing …" Silence again. "Preston? Are you still there?"

"Yes. I'm trying to process all this …"

"Okay, they're back with the tapes. Gotta go. I'll call you. Thank God we really don't need this money."

Detective Jones, the bank manger, and a bank security officer entered the small conference room in the back offices of the bank. While the security man set up the video, Detective Jones set the stage.

"Okay. Here is what we've got. We've got a huge wire transfer completed based on what appears to be a forged signature. The wire transfer was recorded into the system at nine-fifteen a.m. on Friday. So this tape will show everyone who entered and exited the bank for the fifteen minutes before and the hour after the time of the wire transfer. The bank opened at nine a.m. on Friday. We are going to watch this in fast forward so we don't have to sit here for an hour and fifteen minutes. So please watch closely and speak up if you see someone you recognize. Then we'll stop the tape and take a closer look."

"Everyone ready? Okay, go."

Laura watched closely as the grainy black and white images zipped across the screen. Suddenly she saw someone she recognized.

"Oh my God! Oh my God! Stop the tape!"

The security man rewound the tape to the point just before a man and a woman entered the bank. The man and woman had triggered Laura's outburst. He then played the tape at normal speed. To her utter disbelief, Laura was staring at the image of her husband Bill, accompanied by an unknown woman.

"Oh my God! It's Bill! I can't believe it! I ... I ..."

Laura stared at the monitor in stunned disbelief. A million things were running through her mind all at once. Really? Did he hate me that much? To go to these lengths? Or maybe once he knew the marriage was over, he just snapped? Or was it just about the money? Her mind was trying to come to grips with both a tsunami of questions and an avalanche of emotions. She was confused, disgusted, angry and scared all at once. She could feel a major headache coming on.

Dmitri Jones had recognized Bill also. And it was obvious to Dmitri that Mrs. Ferguson had not been accompanying Mr. Ferguson at the time the video was taken. The women looked similar, but the hair was wrong. And the build wasn't quite right either. Of course, he had the benefit of having the real Mrs. Ferguson sitting right there with him. The bank manager who handled the transaction couldn't really be faulted, Mr. Ferguson had done a good job of finding a look-a-like.

"Do you recognize the woman that he's with Mrs. Ferguson?"

"No ... no, she doesn't look familiar. But with those sunglasses on ... even then, oh no, I'm sure that I don't know her."

"Well, the evidence unquestionably points to you being the victim of a huge fraud here, Mrs. Ferguson. It appears that the woman in the surveillance tape presented herself as you and forged your signature. Forged your signature on a wire transfer, and the money was transferred to another account. An account controlled by your husband, most likely."

"Well, I'll be speaking to my superiors, but there is a ninety-nine percent chance we will be bringing in the FBI on this one. With a crime of this magnitude, we'll need their resources."

Plus, unless he was coerced into this, Bill Ferguson now has three million dollars at his disposal, Dmitri thought to himself. And a seventy-two hour head start. He could be anywhere by now. Most likely, the trick will be to follow the money. And the Hartford police didn't have those kinds of resources.

There was a part of him, however, that was delighted with this development. His instincts had been vindicated. Something didn't add up at the "crime scene," but he had been called off the fake death angle before he'd had a chance to sink his teeth into it.

Something was gnawing at him now ... what was it? There was something he wasn't remembering right now, something germane to the case. Bah. He couldn't put his finger on it. He'd have to get back to his office and review his notes. This was one of those cases where there were going to be a lot more questions before there were many answers. But surely now, with a fraud case of this magnitude, the Bureau would be taking over. Probably before sundown. And that was fine with him. He'd been hamstrung from the beginning by Hartford politics on this one. But that wouldn't happen to the Feds.

Chapter Sixty-Three

Friday, November 6, 2009 – 3:00 p.m.

THE TWO FBI investigators looked at each other knowingly. This meeting was going to be very ugly. There was no two ways about it. Their boss, the Special Agent in Charge of the New Haven, Connecticut field office, didn't like bad news. And they were about to deliver bad news in spades.

Special Agents Charlie Bragg and Steve Robey had been working together in the New Haven field office for many years. Having both been assigned to the Criminal Investigation Division early on, they were always the team chosen for big money fraud cases. They reported directly to the Special Agent in Charge, hence, they had grown accustomed to, if not fond of, their bombastic boss.

"Got your earplugs, Charlie?"

"Wish I had them, Steve. But we've weathered the fury of Hurricane Braddock before. It'll be okay."

Steve smiled. Nothing to do but grin and bear it.

The two agents entered Winston Braddock's office.

"All right boys, give me some good news. It's been a long goddamn day."

Charlie Bragg was the lead investigator in the case of Laura Ferguson's missing money. He responded to his boss's request.

"Well sir, we traced the money from the Worthington Bank and Trust in Hartford, Connecticut to a numbered account in Switzerland, which was set up through a broker in the Caymans. On Monday, the Swiss confirmed a deposit in the amount of just under three million dollars into the Swiss Bank from the bank in Connecticut. The deposit was initiated on Friday morning from Hartford, and accepted into the Swiss bank an hour later, which was about four-fifteen in the afternoon, Swiss time."

Bragg continued. "Then on Tuesday the money was transferred out of the Swiss bank and into a privately owned bank in Padai."

"Padai … Refresh me, where the hell is Padai again?"

"It's a tiny island in the Pacific that is its own country. It's only about twenty thousand people. It's been on the radar for a number of years because a lot of shady banking goes on there."

"Right, right, right. I remember now."

"Well, that's it sir. After the money reached Padai, it was transferred out again. And that's when we lost the trail."

"What the hell do you mean, lost the trail? We've been through this with these fuckers from Padai before, have we not? Are you telling me they aren't cooperating?"

Here we go, Charlie thought to himself. His boss was already losing it, and they hadn't even gotten to the "good" part yet.

"We believe they are cooperating fully sir. Our contact at the field office in Manila deals with the Padai authorities on a regular basis."

"And?" asked Braddock. As his anger was building, his face grew redder by the second.

"The bank in question, the one in Padai, is called Driftwood Mutual. It was established just last Monday, the next business day after the money reached the bank in Switzerland. The Padai banking authorities gave the Manila office a copy of all the paperwork regarding the formation of the bank. And they sent police officers to the one branch office listed in the paperwork, but it was just an empty office. Not even a sign on the door. The thing of it is sir, the bank is owned by a Troy Stevens of Myrtle Beach, South Carolina."

"Troy Stevens? Who the hell is Troy Stevens? I thought we were after Bill Ferguson? And what kind of name for a bank is Driftwood?"

"The details are sketchy sir. But it appears that Ferguson and Stevens are the same man. Fred Williamson in the Columbia, South Carolina office faxed me this copy of Troy Stevens' South Carolina driver's license. Looks just like Bill Ferguson."

Bragg handed over the pictures to Braddock.

Braddock stared at the pictures for a second or two as the information sunk in.

"Wait just a bloody minute here. Are you telling me this motherfucker Ferguson created an alias, Troy Stevens, and then used it to set up his own goddamn bank! What the hell! I thought this guy was an insurance salesman, not some criminal fucking mastermind!"

He stopped and gathered himself for a few seconds, presumably so that his head wouldn't actually explode. Those few seconds felt like a few minutes for the senior investigators.

"Okay, I'm afraid to ask this, because I think I already know the fucking answer, and I already know I'm not going to like it. So … Do you have any idea where the money is now?"

"I'm sorry, sir, but we don't know. As I mentioned, the trail went cold in Padai. The Driftwood Mutual account that held the money has been emptied."

"Emptied? Already? Are you telling me the money is gone? All of it just gone? This is insane."

"It looks like Stevens, or Ferguson, whatever you want to call him, set up Driftwood Mutual for this purpose, sir. Once the money was in a bank he controlled, he could ship the money anywhere he wanted. It would be pretty easy to set up a SWIFT wire transfer to any bank on the SWIFT network. And there would be no records, at least not from the sender."

"Why the hell wouldn't there be any records?"

"Because Mr. Stevens wouldn't keep any. The receiving bank would have a record, but you'd have to know what bank the money was transferred to in order to be able to confirm it."

Chief Braddock rubbed his furrowed brow with enough vigor that one could see the imprints of his fingers when he stopped rubbing. "Wait a minute. I know you guys think that the folks in Padai are on the up and up, but weren't we specifically tracking transactions from that country at some point?"

"Yes, I think you're right boss."

"Well, of course I'm right. Anyway, find out if we are still doing that. It might be that easy. If he transferred the money from his bank in Padai to a domestic bank, we can nail him that way."

"Good point. We'll get right on it boss."

The next morning the agents confirmed that transactions from Padai were still being tracked, but there were no deposits from Troy's bank coming into the States.

"Jesus fucking Christ. We CANNOT allow some insurance fuck from Hartford friggin' Connecticut to get the best of us here. You know what? I'll tell you what. We are going to figure this

A DEVIOUS PLAN 341

out, boys. He transferred that money somewhere, and is probably living at the goddamn beach somewhere. I don't care if I get to be one hundred friggin' years old, I'm not retiring until we get this ass-wipe. I want his head on a goddamn platter."

Braddock paused for a couple of seconds.

"So go find him."

Chapter Sixty-Four

Saturday, November 7, 2009 – 2:00 p.m.

TOES BURIED IN the sand, Bill sat in a beach chair, sipping his second Mai Tai. There was nothing like fresh pineapple juice to make a tasty drink even tastier. The eighty-degree sun splashed his shoulders as he watched the surfers battle epic waves. This was exactly what he had envisioned when earlier in the year he had come up with this scheme. He thought maybe he'd like to try windsurfing next week.

Never in his wildest dreams did he think he would come to Hawaii and not play golf. But this was day five as Miles Goodman and he had no interest in picking up a club. Golf had been his last job, and he was on vacation now. He was sure he'd play a few rounds before he left Oahu, whenever that was but it wasn't on the radar right now.

How long to stay in Hawaii? He hadn't decided, but he was thinking a month would be just about right. He didn't want to burn through too much of the money before he invested it. Three million dollars was a lot of bread, but it wasn't like he had three hundred million. It was possible to burn through three million dollars pretty quickly if you went bananas. Bill felt blessed he wasn't so inclined.

He hadn't realized how tense he'd been these path months, until he finally relaxed. After almost of year of very intense planning and activity, it was time to decompress. There was no scheming or planning to be done. Just go with the flow. The biggest decisions each day involved what to eat and what to drink. And he had a vague notion that maybe he'd check out California next, after he'd finished with Hawaii.

So, here he was. The idea for creating Driftwood Mutual in Padai came from reading about international banking online. He'd been reading about Swiss numbered accounts and banking in the Caymans when he stumbled on the information that for about ten thousand dollars, one could go to Padai and start your own bank. That was an eye opener. He realized he could create a bank and use it as a temporary way station for the cash. And without anyone to answer questions at Driftwood Mutual, the money would disappear into the ether. And along the way, the moola would change hands from Troy Stevens to Miles Goodman.

The masterstroke, he felt, was transferring the money from Padai back to the Caymans before depositing it in a Miles Goodman-controlled domestic account. He had read online that the U.S. authorities had experienced lots of problems with banks in Padai being used as laundries for criminal enterprises. At one time, the U.S. was tracking all currency coming in from Padai. And they might still be. The solution? Don't have the cash come in directly from Padai. Hence, while he was in the Caymans, Bill set up a Swiss account for Miles Goodman as well. He assumed it would be very difficult for the U.S. government to track the transfer from Troy Stevens' bank in Padai to Miles Goodman's account in Switzerland.

If the FBI, or whoever was looking for the missing money by now, was able to follow these transfers and catch up with him, then so be it. That would mean they simply had resources beyond what he had been able to envision. And he'd go to jail, and he would have been better off simply getting a divorce.

He'd worked out this morning, vigorously, and followed it with a very light breakfast. Now he was having a liquid lunch. Later he'd have a decent-sized, yet healthy dinner. Then rinse, repeat. It was time to get in shape and get down to his college weight. He needed to change his appearance, just in case. He figured he'd look a lot different if he dropped thirty pounds and grew a beard.

This morning, before his workout, he'd sent Jennifer a quick email using the Johnson email account. All the email said was, "All is well. I'll be in touch." He wanted to let her know he'd gotten the cash, and would eventually make a play for her. Granted, that was way down the road. But at this point, he couldn't imagine who else on earth he might want to be with.

Chapter Sixty-Five

Thursday, November 12, 2009 – 8:00 p.m.

JENNIFER WAS ANGRY, irritated, nervous and scared. But she'd made a choice, the best one she could make. She'd decided to walk a fine line with one foot firmly on the side of truth, the other foot shading to the side of lies. Hers were sins of omission. She made sure not to tell any blatant untruths. But she was guilty of non-disclosure of all the facts, which she felt she could explain away later by claiming confusion, I don't remember, the whole thing was so crazy. She could cry. No one would fault her.

But she was angry at Bill. He should have never put her in this position. What an asshole he'd been for coming to see her. I mean, what had he been thinking? That she would drop everything and help him steal three million dollars and then run off to Tahiti with him? With virtually no warning? Meanwhile for months and months and months she'd thought he was dead. Insane.

She was irritated because of her conflicted feelings. Part of her was flattered that Bill had stuck his neck out to ask for her help. He'd taken a huge risk in coming to see her. And she did have feelings for him. A small part of her regretted not signing on to be his accomplice. It could have been a really fun adventure. But she figured the chances of it ending well were slim to none, with slim having already left the building. He was bound to get caught eventually, wasn't he?

She was nervous and scared because she hated lying. Even though she hadn't blatantly lied, she knew she hadn't told the whole truth, and she felt guilty. She knew there probably wouldn't be any consequences, but there was no way to guarantee that. The whole thing felt very unfair. But, if she told everything, it could hasten Bill's demise. And she didn't necessarily want that.

Part of her felt relieved as well, but she suspected it was only temporary relief. She'd gotten the call on Tuesday from Special Agent Steve Robey. He'd explained that now that it had been confirmed that Bill Ferguson was still alive, the FBI planned to re-interview everyone involved with the case. Oh, of course. Yes, of course I'll agree to an interview. And her stomach had been in knots for two days. She had barely slept. Could she protect Bill without lying? Not really. So she'd told Agent Robey most of the truth, but not all of it.

She admitted that Bill had come to see her. That he'd tried to make her an accomplice in his scheme. And that she'd turned him down. But weren't you at a hearing where he was declared dead? Why didn't you report this? And she'd turned on the waterworks. I was scared, he sounded crazy, I wasn't sure what he was going to do. I didn't know what to do. Did he threaten you? He didn't have to, she said cleverly. I was scared of him, he seemed crazy. And nobody but Bill could dispute that statement.

When Agent Robey asked how Bill had gotten in touch with her, she gave a non-answer. Oh, it was crazy, he just came to see me with this crazy idea about stealing the money. I don't know why he thought I would go along with it. The whole thing, faking a death, stealing millions, who does that? So, he just came by without any warning? Yes, there was a no warning. And she could argue later that she meant there was no warning regarding Bill's kooky scheme.

Agent Robey looked skeptical, but didn't press any further. She'd put on a good performance. She was a victim, and she'd been too scared to call the authorities. Robey thanked her for her cooperation and said he'd be in touch.

So, not mentioning the email from the fake email account might come back to bite her. But she figured disclosing that would absolutely hasten Bill's getting caught. She really had no interest in joining Bill on his "adventure" at this point, but didn't necessarily want to see him go to jail either. So, she chose the route she chose.

Chapter Sixty-Six

<u>About One Year Later</u>
Wednesday, November 24, 2010 – 9:30 p.m.

JOHN AND DMITRI sat down at a table at the Wing Joint, ready to indulge in post basketball wings and beer.

Dmitri spoke. "Very sorry to hear about Andy. I mean, we figured after you didn't hear from him something bad had happened. It's still a shock though, when these things are confirmed."

"Yeah. It sucks. But the closure will actually be a good thing. Can you fill me in on some of the details? The cops who told me about it have been pretty vague."

"Well, some deer hunters found him in the woods near a lake in South Carolina. A pretty remote place. Could be a tie-in with the Ferguson case, I guess. After the money disappeared, they discovered that Ferguson had taken an alias, Troy Stevens, and was living in Myrtle, working as a golf pro. But you knew all that already. The body was found about ninety minutes away from Myrtle. Any chance Andy fibbed when he said he didn't find anything regarding Ferguson?"

"I haven't wanted to believe that, but it's the only thing that makes any sense. Why else would he be in South Carolina? Maybe somehow he found out about Troy Stevens and the money and wanted to cut himself in. Do you think Ferguson killed him?"

"That's a really good question. He doesn't seem like the type, but he also doesn't seem like the type who would fake his own death and steal three million dollars."

"If not Ferguson, then who?"

Dmitri just shrugged. He didn't have any idea.

The wings arrived, the men dug in. Neither spoke for a good five minutes as each man was thoroughly enjoying his post workout meal. This whole evening was a nice diversion for John, who had just been to the funeral a couple of days before. After they took the edge off their hunger, Dmitri spoke.

"One thing that was interesting was the cops found a slip of paper in Andy's front pocket."

"Oh?"

"Yeah, it had a Greystone Mutual email address on it. Harry Johnson or something like that. So, it's another tie-in with Ferguson."

"You mean because of Greystone?"

"Yep. Why else would he have a Greystone email address in his pocket?"

"Weird. He must have had a hell of a lot more information than he let on."

"I guess people start seeing dollar signs and lose their perspective. Ferguson and Andy both."

"Well, say what you want, but it seems like Ferguson has gotten away scot-free with the money."

"Yeah, for now. But almost all of them make a mistake along the way. We, law enforcement, I mean, usually catch them eventually."

"I hope you do catch him. Even if he didn't kill Andy, ten to one says Andy's dead because of him."

"Well, I sent the cops an anonymous tip about the email address. Hopefully they act on it. If not, the fucker might get away with three millions bucks and a murder."

"Anonymous tip? Why anonymous?"

"Remember, your firm's involvement was strictly on the down-low. So from the Fed's perspective, there's no tie-in between Andy and Ferguson. And the cops in SC weren't going to connect that email address to the Ferguson case up here. I'm sure most of them have never heard about it."

"Okay. Makes sense."

"Don't worry, I'll try to make sure someone pays attention. If the Feds don't act, I'm sure Greystone themselves will. And they have enough juice to get the Fed's attention."

"Okay. Please keep me posted. I really want to see that guy get nailed."

"Will do, brother, will do."

Chapter Sixty-Seven

Friday, November 26, 2010 – 10:00 a.m.

IT HAD BEEN almost a year since Bill had first laid eyes on Puget Sound. He'd been on his way to Alaska and decided to check out Seattle for a few days. On a whim he'd taken a four-hour whale watching tour. It had been intoxicating. The views of the Olympic Mountains were stunning and he was taken with the beauty of the San Juan Islands. Who knew Orca whales could jump like that? He'd even seen a bald eagle.

Smitten, he decided to stay for a while. The ultimate goal was to live on a beach somewhere, but this felt like a good intermediate step. Plus, he had wanted to alter his appearance before picking a final destination. And he'd done a pretty good job of that. Not having to work made it easy to eat well and work out vigorously five days a week. He was relentless and focused when it came to health these days, and eventually reached his college weight of 165. The full, lush beard looked good on him, he thought. He'd started wearing glasses, even though he didn't need them to correct his vision.

He bought a luxury condo on the Alaskan Way on the west coast of the city. For half a million dollars he got one thousand square feet and gorgeous views of the sound. From his balcony, he could watch the many cruise ships that used Seattle as a port of call. In addition to the condo, he purchased a white Saab 9-3 convertible to tool around in. Morning workouts were followed by a stop for designer coffee. Weather permitting, there might be an afternoon round of golf. He joined a local chess club. He'd read lots of books, watched lots of movies. It had been a good year. He'd been very much enjoying the solitude after the insanity of the year before.

But now he was beginning to get bored. Given his situation, and not being sure how long he was going to stay, he had been extremely reticent to make any friends. But the longing for meaningful human contact, which had started as a mere whisper in his subconscious, was now bellowing to him. At some point soon, he'd have to fully commit to being Miles Goodman and create a full, balanced life. Somewhere.

He missed women. He hadn't been with one since that last time with Candy, which seemed like decades ago. He'd thought of hiring escorts to go out with him, so he could enjoy some company without any of the effort needed for dating. But he never pulled the trigger.

During the past year he'd thought often of Jennifer and that last kiss they had shared before he became Miles. He remembered her charm, her sense of humor. Her sexiness. He wished he'd seen her in that way a lot earlier in their relationship. She would be perfect for him. Plus, she knew his history; he wouldn't have to keep any secrets from her. He'd sent her a couple of quick emails, but never got a response.

He had tried to call her last month from a pay phone. There was no answer. Probably just as well as he had a few drinks in him. Besides, he didn't really know what he was going to say had she picked up. He'd called partly because of the desire to hear a familiar voice. But mostly because he wanted to know what she was up to. Was she seeing someone? Or was she available? It was time to reach out. Maybe she could be convinced to join him. If not, then he could move on without wondering what might have been.

Grabbing a good fall jacket, he left the condo and took the elevator down to the street. It was a beautiful November morning. Walking south, then east, he headed for a little Internet cafe he'd discovered one morning while exploring the neighborhood. The place was hopping. He ordered a cappuccino and sipped it while he waited for one of the terminals provided by the cafe to open up. After about ten minutes, someone packed up their things and vacated one. He jumped in.

After he got situated, he typed the Internet address for Greystone Mutual into the browser. Once the Greystone web page loaded, he clicked on the link for the employee portal. The login page appeared. He typed in the user name and password for the fictitious employee, Henry Johnson. It always tickled him that he had come up with that idea in the first place. It was one of the many things that had gone right with his plan. After a second, Henry's company email account dominated the display. Bill clicked the "New Message" button.

In the message body he typed simply. "Need to talk to you. Let me know when is a good time to call." It was cryptic but he thought it would be sufficient. She would know who it was. Then he clicked on the email program's contacts button and searched for Jennifer Weaver. Another click loaded her email address in to the "To" field. He clicked send.

It felt good to have sent the email. It was a step toward moving forward. Once things were resolved with Jennifer, one way or another, he could plan his end game. He decided he'd wait a day or two before checking the account. No real reason, but he just thought that would be enough time for her to respond.

Okay. Mission accomplished. Email sent. Good day to play some golf.

Chapter Sixty-Eight

Monday, January 10, 2011 – 10:30 a.m.

THERE WAS A knock on the door. Special Agent Charlie Bragg looked up from his computer screen.

"Come in."

The door inched open and Agent Joel Timmons from Computer Forensics stuck his head in.

"I've got something interesting here, if you've got a minute."

"Sure, come on in. I've always got a minute for you, Joel."

Joel walked in and sat down in one of the chairs across from Charlie's desk.

"Remember that email address from Greystone Mutual you asked me to trace about six weeks ago?"

"Sounds familiar … what have you got?"

Joel handed Charlie a copy of the original tracking request, which included a photocopy of the slip of paper that had been in Andy Jacobsen's pocket.

"Oh yeah, right, the Ferguson case, what was that guy's name, Bruce? This was that anonymous lead that we got. Did you get a hit or something?"

"Uh, I think the guy's first name was Bill. And yes, we got a hit. There was activity involving that account yesterday morning. There was a transmission that traces back to an Internet cafe in Seattle, Washington."

"Very interesting ... this is coming back to me now. When we talked to Greystone about this email account, they came to the conclusion that Ferguson set it up himself. There was no actual employee named Henry Johnson. So this might be a big break, Joel. It might mean Ferguson is in Seattle. Or at least maybe he was yesterday."

Bragg continued. "So, good work my man. I'm going to contact Greystone and have them send me any recent emails from the Johnson account. They seemed very willing to cooperate. They feel burned by this whole thing, also. It's been bad publicity for them. Plus they are out three million bucks."

It was more information than Joel needed, but there was no harm. When Charlie got excited he talked more. And it was good for the techies to hear about the bigger picture sometimes. It gave their work more meaning.

"Oh, and Joel?"

"Sir?"

"I'm sure I don't have to say this, but if you see anything else involving that account, it's a top priority now."

"Got it."

Charlie put in a call to Elliot Bloomfield, the CEO of Greystone. He reminded Bloomfield of whom he was, the special agent in charge of the Ferguson fraud case. Once Bloomfield's memory banks had been activated, Charlie explained that they'd seen some activity that suggested the Henry Johnson email account had been used recently. Remember that email account? The phantom account that we think Ferguson set up? This could be a break in tracking down Ferguson. Bloomfield promised to get Charlie a copy of any Henry Johnson emails within the hour.

As soon as he hung up with Bloomfield, his phone rang.

"Special Agent Bragg."

"Agent Bragg, this is Jennifer Weaver from Greystone Mutual Insurance. Do you remember me?"

"Of course I remember you!" Charlie fibbed. If he hadn't talked to Joel Timmons and Elliot Bloomfield within the last half an hour, he wouldn't have made the connection so quickly.

"Jennifer, what can I do for you?"

"Well, I got kind of a weird email yesterday. I think it might have been Bill trying to contact me."

Jennifer's guilt about lying the first time had gotten the best of her. She had no idea how her sudden urge to tell the truth now would save her bacon.

"Okay, talk to me. Who was the email from, and what did it say?"

"It just said he needed to talk to me. And he wanted to know a good time. That's it, that's the whole email. But the weird thing is it came from someone named Henry Johnson. I don't know a Henry Johnson. So that's why I think it's Bill."

Charlie remembered now that his team hadn't talked to Jennifer when investigating the Henry Johnson lead. There didn't seem to be a reason to. When they had looked at the account activity, it appeared to be only incoming emails regarding fraud cases.

"Jennifer, thanks for calling. I tend to agree, it could very well be Bill Ferguson reaching out to you. Are you willing to work with us on this? There may be something easy that I'll want you to do."

"Okay, I guess so."

"Okay, good, I'll be in touch. And please don't respond to that email until you hear from me."

Bragg continued. "And I really do appreciate the call. It's good to know there are some solid citizens left out there."

As he hung up the phone, he felt like a complete and utter nerd. Solid citizens left out there? What a dork! He must have sounded like he was straight out of a 1950's movie.

Two hours later, Charlie got a small zip file from someone in tech support at Greystone. The zip file contained a copy of a single email from the Henry Johnson account. It was the email that "Henry" had sent to Jennifer.

So now he needed to come up with a strategy for catching Bill Ferguson, assuming it was he who sent the email. Would it be better to have Jennifer respond? Have her try to set up a meeting somewhere? Or would it be better to let Bill stew a little bit?

If I was Bill, thought Bragg, I'd probably check the account a couple of times to see if she responded. If there was no response, I'd give up. If Jennifer responded, then they might just start communicating over the phone. They wouldn't need to use the email accounts anymore. And Charlie already had a court order to monitor the Henry Johnson email account. If a telephone correspondence developed, they'd have to get a judge involved and ask permission for a phone tap on Jennifer's phone.

So, the most practical thing to do was to instruct Jennifer not to respond. And they'd try to nail Ferguson as he looked for her responses. That plan hinged on the idea that he would use the same Internet cafe to check the email account. And that he'd only check it once or twice. So Charlie needed to get his butt out to Seattle, pronto.

Chapter Sixty-Nine

Tuesday, January 11, 2011 – 4:00 p.m.

CHARLIE BRAGG AND his partner Steve Robey had arrived in Seattle the night before. The Special Agent in Charge of the Seattle field office, Angelo Rocca had arranged for two more agents to work with them on the Internet cafe surveillance. It was time for the briefing with the other agents, with Rocca sitting in on the meeting. After introductions all around, the meeting started.

"Okay guys, it's great to meet you. Let's go over what we've got and what we are going to do. And not do."

While Steve passed around a manila folder to everyone, Charlie continued speaking. "In the folder you're being handed is the latest picture we have of Bill Ferguson, AKA Troy Stevens. And we think he must be going under yet another alias now as there are no records of a man moving to Seattle with either of those names within the last year. He's about six feet, two hundred pounds. He has a history of keeping himself in decent shape. We are treating him as armed and dangerous. We think he may have killed a PI in South Carolina who had picked up his trail."

Bragg continued, "We have reason to believe that he sent an email from the Internet cafe at the intersection of Pine Street and Fifth Avenue. We also have reason to believe he will log into the same web account again this week. We are hoping he'll log in from the same location. A picture of the establishment is in the folder. The plan is to stake out that location for the next three mornings, from seven in the morning until noon. The original email was sent at nine am, Seattle time, so we want to cover the cafe for a couple of hours before and after that time, to allow for a variance. Myself and Steve will be in the cafe. I want you two in cars in the parking lot. One of you on the east side, and one on the west. There is an entrance to the cafe on either side. In addition to our hands-on surveillance, we've got electronic surveillance set up on the web account in question. If activity is detected on the web account, I will be notified. We will all be equipped with the standard issue earpieces and microphones. So if you see Ferguson, give the code 863 and the location where he was spotted."

Bragg was purposefully using the generic term "web account" when talking about the Henry Johnson Greystone email account. These guys didn't need to know those details, they were just there to assist with the stakeout of the Internet cafe and report if they saw Bill Ferguson.

"Now, there is one key point I really want to stress. This stakeout is not about taking Ferguson down just yet. We are still building a case and want more information. What we really want is a license plate number so we can use that to find out his current alias, his current address, etc. Plus, then we can access bank records and the like and tie up other parts of the case. If he happens to be on foot, then we can tail him to his home address. Hopefully. Okay, does anybody have any questions?"

No one spoke.

"Good. It's a pretty straightforward assignment. Remember the goal is a license plate number. And if he does turn up, proceed with caution. He may well be armed, and I want a whole team in place when we go to arrest him. Which will be at some point in the near future. We'll meet here in the morning between six-fifteen and six-thirty for coffee and donuts, or danishes or something, and roll to the cafe about six forty-five. Make sure you are here by six-thirty though, in case there is a change in the plan."

Chapter Seventy

Friday, January 14, 2011 – 9:30 a.m.

CHARLIE WAS GETTING frustrated now. The first two days of the stakeout had yielded no results. This was the last scheduled day, and it was now past the time in the morning when Bill had sent that original email. He really didn't want to go back to Braddock and ask for an extension on this stakeout. If this tack failed, he might have to have Jennifer Weaver respond to Bill's inquiry, just to get some traffic going.

But now, he was second-guessing this approach all together. There was no evidence Ferguson used the same Internet cafe each time, was there? It was only the notion that people are creatures of habit that led them to stakeout this location. What if he used a different Internet cafe every day? Or maybe three days wasn't long enough. But surely, he would be looking for a response from Jennifer soon. His email indicated he wanted to talk to her, and it was rather urgent. Perhaps he was in trouble in some way? Who knew? It didn't matter.

He scanned the crowded coffee shop again. No sign of Ferguson. Charlie was primarily focused on the seven public Internet terminals the coffee shop made available. His theory was that Ferguson would use a public terminal as opposed to his own laptop. Less traceability. He had Steve monitoring the rest of the cafe, just in case. There were a number of people scattered throughout the cafe at various tables and booths working on their personal laptops. Steve's job was to watch the laptop people and alert him if any of them was Ferguson.

All seven of the public terminals were taken, with another guy sort of milling about near them. He seemed to be waiting for a terminal to open up. Since he was African American, he was quickly ruled out. None of the other seven looked anything like Ferguson either. Three of the people were women, two were young college guys, another was too young and much too heavy. The guy could barely fit on the stool, he was well over three hundred pounds, possibly three fifty. The seventh person was a man, about the right age by Charlie's estimation, but too thin to be Ferguson. Plus, he had a thick beard and glasses.

Suddenly, Charlie's cell phone started vibrating. It was Joel Timmons back in New Haven.

"Joel, what's up," Charlie practically whispered into the phone.

"We've got some activity on the Johnson account."

"Oh really? Can you confirm the location?"

"Not yet, I've got a trace route running now."

"Okay. Call me back when you've got it."

"It will just take …"

Charlie cut off Joel by hanging up the phone. He immediately sent a text to Steve and the guys in the parking lot. The text was merely the code, "735." They had worked that out to mean, possible siting, be on the lookout. Be on full alert. He could feel them all pop into straighter sitting positions, instantly activating all their senses. One of the girls left her terminal, and the guy who had been waiting jumped in.

A few seconds later, the skinny guy with the beard and glasses left his terminal. Right height, wrong build, thought Charlie. About ten seconds later, his phone was buzzing. Joel again. He was excited.

"Have you got him? The trace route confirmed the communication with the Greystone server was coming from the Internet cafe where you are."

"What? That makes no sense. Ferguson isn't here."

"Really? That's weird. IP addresses don't lie, it's exactly the same IP as Monday's transmission."

"I don't know what to make of that. Thanks, Joel."

Charlie, texted "588." It meant for everyone to quickly meet at the northern most squad car, in this case Susie Walter's car. About thirty seconds later, the four agents gathered in the parking lot.

"Did you guys see anybody? Anybody that looked like Ferguson? Our tech guy is saying he sent another email from this location."

Seattle agent Phil Harmon spoke. "I only saw that guy with the beard. Nobody that looked like Ferguson."

"Okay. Let's not waste any more time here. Somehow, we missed him. My guess is we got a bum steer from the Internet provider and they matched the wrong IP address with the wrong building. Or a network switch got reloaded at some point and now the IPs are assigned to different physical addresses than they were originally. Either way, he's gone."

As they drove back to the field office, Steve Robey spoke.

"Frustrating, isn't it?"

"Yeah, I'm guessing we'll have to ask Jennifer Weaver to respond now, to get some more traffic going. Get those two corresponding. That is, after we straighten things out with the Internet provider."

The partners didn't speak for a minute while the car rolled on toward the field office.

Then, Robey spoke again. "Charlie, let me ask you something. How well would you remember the faces we saw today? You know, in the cafe?"

"Pretty well. A number of them were there every day. Why? What are you thinking?"

"Well, it has been about a year and half since that picture of Ferguson was taken for that golf course website. What if he's altered his appearance since then?"

"Hmmm. Good thought. I guess that's possible. Think we should sit down with a sketch artist this afternoon?"

"Can't hurt, can it?"

"No, it can't. I'll work with Rocca and line something up for after lunch."

After lunch, Rocca led Charlie and Robey to the office of Alicia Chou, sketch artist extraordinaire. They showed her a copy of the most recent picture they had of Ferguson, and she deftly reproduced an accurate facsimile in the Suspect ID software. They then peppered her with different variations, make the hair a little grayer, add twenty pounds, take away twenty pounds. Add forty pounds, add a mustache. Take away forty pounds, add a mustache. Hey, wait a minute! Make that mustache a full beard …

"Crap!" shouted Charlie. "That's him! He was there!"

Charlie stopped to catch his breath. He was quite aggravated at that moment.

"Okay. Okay," he said, pacing now. "Too bad we missed him. But at least we have an up-to-date composite now. And we know for sure he's in Seattle, and the IP address was right, and it's just a matter of time. Would you mind printing out about ten copies of this picture? And thank you, great work. I guess I'll call New Haven and give Braddock the pretty good news. Although I'm sure he won't take it that way."

Robey chuckled, and was happy Charlie was the lead investigator on this case. He then asked, "So what's the plan now?"

"Well, I guess we can just keep the same game plan. He'll probably check the Johnson account a few more times looking for a response from Jennifer. We should have him in custody by the middle to the end of next week."

"Sounds reasonable. Good luck with Braddock."

"Yeah, thanks. I think …"

Both men chuckled.

At three a.m., Charlie woke up with a start. Alone in his hotel room, he just sat in his bed beaming. He'd thought of a better, faster, more surefire way to catch Ferguson. Some risk, but a lot less passive than staking out that lone Internet cafe. Unable to get back to sleep, he got out of bed, found a notepad, and began detailing his new plan.

Chapter Seventy-One

Saturday, January 15, 2011 – 12:30 p.m.

"OKAY, CHARLIE, WHAT'S got you all hot and bothered this morning? Or, this afternoon I should say," Robey asked, after he and Bragg had placed their lunch orders at the Bob Evans nearest their hotel.

"I know how to catch him. And it's better than the Internet cafe stakeout."

"Okay. Shoot."

"Coffee. The guy loves his fancy coffee. And he can certainly afford it now."

"Are you saying we stake out fancy coffee shops? Lots of those in Seattle. Isn't this where Starbucks got started? And isn't there a Seattle's Best chain also?"

"I think so. That's okay. Chances are that Internet cafe is within shouting distance of where he lives. So we pick the ten coffee shops closest to the Internet cafe, put two people on each, and we should be able to nail him within a week."

"Twenty people now? Do you think we can get that many?"

"Braddock said he would back us. Besides you and me, we'd need eighteen additional people, each for three hours a day, for a week. Shouldn't be that big a deal for a catch like Ferguson."

"Wait a minute, Braddock said he would back us? When did you talk to Braddock?"

"About a half an hour ago."

"On a Saturday?"

"Well, he told me if anything came up, to call him at home. He seemed okay with it, it was nine a.m. Eastern when I called."

"Wow. Good for you. I don't think I would have had the guts to call him on the weekend."

"Well, back in the day he used to be a field agent. So he's pretty supportive of guys when they are out in the field."

"Hmmm. I never realized."

"Anyway, I'm thinking we'll go for these ten locations," said Charlie, pulling out a map of Seattle.

He showed Robey the map with the locations he wanted watched. He'd marked them with a felt tip pen.

"Damn, you've been busy! Did you sleep at all last night?"

Charlie chuckled. "Not after three. The coffee idea came to me in the middle of the night."

"Tuesday time frame, I guess?"

"Exactly. A day to bring Seattle up to speed on the new plan and to identify resources. We want to be in position everyday by seven a.m., so Monday isn't reasonable. It's not enough of an emergency to bring guys in this weekend for briefings. Ferguson is a big fish, but not that big."

Charlie smiled, then continued. "I'm thinking one person inside each Starbucks, or whatever, and one outside. Once Ferguson is identified, the two agents, and anyone else in the vicinity, will tail him. Hopefully we'll get a license plate number and/or address from the tail."

"Why bother following him? Why not just grab him up right there?"

"Just in case it's not him. We're going off a composite sketch right now, and it's probably right, but I'd feel better if we found out his new alias, his address, could check his bank accounts, etc. If we grab the wrong guy, it will be a big waste of time. Or if we grab the right guy, and he clams up, then what have we really got?"

"Makes sense. Assuming he doesn't figure out how close we are."

"The guy is pretty sharp, but he is, or was, an insurance executive. I'd be shocked if he could spot a two-man stakeout."

They held the full briefing on Monday afternoon. At the behest of the New Haven field office and a call from FBI Headquarters in Washington, D.C. Rocca had identified sixteen new agents to help. This was in addition to Walters and

Harmon, who'd worked with Bragg and Robey the week before. Rocca assigned the sixteen to eight pairs, in order to support the two-man stakeout plan. The twenty agents, in addition to Rocca and his deputy, attended the briefing. Charlie took the lead.

He went over the overall concept, that Ferguson was known to indulge in a fancy coffee every morning, so they would be staking out ten coffee shops near the Internet cafe where he had been spotted. An agent inside, an agent outside, at each of the locations. The stakeouts would run for three hours, from seven a.m. to ten a.m., when they guessed Ferguson would be up and about getting his coffee. He speculated that nine a.m. was prime time. For a guy to slim down that much he probably worked out most mornings. That was an educated guess, based on the assumption Ferguson wasn't working these days, and probably got up and worked out first thing.

He reminded them all this was a surveillance, and if he was spotted the agents who saw him were to alert the team and then follow him. Try to get a license plate or an address. Don't get too close and don't try to arrest him. The surveillance was to run from Tuesday through Saturday, and then the results would be evaluated, if they hadn't already caught Ferguson.

Chapter Seventy-Two

Tuesday, January 18, 2011 – 9:00 a.m.

"THIS IS BRAGG."

He had specifically assigned himself as the agent in the parking lot of the Seattle's Best Coffee that he and Robey were working. If he'd had it to do again, he'd have asked for one more man so he could just coordinate and not have to take calls and perform stakeout duties at the same time.

"Yeah, this is Stone at location number four. We've got him."

"Got him? You've seen him? You're tailing him?"

"No, sir. We've got Ferguson in custody. We just grabbed him up."

"What do you mean, grabbed him up? Were you not at the briefing the other day?"

"Yeah, I was there," Stone said indignantly. "But Smith and I decided not to wait. We didn't want the opportunity to pass, sir."

Bragg could feel his blood pressure rising. He wanted to reach through the phone and strangle Stone, whoever he was. He took a moment and tried to calm himself down.

"Sir?"

"Agent Stone. You better hope that is really Ferguson. You were instructed to tail him and get an address, not arrest him. But I guess you took matters into your own hands, didn't you? So let's meet back at the field office and sort this thing out. Oh and by the way, if it's not him, you are off this detail." Bragg hung up without waiting for a response.

The interrogation started off badly and didn't get any better. Tom Forney looked a lot like the composite, but it quickly became obvious he wasn't Bill Ferguson. A quick background check showed he had lived in the greater Seattle community his whole life, and was a respected member of the community. He owned a small software company that wrote device drivers for specialty hardware. Forty-two years old, he'd lived in the same house for the last ten years with his wife and three kids. The Forney's went to church every Sunday.

Forney was incensed at having been taken in; he was missing a critical business meeting. He claimed being illegally grabbed like this was costing him thousands and promised to sue. Bragg didn't think the FBI could be sued, but that was beside the point. Stone's mistake had diverted their attention from finding the real Ferguson.

On behalf of the department, Bragg apologized profusely to Mr. Forney, explaining that unfortunately, he resembled a dangerous fugitive. The department had made a mistake, but it was in the interest of keeping Seattle, and the country, safe. Forney seemed to calm down somewhat. They released him, and Bragg had Stone and Smith replaced with two new agents. And he then called all the agents on his detail back that afternoon and re-briefed them on the procedures he expected them to follow.

Chapter Seventy-Three

Wednesday, January 19, 2011 – 8:15 a.m.

BRAGG'S PHONE VIBRATED with a new "755" text message. A few seconds later his phone vibrated with a call.

"Agent Bragg."

"Agent Bragg, this is Donnelly at location number seven. I think we might have just spotted the subject, sir."

"Are you following him?"

"Negative, sir. I was positioned in the parking lot. I saw someone fitting the suspect's description driving a late model white Saab through the drive-thru. I was all set to tail him, but another car pulled out of his spot and was involved in a fender bender right in front of me. By the time I got around them, the Saab was gone."

"Damn! Sounds like really bad luck."

"It's frustrating. But there wasn't anything I could do. The guy driving that car, however, did look just like the composite."

"Did you get the license plate?"

"No. I'm sorry, I never got a good look at it."

"Well, okay. Sounds like you did the best you could. Keep on the lookout until ten a.m. though. I'm sure you heard about yesterday's fiasco. Apparently, there is more than one thin guy with a dark beard wandering around Seattle."

Donnelly chuckled. "Yes, sir, you got it."

At ten-thirty, Donnelly and his partner Wilson met with Bragg, Robey and Rocca at the field office. Bragg asked how closely the person Donnelly had seen resembled the composite sketch. Donnelly thought the composite was very close, and wouldn't suggest any changes to it. But he was a good fifty yards away, and wasn't exactly looking into the whites of the suspect's eyes. After that, using pictures from the Web, they were able to identify the Saab as a model 9-3 convertible.

"Okay," said Charlie. "I think we should double down on this location. Get two people inside, and get a second car in a second position, maybe even out on the street. That way if he comes by there again, we won't have the problem of getting out of the lot for tailing purposes."

"Okay, what location do you want to pull the other two from?" Robey asked.

"Well, any chance we can have two more people for a couple of days?" Bragg asked Rocca.

"Sorry, but there is no chance. My people are spread too thin as it is."

"Okay. Then I say we pull from location number one. It's the furthest one from number seven. If it was Ferguson this morning, he probably won't be showing up at number one."

"Sounds reasonable."

Charlie informed the agents who had been working location number one of their new assignment. He knew this lead wasn't super solid, but it was something. Maybe there was a pattern. Maybe he frequented that particular drive-thru every morning. Or on certain days. Probably after some kind of a workout. At least today's stakeout had ended a lot better than yesterday's.

***

As Bill pulled out of the drive-thru at Starbucks earlier, he'd noticed the fender bender in the parking lot. He was glad his beautiful Saab had remained accident-free so far. He loved driving that car on sunny days, but Seattle didn't provide a high percentage of those. Oh well, he'd just have to have a convertible at his next destination. And the next destination would be sunny and warm, a lot. Yes, it was time to start thinking about that. He'd enjoyed Seattle immensely, but now felt he was ready to pick a final destination. It would mean making a few scouting trips. Fiji was first on the list.

He'd scheduled a flight from Los Angles to Fiji for Saturday night. He'd stay there a week, scout it out, take some tours. Get a feel for the place. In the meantime, he'd fly from Seattle to Los Angeles on Friday morning. That flight was scheduled for nine o'clock in the morning. He'd skip his normal seven a.m. Friday workout and leave for the airport around six-thirty a.m.

Since he'd never been there, Bill thought of taking a tour of Los Angeles while he was in town. Why not see the sights? So he scheduled an extra day there. He had no desire to live in a big city, but he was sure it was a fascinating place. Plus, it would have been a very long day to go from Seattle to Los Angeles to Fiji with no break. He could afford to take a break. There was nowhere he had to be.

It was drizzling today, but he had a hankering to play golf. So he'd do that and then enjoy a nice dinner at a little Vietnamese place around the corner from his house. Maybe he'd catch a movie at a theater tonight. Or he could use that Chessmaster software he'd just bought and review his lost match from the chess club on Sunday night. He wouldn't be up too late though. He wanted to take his normal five-mile run at six the next morning.

Chapter Seventy-Four

Thursday, January 20, 2011 – 6:55 a.m.

BRAGG'S CELL PHONE vibrated with the receipt of a new text message. The code was "755." Hmmm. A bit early, but a least someone was following protocol. Looked like the re-briefing after Tuesday's debacle had gotten the message across. Ten seconds later his phone rang.

"This is Bragg."

"Possible sighting, sir," said someone a little short of breath. "I'm following the subject on foot right now."

Bragg wondered why there was a sighting before the stakeout was supposed to start. But they could straighten that out later. "Okay. Who am I speaking with?"

"Sorry, sir, this is Hayes, location six."

Location six made sense to Bragg. It was just a few blocks over from location seven. So it was possible that the same person, if he lived nearby, could frequent both locations. "Which way are you headed?"

"I'm following the suspect southwest on Virginia Street."

"Okay. Keep following him. I'm on my way."

Charlie sent a quick text to Robey, "588," indicating he wanted Robey to come out and meet him at the car. Within seconds, Robey emerged from the Starbucks they were watching.

"Hey, what's up?"

"Possible sighting over on Virginia Street. Let's roll."

"Okay. Wow, it's early, it's not quite seven yet."

"Well, maybe we should have been starting at six and we just got lucky," said Charlie, as he eased the cruiser out of the Starbucks lot. He steered the car northwest on Fourth Avenue toward Spring Street at a smooth clip.

When they got to the intersection of Fourth and Spring, they were in for a surprise.

"Crap! Spring Street is one-way the other way!"

Just then, his phone vibrated.

"Bragg."

"Sir, this is Hayes again. Subject has just entered the lobby of a high-rise apartment building at Spring and Western Avenue."

"Okay. Good work Hayes. Stay put outside that building. Maybe he's making a quick stop. Where is your partner?"

"He's on the way. He had to make a detour, he forgot Spring was a one-way street."

"Right."

A couple of minutes later, Bragg and Robey pulled into the parking lot of the Sand Dollar Condominiums. Charlie recognized the tall, lanky Hayes from the briefings. He was sitting on a bench near the condo entrance, reading a newspaper, doing a great job of feigning disinterest in who was coming and going from the condo building. Bragg figured Hayes was probably a pretty good agent. As they were getting out of the car, they saw Andy Frost, Hayes's partner pull up in a green Ford Sedan. The four agents had a quick meeting at Hayes's bench.

"Okay, Hayes, you stay here in case the suspect comes out of the building. If he does, let me know and continue to tail him. Frost, I want you on the other side of the building in case he exits on that side. Robey and I will go and talk to building management."

Bragg and Robey entered the lobby of the high-rise condominium building. The lobby was decorated with comfortable-looking chairs and sofas with solid wood tables in between them. There were a lot of pictures of the Puget Sound hanging on the twenty-foot high walls. Bragg thought it was a nice place--a great place for a fugitive millionaire.

Bragg and Robey approached the concierge desk. They asked to see the manager on duty. The clerk at the desk scurried off to the office behind him. A large, heavyset man, about six foot two, emerged from the office.

"I'm the manager. How can I help you gentlemen today?"

Bragg pulled out his badge and showed it to the manager. "We're FBI agents here on official business. What is your name, sir?"

"Lamar Goodburn. What is this about?"

"Do you know this man?" asked Bragg, showing the manager the composite of Ferguson.

"Kind of looks familiar …"

"We'd like to know his name, and what unit he lives in."

"Well, I wish I could help you, but he doesn't live here."

Bragg and Robey looked at each other skeptically. "Are you sure he doesn't live in this building?"

"I'm quite sure. It's my job to be familiar with all the tenants in the building."

"Okay, how do you know him?"

"I'm not sure, he just looks familiar is all."

"He just entered this building a couple of minutes ago."

"Well, I don't know what to say. He doesn't live in the building. Maybe he uses it as a pass-through. Although he shouldn't. Let me get Barker, he's the security guy on duty today. Maybe he knows this jamoke."

A minute or two later, Goodburn returned with Barker. Bragg and Barker shook hands.

"I'm Special Agent Bragg with the FBI."

"Jerome Barker."

After seeing the composite, Barker spoke. "Sure I know that guy. He's Mr. Miles. Well, Miles is his first name. We play in the chess club together."

Bragg was confused. "Okay. So you play chess with him. Any idea why he came here this morning?"

"Since I know him from chess, and he seems like a good guy, I let him pass through the lobby a couple of times a week. He uses it as kind of a shortcut on his way back from his morning run."

Bragg was a still a little puzzled, and a little irritated. "How many times a week does he pass through the lobby?"

"Usually Tuesdays and Thursdays that I've seen. Wouldn't know about the weekends. I work Monday through Friday."

"Okay. You say he is passing through. Any idea where he's going?"

"I think he lives in one of those high rises over on the Alaskan Way. There's three in a row over there. If I were to guess, I'd say check those buildings. Has Mr. Miles done something wrong?"

"Not that I'm aware of," lied Bragg. "We just want to talk to him as a possible witness in a case we are working. Do you know his last name?"

"No, I'm sorry, I don't."

"When does the chess club meet again?"

"We meet on Sunday evenings."

"Where?"

"Over at the Turn of the Page Bookstore on Sixth Avenue."

"What time?"

"About seven p.m."

"Is Miles there every week?"

"Not every. Three out of four, I'd say."

"Okay, Mr. Barker. Thanks for your help. I need to ask you one favor."

"Okay, shoot."

"If you see Mr. Miles at the chess club on Sunday evening, or any other time, please don't mention this little meeting. We like to talk to witnesses when they aren't expecting to talk to us. That way the responses are more natural."

"Uh, okay."

"Thank you. It's important, okay?"

Barker nodded.

And with that, Bragg and Robey headed through the lobby to the exit closest to the Alaskan Way, and the three high-rise buildings. But when they exited the building onto the street, they saw six high-rise buildings.

"What do you want to do?" asked Robey.

"Not sure. Let me think for a minute."

After a full three minutes, Bragg spoke. "Okay. Fuck canvassing those six buildings. For now. We'll use that tactic as a last resort. Tomorrow we'll scale back to eight guys, and go four each at the two locations where we think we've spotted Ferguson. Two guys inside, two guys outside at both locations. My bet is on location seven, because that's where he was on Wednesday. He's probably got an alternating schedule: Monday, Wednesday, Friday one activity, Tuesday, Thursday something else. Running, according to Mr. Barker."

"Sounds like a plan. I'm not as sure as you are about abandoning the other sites though."

"Well, we've got several options, which is a good thing. We can always scale back up, if we can prove it's a good plan. In the meantime, I've got another idea."

"Oh yeah?"

"Yep. I want you to find out from Rocca if anyone on this detail plays any chess."

Chapter Seventy-Five

Friday, January 21, 2011 – 6:30 a.m.

BILL WAS PACKED and ready for his trip to Fiji. He'd just finished throwing his bags into the car. The average temperature in Fiji for this time of year was about eighty-nine degrees Fahrenheit. The balmy temperatures would be a welcome change from the forty-degree dampness of Seattle in January. It had rained on sixteen of the twenty-one days so far in 2011, and there had even been snow flurries a couple of times. He wasn't sure what the annual suicide rate for Seattle was, but it wouldn't have surprised him one bit if it was very high this time of year. The overwhelming grayness could have depressed the happiest person alive. Come on Fiji!

But before landing in the tropics, he would spend a day and a half in Los Angeles, getting the lay of the land there. It never would have occurred to him to do this, but the only flights to Fiji he could find originated in L.A. He hadn't researched it, but he assumed the weather in L.A. would be very nice as well. At least compared to Seattle. Just imagining this trip drove the point home. It was time now for a new home in the tropics.

Just five minutes into his twenty-minute sojourn to the airport, Bill broke into a cold sweat. Crap! Do I have the Miles Goodman passport? He simply couldn't remember putting the passport into the carryon bag after placing it on the kitchen counter. Abruptly, he swerved into a nearby parking lot. After pulling the lever to pop the Saab's trunk, he leaped out of the car and dashed around to the back. Cold raindrops bounced off his rain slicker as he opened his carryon bag. Rifling through his assortment of airline itineraries, hotel reservations and bus tour pamphlets, he found no passport. Shit. Need to head back to the condo.

Finally, back in the apartment. It had been painful to get going back in the direction of his building. He'd had to wait through a couple of lights. But, sure enough, there was the passport, right on the kitchen counter where he'd left it. Okay, at least it hadn't cost too much time. It felt like he had grabbed the passport and turned and bounded out the door all in one motion. He got an elevator quickly, and was back in his car by six fifty-two.

***

"Okay, time to roll!" said Charlie as he led the other seven agents out of the field office. It was six-fifteen a.m. While it was only three blocks due north from the field office to location six, and four blocks northeast to location seven, the agents fought the rush hour traffic in their sedans to get to their respective locations. Not because the cold pelting rain discouraged them from walking, but because if Ferguson was in a car, they would need cars to tail him. It took both teams an absurd twelve minutes each to reach their destinations. Such was life downtown during rush hour. Both crews were on time for the scheduled six-thirty a.m. start. Two men inside each coffee shop, two vehicles outside, positioned more strategically this time so as to easily follow someone leaving either the drive-thru or the parking lot.

But nothing happened. Charlie would have put money on location seven and assigned himself to one of the cars at that location. It made sense to him that Ferguson had some sort of Monday, Wednesday, Friday schedule that would bring him back to the same place for coffee on those days. But the only white Saab convertible was driven by a comely thirty-something female. And the agents doubted that Ferguson had gotten a sex change overnight.

At ten a.m. they wrapped it up and headed back to the field office but the week hadn't been a total bust. They had two possible sightings of Ferguson at two logical locations. Potentially, they knew what kind of car he drove, and they may have learned his new first name, Miles, and that he played at a local chess club. The chess club was Charlie's next move.

Chapter Seventy-Six

Monday, January 24, 2011 – 12:00 a.m.

CHARLIE AWOKE TO the feel of his phone vibrating in his hand. <u>Damn. I guess I dozed off</u>. He righted himself in the chair in his hotel room, quickly turned down the volume of the TV, and answered the call he had been waiting for.

"Agent Bragg."

"Sir, this is Agent Richter."

"The chess player, I presume?"

"Well, sort of. Got my ass handed to me tonight."

"Rusty, are we?"

"I was never as good as most of those guys."

"Well, I guess most of them play every week and study in between."

"Yeah, I think most of them play online as well."

"So, any luck?"

"In terms of seeing Ferguson, no. But I may have stumbled on to something else. That's why I'm calling a bit late."

"Okay. Shoot."

"Well, this chess club has its own website. So after I got done getting crushed, I went home and checked out the site. There is a discussion forum, and you can see someone named Miles posted some information. Asked some questions, answered some. But what could be valuable is what I found in the Selected Games section. In that section, there are about ten games or so that are annotated, meaning, the moves from the game are shown along with commentary from the players. One of the games is between a J. Barker and an M. Goodman. Interesting game."

"Do you know when that game was posted to the site?"

"About two months ago."

"Okay. Okay. Good work Richter. Let's keep our fingers crossed that M. Goodman is Miles Goodman, AKA Bill Ferguson. This could be a huge break. If you think of anything else, don't hesitate, call anytime."

"Will do, sir."

"Okay, get some rest. I might need some help from you tomorrow also."

Charlie tossed and turned, finally falling asleep in the wee hours. For much of the night he hadn't been able to turn his brain off. He was too excited. He was hoping beyond hope that M. Goodman, was Miles Goodman. It would make sense since he was apparently friendly with Jerome Barker, the security guard at the Sand Dollar Condos. It would make sense that the two friends played a match, and it wound up getting posted on the site. He'd have one of the agents follow up with Barker. Barker could confirm that the M stood for Miles.

With a possible full name, they could really start searching. There were databases to check, credit bureaus, government agencies. But, there wasn't anything he could do in the middle of the night. In the morning, the search for Miles Goodman would begin.

***

After his fitful night, Charlie arrived at the office at eight and got straight to work. By eight-thirty Richter had found Barker at his job at the Sand Dollar Condominiums and confirmed that the game from the website was one he played against his friend Miles. Bingo! Now he had the full name, Miles Goodman, and a composite picture. And a probable make and model of what Goodman/Ferguson was driving. The question was could they gather enough evidence to convince the bosses that Miles Goodman was the same person as Bill Ferguson?

With help from their friends at the Washington State DMV, the agents were able to discover several encouraging facts. First, there were only two people named Miles Goodman in the greater Seattle area and only one of them lived on the Alaskan Way in downtown Seattle. Second, the car registered to Miles Goodman who lived downtown was a white Saab 9-3 convertible. And last but not least, the DMV picture for Miles Goodman greatly resembled their composite sketch. The problem was the DMV photo was taken before Ferguson had grown the beard. So Charlie worked with Alicia Chou once again, and had her draw up a picture of what Ferguson would look like now, forty pounds lighter, with no beard. And he also had her add a full beard to the DMV picture. The pictures all matched very, very closely. This was their guy, and now they had an address.

By late morning, they had the credit bureau information for Miles. This guy seemed to have appeared out of the ether only eighteen months ago. No credit history before then. For a forty- year old man? Exactly what Charlie expected. Good stuff.

By the afternoon, they knew about his bank accounts. There was over a half million dollars in a local Seattle bank. A nice chunk of change. Where was the rest, assuming it hadn't been spent? Probably in the Caymans. Or in a Swiss numbered account. If it was still controlled by Goodman, they would find it.

By the end of the day, the agents knew why Miles hadn't shown up at one of the coffee shops they had staked out. Through his credit card statements, they were able to see that he had recently bought plane tickets with Air Pacific. A contact at Air Pacific clued them in. Miles hadn't bought coffee in Seattle on Friday morning because he was on his way to Fiji. The agents were very happy to learn that Miles had a return flight scheduled, although Charlie could think of worse duty than to try to track down a fugitive in Fiji. Nothing wrong with a quick trip to the tropics in January. And a guy like Ferguson would probably stand out like a sore thumb. But that was a moot point. He had a return ticket, and they knew where he lived now. They'd be waiting for him when he came back from Fiji. After calling Braddock, Charlie went to talk to Rocca about getting the warrants in place.

Chapter Seventy-Seven

Sunday, January 30, 2011 – 12:00 p.m.

"ANYBODY SEE THE Saab in the parking lot?" Bragg asked quietly. According to Pacific Air, Ferguson's plane should be landing right now, so he shouldn't be home yet. But it was better to be safe than sorry. He had five men stationed in different places in the parking lot of the Sound condominiums. Three were in parked cars spread strategically throughout the lot. Robey was sitting on a bench right next to the lot, pretending to read the newspaper while scanning for Bill Ferguson, AKA Miles Goodman, or his late model Saab. The fifth agent was simply making slow loops around the parking lot on foot, coffee cup and newspaper in hand, as if he was out for a morning stroll. Bragg himself was in a car in the part of the parking lot that was under the building. These spots were the most popular, because they were out of the weather, but there were several spots available now as people were out and about.

One by one, Bragg heard five "no" answers in his earpiece in response to his question.

"Okay, people, just hang tight. He should be along shortly."

Bragg had picked this time to wait for Ferguson because it seemed logical. He was banking on Ferguson coming straight home from the airport after his jaunt to Fiji. But twelve-thirty came and went with no sign of him. Then one p.m. passed. Bragg was starting to get nervous. Maybe Ferguson caught another flight out? No, hopefully he was just making a stop or two along the way home. Too early to panic or even reevaluate, for that matter. He urged himself to stay patient.

Surveillance like this, open-ended, with no time constraints, could be tough duty. You had to balance paying attention with over-straining. Grinding too hard could wear you out. Bragg allowed himself to glance at the headlines in the newspaper, but he couldn't allow himself to get too wrapped up in reading any articles. It would be a huge waste of time and resources to miss Ferguson when he finally did show up. The last thing Charlie wanted to do was go knock on the door of a potentially dangerous fugitive. Given the chance, Ferguson might choose to go down fighting.

Finally, at about one-thirty, Bragg heard a voice in his earpiece. "White Saab entering the lot. Bearded man driving." The notification had come from Robey. Okay, this was it. The timing of the next few moves had to be right. Once Ferguson parked, everyone would have to hustle to the car and surround it before he got out. But it was impossible to predict exactly where he would park. Luckily the lot wasn't THAT big. The first guy to the Saab could control the situation for a few seconds while the others arrived.

The Saab angled into Bragg's section of the parking lot.

"Okay, looks like he's parking over here, under cover. Quick! Start moving!"

After the Saab passed Charlie's location, moving from his left to his right, he edged his car door open. He slid out and crouched down beside the vehicle on the driver's side. As soon as he saw the brake lights go out on the Saab, he sprang into action, sprinting the fifty feet to a position just behind Ferguson's car. Then he immediately crouched down again to stay out of sight. The other agents, who had been en route for a few seconds, took up positions hiding behind nearby cars.

Bill, using the lever just under the dash, popped open the trunk, planning to grab his suitcases on the way to the condo. After stopping for a nice lunch on the way back from the airport, he'd cruised through a drive-thru Starbucks for a cup of his coveted latte. It had been a whole week and he was craving it. With his left hand, he opened his car door, Starbucks coffee cup in his right hand. He wasn't sure how he would manage the coffee and bags yet.

To his shock, he heard someone yelling, "FBI! Hands on your head! Hands on your head, NOW!" Turning around, he saw five guys, spread out across his field of vision behind various parked cars. Each one had a gun trained directly at him. Completely stunned, he could barely comply with the order. Almost subconsciously, he placed his hands on his head. He didn't even realize he had dropped his coffee cup, fresh coffee splattering everywhere.

"Okay, on your knees asshole! NOW!" Bill, still in a state of shock, sank to his knees, not fully comprehending what was happening yet. "On your stomach! Hands behind your back!" He sheepishly complied. Next, he felt cable ties cutting into his wrists and ankles as an agent restrained him with a knee in the back.

Okay, he was starting to get it. Somehow, he'd been caught. But why all the precautions by the FBI agents? It didn't seem to make any sense. All they had to do was show him a gun and a badge and he would have come quietly. He'd defrauded an insurance company and was on the run, so to speak, but he'd never been violent.

Three agents grabbed him and tossed him into the back seat of a sedan. With the car door still open, Bragg addressed him.

"Bill Ferguson? You are under arrest for fraud and murder. You have the right to remain silent. Anything you say can be used against you in a court of law. You have the right to have an attorney present during questioning. If you cannot afford an attorney, one will be appointed to you, free of charge. Do you understand these rights?"

Bill stared blankly at the FBI agent. His mind was racing. Murder? Murder of who? This is crazy. I've never killed anyone, never even threatened anyone. Maybe they've got me mixed up with someone else. But they knew my real name …

"Okay, let's roll. We'll talk about this downtown."

***

Over the next few weeks, Bill and a well-paid lawyer were able to hammer out a deal. He agreed to return all the remaining money, about two million dollars, to the insurance company. The Saab and the condo would be sold at auction. That still left a half a million dollars unaccounted for. Bill said he had spent it on luxury travel. The FBI was forced to back off the murder charge. There simply wasn't enough evidence to prove that Bill had killed Andy Jacobsen. All the evidence was circumstantial. And of course, Bill vehemently denied he had killed anyone. If the Bureau had been able to prove the rug that Andy was wrapped in when he was found had come from Bill's apartment in Myrtle Beach, it might have been different. Ultimately, Bill agreed to a three-year sentence in a minimum-security prison, and he would most likely be out in two years for good behavior.

Epilogue

BILL FERGUSON IS currently in a minimum-security federal penitentiary, serving out a three-year plea deal for insurance fraud and money laundering. The FBI was able to recover two million of the original three million dollars, with Bill's cooperation. The money had been sitting in various Seattle banks in accounts held by Miles Goodman. The missing five hundred thousand is sitting in a Seattle bank account and will likely still be there when Bill gets out of jail. The FBI looked for bank accounts in the Seattle area for Miles Goodman and Troy Stevens, but didn't look for any accounts in the name of Bill Ferguson.

Given his relative youth and fairly light sentence, Bill is at peace with the decisions he's made. Ultimately, he feels he never would have come close to the level of adventure and sense of freedom he enjoyed for those eighteen months if he had just gotten a standard divorce. And now he'll have a pile of money waiting for him when he gets out.

***

A DEVIOUS PLAN 407

Laura Ferguson officially divorced Bill, and is engaged to Preston Malloy. They both quit their jobs in Connecticut and moved to Boston, where they are power lawyers for a prominent Boston law firm. They purchased a vacation home in Narragansett, and relax there almost every weekend.

***

Jennifer Weaver still works for Greystone Mutual. She is finally in a serious relationship with a man she thinks is Mr. Right. She is now very happy that she opted out of Bill's fraud scheme.

***

The Stapleton Detective Agency is thriving under the stewardship of John Stapleton. But Andy Jacobsen is missed. One of a kind, he could never really be replaced. John still plays basketball on Wednesday nights with his old buddy Dmitri Jones.

***

Dmitri Jones is still working as a detective for the Hartford Police Department. He's looking forward to retiring from the force in a few years and then going to work for John Stapleton.

***

Based on his work tracking down Bill Ferguson, Charlie Bragg is next in line to be promoted to Special Agent in Charge of the New Haven field office once Hurricane Braddock retires.

CPSIA information can be obtained
at www.ICGtesting.com
Printed in the USA
LVOW04*1026081215
465925LV00009B/32/P